YESTERDAY'S NEWS

YESTERDAY'S NEWS

A CLARE CARLSON MYSTERY

R. G. BELSKY

WITHDRAWN

OCEANVIEW PUBLISHING
SARASOTA, FLORIDA

ISBN 978-1-60809-281-9

Cover design by Christian Fuenfhausen

Published in the United States of America by Oceanview Publishing
Sarasota, Florida

www.oceanviewpub.com

10 9 8 7 6 5 4 3 2 1

PRINTED IN THE UNITED STATES OF AMERICA

For Laura Morgan

One misfortune is worse than murder. It is to lose someone you love, without ever knowing that person's fate.

—Edna Buchanan
The Corpse Had a Familiar Face

"I wish you wouldn't keep appearing and disappearing so suddenly," Alice told the cat.

"All right," said the cat.

And this time it disappeared quite slowly, beginning with the tail and ending with its grin, which remained some time after the rest of it had gone.

—Lewis Carroll
Alice in Wonderland

PROLOGUE

School was always special to her.

Some children hated to go to school. But she always looked forward to going back to school each morning. She loved her friends. She loved her teachers. And most of all, she loved to learn.

For her, it was a time of excitement, a time of adventure, a time of new beginnings each day she sat in the classroom—like a butterfly emerging from a cocoon in a field of flowers underneath a blue, cloudless sky.

And so, on this sunny morning, like so many others, the mother and daughter leave their house and walk together toward the school bus that will pick up the little girl.

"What about your lunch?" the mother asks.

"I'm buying it at school today, remember?"

"Do you have enough money?"

"Yes, you gave it to me last night."

"Right," she says.

The mother knows that, but she's forgotten.

"And remember to come home right after school."

"You worry too much, Mom. I'm not a baby anymore."

That's all too true, of course. She is growing up. Just like they all do.

But today she is still her little girl.

The mother hugs her and puts her on the school bus, watching her in the window until the bus disappears from sight.

A little girl who has everything in the world ahead of her.

A lifetime of memories to come.

And all the time in the world to enjoy it.

OPENING CREDITS

THE RULES ACCORDING TO CLARE

I ALWAYS TELL the same story to the new reporters on their first day.

It goes like this: Two guys are sitting in a bar bragging about their sexual exploits. As they get drunker and drunker, the conversation becomes more outrageous about how far they'd be willing to go. Would you ever have sex with an animal, one of them asks? Of course not, the other guy replies angrily. What if someone paid you $50 to do it with a dog? That's ridiculous, he says. How about $500? Same answer. Okay, the first guy says to him, would you have sex with a dog for $5,000? The other guy thinks about that for a while, then asks: "What breed?"

The point here is that once you ask the question "what breed?" you've already crossed over a very important line and can never go back.

It's based, I suppose, on the famous old Winston Churchill story. They say Churchill was seated at a dinner party next to a very elegant and beautiful lady. During the meal, he turned to her and asked if she'd be willing to have sex with him if he gave her $1,000,000. The woman laughed and said sure. Then he asked if she'd have sex with him for $25. "Of course not, what do you think I am?" the indignant woman replied. To which Churchill told her, "Madame, we've already established what you are. Now we're just haggling over the price."

This is a crucial concept in the news business where I work. Because there is no gray area for a journalist when it comes to honesty and integrity and moral standards. You can't be just a little bit immoral or a little bit dishonest or a little bit corrupt. There is no compromise possible here.

Sometimes I tell a variation of the dog story.

I call it the Woodstein Maneuver.

The idea is to come up with a new scenario for the Watergate scandal. To speculate on what might have happened if Bob Woodward and Carl Bernstein ("Woodstein!" in the Robert Redford–Dustin Hoffman movie) had not written their stories that led to Richard Nixon's ouster, but instead gotten hush money to cover up the scandal. What if Nixon had paid them to make it all go away?

I ask a new reporter to put themselves in Woodward and Bernstein's place and think about what they would do if offered such a bribe.

Most of them immediately say they would never take money under any circumstances to compromise a story. I'm not sure if they say it because they really mean it or simply because they believe it's the answer I want to hear. A few laughingly say they'd go for the money, but I'm not sure I believe them either. I figure they're just trying to be outrageous or different.

Only a few reporters ask the key question.

The "what breed?" question.

"How much money?" they want to know.

Those are the ones I worry about the most.

PART I

LUCY

CHAPTER 1

"IT'S THE FIFTEENTH anniversary of the Lucy Devlin disappearance next week," Maggie Lang said. "Little eleven-year-old girl leaves for school and just vanishes into thin air. It's a legendary missing kid cold case. We should do a story for the anniversary."

"Lucy Devlin is old news," I told her.

"The girl's never been found, Clare."

"And after a while people just stopped caring about her."

"Well, you sure did all right with it. You won a damn Pulitzer."

Maggie Lang was my assignment editor at the TV station where I work as a news executive these days. She was a bundle of media energy—young, smart, ambitious, outspoken, and sometimes a bit reckless. I liked Maggie, but she scared me, too. Maybe because she reminded me of someone I used to know. Myself when I was her age.

Back then, I was Clare Carlson, award-winning reporter for a New York City newspaper that doesn't exist anymore. When the paper went out of business, I moved on to a new career as a TV reporter. I wasn't so successful at that. They said I came across as too intense on the air, too grating, too unlikeable to the viewers. So, they offered me a job in management. I was never quite sure I followed the logic of that, but I just went with the flow. I started out as an assignment editor, moved up to producer, and then was named news director for Channel 10 News here in New York City. It turned out that I really like telling other people what to do instead of doing it myself. I've always been a bitch. I guess now I just get paid for being one.

Maggie looked over at the Pulitzer Prize certificate I keep prominently on my desk at Channel 10. Hey, you win a Pulitzer—you flaunt it.

"You helped make Lucy Devlin one of the most famous missing child stories ever in New York City fifteen years ago, Clare," she said. "Imagine if we could somehow find her alive after all this time . . ."

"Lucy is dead," I told her.

"How can you be so sure of that?"

"C'mon, you know she's dead as well as I do. Why else would she never have turned up anywhere?"

"Okay, you're probably right. She is dead. And we'll never find the body or catch who did it or know anything for sure about what happened to her."

"So, what's our story then?"

"There's a new angle."

"Believe me, I covered all the angles on this story a long time ago."

"Anne Devlin, Lucy's mother, is telling people she has some new evidence about the case," Maggie said.

"Anne Devlin always claims she has some evidence. The poor woman has been obsessed with finding answers about her daughter for years. I mean, it's understandable, I guess, given all the pain and anguish and uncertainty she's gone through. But none of her so-called evidence ever goes anywhere."

"Doesn't matter. We go to the mother and say we want to hear about whatever new evidence she thinks she's come up with. I tell her we want to interview her about the case for the anniversary. That maybe someone will see it and give cops some new information. It'll be great TV. And that video—the heartbroken mom still pleading for someone to help her find out what happened to her daughter fifteen years ago—would go viral on social media."

She was right. It was a good idea. A good TV gimmick. A good social media gimmick.

And that was my job now, whether I liked it or not. I was a long way from winning Pulitzer Prizes or writing thoughtful in-depth journalism. In television, it was all about capturing the moment. And an emotional interview like that with Lucy's mother on the anniversary of her disappearance would definitely be a big media moment.

I looked out the window next to my desk. It was early April, and spring had finally broken in New York City. I was wearing a pale-pink spring pantsuit to celebrate the onset of the season. I'd bought it at Saks one bitterly cold day during the depths of winter to cheer myself up. But right now, I didn't feel very cheerful.

"Okay," I finally said reluctantly to Maggie, "you can reach out to Anne Devlin and see if she'll sit down for an interview with us."

"I already did."

Of course. Knowing Maggie, I should have figured she'd already set it in motion before checking with me.

"And?" I asked her.

"She said yes."

"Good."

"Under one condition. She wants you to be the person who does the interview with her."

"Me?"

"She said she'd feel more comfortable talking to you than some reporter she didn't know."

"C'mon, I don't go on air anymore, Maggie."

"She insisted on talking to you. She said you owed her. She said you would understand what that meant."

I sighed. Oh, I understood. Anne Devlin was holding me to a promise I made a long time ago.

It was maybe a few months after Lucy was gone. Anne had become depressed as people stopped talking about the case. The newspapers, the TV stations, even the police—they seemed to have given up and moved on to other things. She felt so alone, she said. I told her that she wasn't alone. I told her I'd always be there for her. I made her a lot of promises that I couldn't keep.

"Let's make a pact," she said, squeezing my hand on that long-ago night. "If I ever find out anything, you'll help me track Lucy down, won't you, Clare?"

"I promise," I said.

"No matter what happens or how long it takes, you can't let people forget about her."

"No one will ever forget about Lucy."

I thought about that long-ago conversation now as I sat in my office looking at the Pulitzer that had come out of my coverage of the Lucy Devlin story in what seemed like another lifetime ago. That story had been my ticket to fame as a journalist. It made me a front-page star; it catapulted me into the top of the New York City media world; and it was eventually responsible for the big TV executive job that I held today.

"She said you owed it to her," Maggie said again.

Anne Devlin was right.

I did owe her.

CHAPTER 2

LUCY DEVLIN DISAPPEARED on a sunny April morning.

She was eleven years old, and she lived on a quiet street in the Gramercy Park section of Manhattan with her parents, Anne and Patrick Devlin. That last day her mother had helped her get dressed for school, packed her books in a knapsack that hung over her back, and then kissed her good-bye before putting her on the school bus.

As far as anyone knew, she was with the other students on the bus when they went into the school. The first indication that something was wrong came when Lucy didn't show up in her classroom for the morning attendance. The teacher thought she was either late or sick, reporting it at first to the principal's office as a routine absence. It wasn't until later that police began a massive search for the missing eleven-year-old girl.

The disappearance of Lucy Devlin exploded in the media when the *New York Tribune*, the newspaper I wrote for, ran a front-page story about her. The headline simply said: "MISSING!" Below that was a picture of Lucy. Big brown eyes, her hair in a ponytail, a gap between her two front teeth.

The story told how she was wearing a blue denim skirt, a white blouse, and cork sandals when she was last seen. It said she loved reading; playing basketball and soccer; and, most of all, animals.

She petted every dog in the neighborhood and begged her parents to get her one. "She was my little angel," Anne Devlin said in the article. "How could anyone want to hurt an angel?"

The whole city fell in love with her after that. The *Tribune* story spared no emotion in talking about the anguish of her parents as they waited for some kind of word. It talked about their hopes, their despair, and their confusion over everything that had happened.

I know because I was the reporter who wrote it.

With my help, Lucy Devlin—just like Maggie had said—became one of the most famous missing person stories in New York City history. Posters soon appeared all over the city. Announcements were made in schools and churches asking people to look for her. The family offered a reward. First it was $10,000. Then $20,000 and $50,000 and as much as $100,000 as people and civic groups pitched in to help the Devlin family.

For many it brought back memories of the tragic Etan Patz case—a six-year-old boy who had disappeared from the streets of New York City a quarter century earlier. Little Etan became the face of the missing child crisis all over the country when his picture was the first to appear on a milk carton in the desperate search for answers about his fate. In that case, the family had finally achieved some closure when a man was eventually arrested and convicted for their son's murder. But there was no closure for Anne and Patrick Devlin.

I sat in the Devlins' apartment—crying with them, praying with them, and hoping against hope that little Lucy would one day walk in that door.

I've never worked a story before or after where I identified so much with the people I was writing about. My access to the parents gave me the opportunity to see things no one else did, and I put every bit of that into my stories. Everyone was picking up my stuff—the other papers, TV news, and even the network news magazines like *Dateline* and *60 Minutes*.

Yes, I did win a Pulitzer for my coverage of this story. The Pulitzer judges called it "dramatic, haunting, and extraordinarily compassionate coverage of a breaking deadline news story" in giving me the award. That was nice, but they were all just words to me. I wasn't thinking about a Pulitzer or acclaim or my career when I covered the Lucy Devlin disappearance. I just reported and wrote the hell out of the story, day after day.

Eventually, of course, other stories came along to knock this one off the front page.

All the reporters moved on to cover them.

In the end, I did, too.

It wasn't that easy for Anne and Patrick Devlin. The police told them that Lucy was probably dead. That the most likely scenario was she'd been kidnapped outside the school that day, her abductor had become violent and murdered her. He then must have dumped her body somewhere. It was just a matter of time before it turned up, they said.

Anne Devlin refused to believe them.

"I can't just forget about my daughter," she said. "I know she's still alive. I know she's out there somewhere. I can feel her. A mother knows. I'll never rest until I find her."

Her obsession carried her down many paths over the next few years. Every time a little girl turned up murdered or police found a girl without a home, Anne checked it out. Not just in New York City either. She traveled around the country, tracking down every lead—no matter how slim or remote it seemed.

There were moments of hope, but many more moments of despair.

A woman who'd seen the story on TV said she'd seen a little girl that looked like Lucy at an amusement park in Sandusky, Ohio. She was standing with a man holding her by the hand near the roller coaster, looking confused and scared. At one point, she tried to break away, but the man wouldn't let her go. The woman told one of the security guards that there was something suspicious about the man and the little girl, but never found out what happened. Anne went to Ohio and talked to everyone she could find at the amusement park. She eventually tracked down the security guard and finally the little girl herself. It turned out that the man was her father, and she looked scared and tried to run away because she was afraid to ride the roller coaster.

Another time a group of college coeds thought they spotted her in Florida during spring break. Some fraternity guys who tried to hit on them had a young girl in the back seat of their car, and she seemed out of place amid the beer swilling Neanderthals partying up a storm in Fort Lauderdale. The coeds told Anne they were convinced it was her missing daughter. That lead turned out to be a dead end, too. She was the daughter of a woman the fraternity guys had picked up the night before. The woman had passed out back in their hotel room, and they were just driving around with the girl because they didn't want to leave her alone.

And then there was the time the body of a young girl about Lucy's age and description was found alongside a highway in Pennsylvania. The state troopers found Lucy's name on a list of missing children and contacted Anne. She drove ten hours through a blinding snowstorm to a morgue outside Pittsburgh, where the body had been taken. The entire time she had visions of her daughter lying on a coroner's slab. But it wasn't Lucy. It turned out to be a runaway from Utah. A truck driver had picked her up hitchhiking, raped and killed her, then dumped the body alongside the road. Anne said afterward she felt relief it wasn't Lucy, but sadness for the family in Utah who would soon endure the same ordeal as she did.

Once a psychic came to Anne and said she'd seen a vision of Lucy. Lucy was living somewhere near the water, the psychic told her. Lucy was alright, but lonely. Lucy wanted to get back to her family, but she didn't know how. Eventually, the psychic said she saw a sign in the vision that said La Jolla. La Jolla is a town in Southern California, just north of San Diego. The psychic offered to travel with Anne there and help search for her. They spent two weeks in La Jolla, staying in the best hotels and running up big bills at fancy restaurants. The psychic found nothing. Later, it turned out she just wanted a free trip to the West Coast and some free publicity for her psychic business.

Worst of all were the harassing phone calls. From all the twisted, perverted people in this world. Some of them were opportunists looking for extortion money by claiming they had Lucy. Others were just sickos who got off on harassing a grieving mother. "I have your daughter," they would say and then talk about the terrible things they were doing to her. One man called Anne maybe two dozen times, day and night, over a period of six months. He taunted her mercilessly about how he had turned Lucy into his sex slave. He said he kept her in a cage in the basement of his house, feeding her only dog food and water. He described unspeakable tortures and sexual acts he carried out on her. He told Anne that when he finally got bored, he'd either kill her or sell her to a harem in the Middle East. When the FBI finally traced the caller's number and caught him, he turned out to be one of the police officers who had been investigating the case. He confessed that he got a strange sexual pleasure from the phone calls. None of the others turned out to be the real abductor either. But Anne would sometimes cry for days after she got one of these cruel calls, imagining all of the nightmarish things that might be happening to Lucy.

All this took a real toll on Anne and Patrick Devlin.

Patrick was a contractor who ran his own successful construction firm; Anne, an executive with an advertising agency. They lived in a spacious town house in the heart of Manhattan. Patrick had spent long hours renovating it into a beautiful home for him, Anne, and Lucy. There was even a backyard with an impressively large garden that was Anne's pride and joy. The Devlins seemed to have the perfect house, the perfect family, the perfect life.

But that all changed after Lucy disappeared.

Anne eventually lost her job because she was away so much searching for answers about her daughter. Patrick's construction business fell off dramatically, too. They had trouble meeting the payments on their town house and moved to a cheaper rental downtown. Their marriage began to fall apart, too, just like the rest of their lives. They divorced a few years after Lucy's disappearance. Patrick moved to Boston and started a new construction company. He remarried a few years later and now had two children, a boy and a girl, with his new wife. Anne still lived in New York City, where she never stopped searching for her daughter.

Every once in a while, at an anniversary or when another child disappeared, one of the newspapers or TV stations would tell the Lucy Devlin story again.

About the little girl who went off to school one day, just like any other day, and was never seen again. But mostly, no one had time to think about Lucy Devlin anymore.

Everyone had forgotten about Lucy.

Except her mother.

CHAPTER 3

I'VE BEEN MARRIED three times. The first time was to a doctor when I was a reporter at the *Tribune.* The second was to an attorney after I left newspapers to become an on-air reporter at Channel 10. And the third was to an NYPD homicide detective that ended not too long ago. A doctor, a lawyer, and a cop—I'd hit the trifecta in divorce by the time I was in my midforties. I think it's safe to say that I don't do marriage well.

Not that I'm blaming any of my ex-husbands for the way it turned out. They were all good guys. Well, mostly good guys. Especially Sam Markham, the cop and the most recent of my ex-husbands. I still felt badly that one hadn't worked out. No, if there was a finger of blame to be pointed for me not living happily ever after with any of these three men . . . it had to point right back at me.

It was my devotion to the job—some might call it an obsession—that ultimately led to all the marital disasters I've experienced. Funny, because with a doctor, lawyer, and a police officer—well, you'd think they would be the ones with the stressful, high-pressure jobs that could bring down a marriage. But it was always me. You see, I could never just walk away from the news at the end of the day. It was always the biggest thing in the world to me. It became the most important thing in my life. And so, in the end, it became my life.

I remembered a conversation I'd once had with Sam about all this. It happened a few months after we met. Before we were married. Maybe I should have realized then that marriage to Sam wasn't going to work any better for me than the previous two.

We were lying in bed at his apartment after having sex when he turned to me and said, "Let's talk about the future, Clare. Our future."

"Oh, that," I said.

While we were talking, I took out my cell phone and checked to see if there were any updates or big stories breaking.

"All you ever think about is chasing the news. Twenty-four hours a day, seven days a week. Why is that?"

"Uh . . . it's my job."

He sighed.

"Have you thought any more about the idea of giving up your apartment and moving in here with me?" he asked.

"I've pondered it from time to time."

"How about marrying me?"

"Also under consideration."

"And how about starting a family?"

"Do I get any kind of a break between all those things? Or do I have to hire the moving van, put on a wedding dress, and go through childbirth all in the same day?"

"I want to marry you, Clare."

"I've been married, Sam. Twice. I'm not the best candidate you can find."

"I don't care about your past. I want to spend the rest of my life with you. I want to marry you. I want to wake up every morning and be able to see you lying next to me."

"I can be a little cranky sometimes in the morning."

"I've noticed that."

"Okay, full disclosure time here, I'm really a lot cranky in the morning. Every morning."

"I understand."

"What I'm trying to say is I'm not exactly a morning person."

"No problem."

"Well, good to know that's not a deal breaker," I said.

Yep, Sam was probably the best of them. The one marriage I really wanted to make work. But it went down in flames just like the previous two because I was always working at the office and hardly ever around for him. He even had our divorce papers sent to me at the Channel 10 newsroom. Figured that way I'd be sure to get them. The envelope with them inside was delivered there while I was running coverage of a big fire at a Manhattan high-rise building. I didn't open them until the fire was out.

Sometimes I think that my only true love is that damn newsroom.

And that . . . my children are all the big stories that I've covered and broken through the years.

I have a scrapbook on my shelf at home where I pasted all the big stories I covered back when I was a newspaper star.

I took down the scrapbook now and paged through it to the Lucy Devlin coverage. There were pictures there of Lucy riding a bike, petting a dog, opening Christmas gifts—having a great time growing up as a little girl in a loving family until that nightmarish morning when someone took it all away. There were pictures of her parents, too—Anne and Patrick Devlin first in happier times with their little girl, then wearing the haunted looks of anguish, despair, and fear that I saw so many times in the days while we waited for some word about what might have happened to Lucy. Of course, that word had never come. And now, fifteen years later, her disappearance was still as much a mystery as it was when she first vanished.

Finally, I forced myself to put the scrapbook down.

I needed to stop thinking about the past.

I really needed to focus my attention on something different than my own marital woes and the long-ago sad saga of Lucy Devlin.

That was the right thing to do.

The smart thing to do.

And so—from long practice of doing the wrong and the stupid thing at critical moments—I picked up my phone and made a call.

"Hi, it's Clare," I said when Sam picked up the phone at the East Side precinct where I'd called him.

There was a long silence.

"Clare Carlson."

More silence.

"Your ex-wife."

"You and I were married?" he said finally.

"Briefly."

"Gee, I hadn't noticed."

"How's life as a police officer on the mean streets of New York these days? Do you still get to ride around in that squad car and scare people with all those flashing red lights and that cool siren?"

"Yes, that's one of the perks of the job."

"How about we take a ride one day and you let me play with the siren?"

"We're not allowed to do that. Only authorized law officers have access to police cars. No one else."

"Not even your ex-squeeze?"

There was a long silence on the other end. One of the problems of being married to someone—no matter how briefly—is they get to know an awful lot about you. You can't fool them the way you do other people.

"What do you want, Clare?"

"What makes you think I want something?"

"Well, I haven't heard from you in months. You suddenly call me up out of the blue and start trying to turn on the charm. I've seen you on a story, Clare. I know how you work. Don't try to work me. Why don't we just cut through all the bullshit and get right to the point of your call?"

I told him my station was doing a story about the fifteenth anniversary of the Lucy Devlin disappearance. And that the mother claimed she'd come up with some new kind of lead that I was going to talk with her about the next day. I asked him if he'd heard of any new developments about the case after all this time.

He didn't know anything, which wasn't really a surprise. He said the NYPD and the FBI still carried it as an open case—a kidnapping case was never closed until the victim was either found or determined definitely to be dead—but this clearly was an investigation that no one spent any time on anymore.

"Anne Devlin claims she's got some kind of new lead," I told him.

"Good luck with that. She still comes to us once in a while with these far-out scenarios about what really happened to Lucy."

"Yeah, I understand. God knows what this latest theory of hers is—she probably thinks the kid got abducted by a UFO or something."

"I guess it's a way for her to avoid confronting the obvious fact that her daughter is long dead. Think about it: If Lucy were alive, she'd be twenty-six years old now. Probably married. Possibly with children of her own. Christ, maybe someone out there really does know that Lucy is alive and where she is. And we just haven't found them. Stranger things have happened."

"Probably not, though," I said.

"Probably not," he agreed.

There wasn't much else to say. I didn't want to just leave it like this between us, though.

"It was good talking to you, Sam. It's been too long. Maybe I'll call you at home sometime soon when you have more time to talk. We'll catch up on everything. I'd really like that."

"That's probably not a good idea for you to call me at home," he replied.

A warning bell went off in my head.

"Why not?"

"I'm living with someone."

"A roommate?"

"My fiancée."

"You're getting married?"

"Her name is Dede. I probably should have told you . . ."

"You sure work fast."

"Well, Dede's ten weeks pregnant."

"Yep, you definitely work fast."

We made some awkward small talk for a few more minutes, and then I got off the phone.

I wasn't sure how I felt about this. I was pretty sure that I didn't want to remarry him or anything. But I suppose that somewhere in the back of my mind I hoped we might get together again.

Now I knew that was never going to happen.

He was moving on with his life, having a child with another woman—and leaving me behind.

Somehow that depressed me.

CHAPTER 4

"YOU LOOK GOOD, Clare," Anne Devlin said to me when she sat down in my office, and she sounded like she meant it.

"So do you," I told her, even though she didn't.

The truth was the years had taken a heavy toll. Her hair was thinning and gray. Her face looked wrinkled and tired. She seemed gaunt, too, almost frighteningly thin. The death of a loved one can do that. It not only kills the victim, but it destroys the family members around it, too. I could only imagine the horror of what this woman had been through since that dreadful morning.

"My, my, look at you," she said. "They tell me you're a real big shot here now."

"I'm the news director."

"The last time we talked you were just a reporter."

"Well, you know what they say: Those who can, do. Those who can't, teach. And those who can't do either become TV executives."

She smiled. We'd always had an easy relationship, the two of us. That was probably one of the reasons I got so close to her and her husband while I was covering Lucy's disappearance for the *Tribune*. We felt comfortable together. I was never quite sure why, since the only thing we seemingly had in common was finding out what happened to Lucy.

Devlin said she still lived in New York City, in a studio in the Chelsea area. She got some money from her husband in the divorce settlement, and worked part-time as a paralegal. There were no men in her life anymore, she said—all that was in the past for her.

"Your husband got remarried," I pointed out. "You could, too."

"Oh, I'm long beyond that. I haven't been with another man in years. I can't even imagine being intimate with someone like that again. I mean, it's been so long I wouldn't even know what to do . . ."

"They pretty much all still do it the same way," I said.

Maggie came into my office to join us. I introduced her to Anne Devlin. She was polite, but not overly friendly to Maggie. She clearly focused all her attention on the woman in the room that she knew—the woman that she trusted. That would be me. And why not? I'd been her friend, her rock, her shoulder to lean on from the very beginning of her nightmare.

"What about your personal life, Clare?" Devlin asked me now.

"Oh, that . . ."

"Are you married?

"Not at the moment."

"But you were?"

"Uh . . . yes. Several times."

"How old are you, Clare?"

"Forty-five."

"What about you? Do you think you'll ever get married again?"

I shrugged. "I have some commitment issues."

There is a pace to being a good journalist. I learned that a long time ago. You had to play the game until the person you wanted to get something from was ready to talk. I didn't plunge right into questions about her daughter. Instead, I just made this kind of small talk with the woman until I thought the time was right to ask about Lucy.

"I understand you have some kind of new lead about what might have happened to your daughter," I finally said.

"Lucy is still alive," Anne Devlin said.

"Okay."

"You don't believe me, do you? No one believes me anymore. Not even you, Clare."

"I think at some point you have to accept the inevitability that Lucy is gone for good," I said, trying to choose my words carefully.

"Mountainboro, New Hampshire," Devlin said.

"Excuse me?"

"That's where I think she is. Or was."

We'd gone through this same thing many times in the months after Lucy disappeared. Her coming to me all excited about some tip or lead. Of course, none of them panned out. Eventually, I imagined she would accept the fact there was nothing more she could do. But here she was, after all this time, still chasing the ghost of her lost daughter.

She handed me a piece of paper. A printout of an e-mail. It was from someone named CONCERNED CITIZEN at a hotmail address. The e-mail said:

Dear Mrs. Devlin:

You don't know me, but I saw a TV special not long ago about your daughter's disappearance. I watched you being interviewed, and my heart went out to you. At the end of the show, they ran your e-mail address in case anyone had any information about Lucy.

That's why I'm writing to you now.

A long time ago, right around the time your daughter disappeared, I belonged to a motorcycle gang. That spring we all met up with other gangs for a convention in a little town in New

Hampshire called Mountainboro. Hells Angels were there, bikers from California—they came from all over the country. One of the guys was from a motorcycle gang in New York called the Warlock Warriors. He had a little girl with him.

It's been a long time, but when I saw the photo of your daughter, I remembered her again. I'm pretty sure it was your daughter. She looked like the pictures I've seen of her. I only talked to her once. She told me how much she loved Cheerios and Oreo cookies.

I remember thinking how unusual it was for a little girl to be there in the midst of all those motorcycle people. I noticed that she had a birthmark on the back of her left shoulder. I don't know if your daughter had a birthmark at all. But if she did, perhaps it was really her that I saw that day.

The other thing you should know is the little girl didn't leave with the same man she came with. On the last day, I saw her on the back of a motorcycle with a guy from a different gang. Someone said his name was Elliott. It was this Elliott that the little girl left with.

I knew something was wrong, and I probably should tell the police. But you didn't do that when you were in a gang like mine. If you cooperated with the authorities, you might wind up dead. So I did nothing. And I never saw that little girl again.

I pray for you, Mrs. Devlin. I pray that my information isn't too late....

I handed the e-mail back to her.

"What do you think?" she asked.

"It seems kind of thin,"

"Lucy loved Cheerios and Oreo cookies."

"So do a lot of kids."

"She had a birthmark on her left shoulder."

"The person who sent you this e-mail might have read that in the papers."

There was more. I could tell it from the expression on her face.

"My husband," she said slowly, "was a member of a motorcycle gang before I met him. Right here in New York City. The Warlock Warriors. The same group as the e-mail said she came with. Patrick and I used to laugh about him once belonging to a motorcycle gang when he was young. But now . . ."

I stared at her. "You think your husband might have had something to do with your daughter's disappearance?"

"I'm not sure about anything anymore. Something happened the last day before she disappeared. I've never told anyone about it, not even the police. I guess I didn't want to even admit it to myself for a long time. I pretended like it never happened. But I've been thinking about it a lot lately. Lucy was very strange that last night. Something was bothering her. I finally asked her what it was. 'Dad wants to have sex,' she said."

"Sex?"

"That's what she said."

"What does that mean?"

"What do you think it means?"

"I've no idea . . ."

"What if Patrick was trying to have . . . well, you know . . . sex with her?"

I closed my eyes and tried to let the enormity of what the woman had just said sink in.

"The note said the little girl at the rally came with one of the guys from the New York gang, the Warlock Warriors," she said. "But she didn't leave with him. She left with another biker gang. On the back of a motorcycle with someone from that gang named Elliott. If it was Lucy, then this Elliott is the last person we know that saw her. Elliott could be the key to all this. Elliott might have all the answers about Lucy that I'm looking for."

"Look," I said, "this all happened a long time ago. The trail is cold—so cold you'd need a miracle to find anything now. I know how hard this is for you, but I think you just have to get on with your life and hope that somehow, before you die one day, you'll get the answers you want."

Anne Devlin shook her head sadly.

And that's when she delivered her real bombshell news.

Sometimes you don't know what's going to happen in an interview until you get to the very end.

That's what happened here with Anne Devlin.

It turned out she had—as the old journalistic expression used to go when I worked in newspapers—buried the lede of her story.

"I'm dying right now," Anne Devlin said. "It's cancer. I have an inoperable tumor in my lung. That's why I look this way. The disease—not to mention the chemotherapy—really takes a toll on you. I don't even recognize myself in the mirror anymore. I figured you would notice. Thank you for not mentioning it. The doctors say I've got another few months, maybe three to six months at the most. So, as you can see, I'm not going to be able to 'get on with my life,' as you put it. This is my last hope, Clare. My last hope to find out what happened to my daughter before I die. You've got to help me."

CHAPTER 5

I TOLD JACK Faron, the executive producer and my boss at Channel 10 News, about Anne Devlin's health condition. How she was dying of cancer. How the doctor had told her she had several months to live. About the e-mail claiming a long-ago sighting of a little girl who looked like Lucy at the motorcycle convention in New Hampshire.

"Anne Devlin is staring death in the face," Faron said excitedly when I was done. "She desperately wants to find out what happened to her long-lost daughter before she dies. She has this one slim hope of a new lead about what happened to her daughter. And Channel 10 News is out there in front of the story trying to help her. Missing girl. Heartbroken mother. A race against time for her to find answers. And all this is happening on the fifteenth anniversary of the day the girl went missing. I like it, Clare. We can even make a poignant plea to the Channel 10 News viewers for anyone to come forward who might have some information about the case."

I nodded.

"So, who will do the on-air interview with her? Cassie?"

"Not exactly."

"Janelle?"

Cassie O'Neal and Janelle Wright were the hot female faces on Channel 10 News. Glamorous, glib, and a bunch of other G-stuff

thrown in, too. Their most recent journalistic achievement had
been going undercover to get jobs at an upscale strip club. By
doing so, they discovered exclusively that A) many beautiful
women worked there; B) the beautiful women danced and took
their clothes off for a living; and C) men paid money to see these
beautiful women do this. Somehow, we managed to stretch this
into a ten-part series for the last sweeps period.

"No, I don't want the Barbie Twins involved in this story."

"Who, then?"

I told him how Anne Devlin only wanted to do the interview
with me.

"You?"

"Yeah, me."

"Are you talking about going on the air again?"

"I've been on the air before."

"Yes, and we all remember how that worked out."

"I wasn't that bad."

"Even if I wanted to let you do this, Clare—and I really don't—
it's been a long time since you've been in front of a camera. Do
you even still know how to do it?"

"Let me see," I said, pretending to think about the question. "I
stand stiffly, hold a microphone in front of me, and say: 'Hello,
I'm Clare Carlson of Channel 10 News . . .' Yes, I think I still
know how to do it."

I pointed out to him my long relationship with Anne Devlin.
My Pulitzer Prize fame for writing about it and breaking the case
fifteen years ago. The publicity bonus we'd get at the station from
my name being attached to this story again. He understood all
that, but he still seemed dubious.

"Look, Jack, it's my story," I told him. "This has always
been my story. If we're going to revisit the whole Lucy Devlin

disappearance again, I want to be the one to do it. I need to do this one myself."

After Faron eventually agreed to the plan, I went next to tell Brett Wolff and Dani Blaine, the Channel 10 news anchors, what was going to happen. Brett and Dani weren't the stereotypical "just a pretty TV face" type of anchors. They were good. Maybe too good. So good that I was constantly worried about losing them to a bigger station.

Brett had come from a syndicated TV show called *Inside Scoop*. I'd competed against him on the street when I was a reporter. And I knew how aggressive and savvy he was. When *Inside Scoop* went off the air, I signed him to be the anchor for the six- and eleven-o'clock newscasts. He was attractive, had a real presence on camera, and knew what he was doing, too. I figured he couldn't miss.

Dani Blaine was another story. Her real name was Nancy Grabowski, and she started out as a reporter at the *New York Post*. Scored a lot of big scoops for them. I met her once at an award dinner and was impressed. She was blond, pretty, and came across as a bubblehead when she was really very smart. Perfect for TV. We changed her name to Dani Blaine—it just sounded better than Nancy Grabowski—and teamed her up as the co-anchor with Brett.

The strange thing is it didn't work at first. The ratings were not good. Faron told me he thought it was a mistake, and he'd have to let them go. It could have cost me my job, too.

But then I came up with an idea for a new concept for the news show. I called it "Go News." The gimmick was to keep Brett and Dani—along with everyone else on camera—moving all the time. Instead of sitting behind anchor desks, I had them walking all over the set. They'd stride over to one of the other reporters, go stand next to a graphic—sometimes even act out in front of the camera some of the physical aspects of a story. No sitting, always keep moving—that was the motto.

It made the whole news show seem energetic and fresh and lively. Of course, it didn't hurt that Dani Blaine was one hot babe. Our demo surveys showed that lots of guys tuned in just to see her legs in a miniskirt, something you couldn't do when she was behind the anchor desk.

The idea worked even better than I had hoped. Ratings soared. So did advertising revenues. One newspaper did a poll that named Brett and Dani as the hottest news team in town. I was hailed as a genius. Believe it or not, it's ideas like this that can make or break a TV executive's career.

I told Brett and Dani now that I was going to be doing the Lucy Devlin report myself on the six-o'clock news show that night.

"Do you really think that's a good idea?" Brett asked.

"Now why wouldn't it be a good idea?"

"Something might go . . . well, wrong."

"What could go wrong?"

"You haven't been on the air for a long time, Clare," Dani pointed out.

"It's not exactly brain surgery."

"I just don't want to see you embarrass yourself."

"Thanks," I said sarcastically. "Maybe I'll have a mental meltdown right there on camera and reveal to the audience that my oh so attractive anchor had plastic surgery tucks done on their last vacation."

"I did no such thing," Dani said.

"Actually, I was talking about Brett."

I was walking a fine line here. I wanted to do the story myself. But I didn't want their noses out of joint. I needed Brett and Dani. My career depended on their careers. That was a part of

TV I didn't like. Depending on other people. I hate to do that. People usually let me down.

"How about this?" I suggested. "You guys introduce the segment. You give the background and do the intro. Then I'll do the report with an interview with the mother of the little girl that didn't come home. How she wants to find out the answers before she dies. Then you come back and do a wrap. That way it looks like you're directing the whole thing. I think it's good for the show to keep it like that. I mean no one knows who the hell I am. And you guys, I mean you're New York idols."

Dani looked over at Brett. He nodded.

"I can live with that," she said.

"Works for me," Brett chimed in.

"See?" I smiled. "I told you we could work this out."

* * *

I spent the next hour making notes on the people who'd been involved with the Lucy Devlin story when I covered it as a newspaper reporter. Lou Borrelli, the cop who headed the task force looking into the disappearance, was dead—from a heart attack five years ago. So was the first officer on the scene, Bill Graham. Cancer, last year. I made a list of the other investigators and law enforcement officials and tried to call as many as I could. I thought about calling Sam again, but decided against it. Nothing to be gained for me— on any level—by going back there.

A lot of the old law enforcement people I tried weren't around anymore or their numbers were no longer any good. The ones I did reach didn't tell me anything I didn't already know. It was an old case. They'd thought about it, just like I had. But there'd been no clues or leads or developments in a long time.

The last call I made was to Patrick Devlin, Lucy's father. After we went through the initial pleasantries, I told him why I'd looked him up.

"Your wife thinks she has a lead on what might have happened to Lucy. She got an e-mail saying Lucy had been seen at a motorcycle convention in New Hampshire right after she disappeared. It's the fifteenth anniversary of Lucy's disappearance coming up. I'm going to do a report on it all. I just wanted to get a response from you."

"Anne just can't let it go, can she?" he said. "She keeps clinging to stories like this so she doesn't have to deal with the truth."

"What truth?"

"That her daughter is gone and isn't coming back, not now or ever."

"She's your daughter, too."

"That was years ago."

"That's right. And she's never gotten over it. She wants to know what happened to her daughter. I would think you would, too."

"You and I both know that Lucy is dead," he said.

"I don't know that."

"Sure you do. You just don't want to admit it. Some pervert took her. That's what happened. We can't change that. I've accepted that. I've got a new life now. Anne, she's still mired in the past. Going over and over things that she's never going to be able to change. Lucy's dead. Tell her that. Tell her it's time to move on."

I hated to hear him talk like that.

"Do you know that Anne has cancer?" I asked. "She's only got a few months to live. That's why she's so desperate to find out what really happened that day. She doesn't have much time left. Can't you understand that? I would think that would be important to you, too."

"What's important to me now is my life here in Boston and my wife and my son and daughter here with me. I know it may sound unfeeling to you, but Anne is not a part of my life anymore. Neither is Lucy. And so, no, I don't have any response for your TV show."

I wondered why he was so upset. I thought about how Anne had said how he was a member of a motorcycle gang himself once —the same gang that the e-mail said had brought a little girl who looked like Lucy to New Hampshire. How Anne even suspected Patrick might have had something to do with Lucy's disappearance. I didn't believe it at the time. I mean, I'd known Patrick Devlin, and he'd loved Lucy with all of his heart. Or at least I thought he did.

But now I wasn't so sure.

Sometimes we don't really know people at all.

That's how I felt about Patrick Devlin at that moment.

CHAPTER 6

SIX O'CLOCK THAT night. Show time. I felt the same butterflies in my stomach that I always used to get before I went on the air. I took a deep breath and reminded myself I was a boss now as the opening credits for the newscast ran . . .

ANNOUNCER: This is the Channel 10 News.

With Brett Wolff and Dani Blaine at the anchor desk. Steve Stratton with sports and Wendy Jeffers at the Accu 10 weather central.

If you want to stay up to date in this fast-paced city, you need to keep on the go with Channel 10 News.

And now, here's Brett and Dani . . .

The camera cut to Brett and Dani.

BRETT: Good evening. We start with an update on a sad story that has haunted New Yorkers for years. The disappearance of little Lucy Devlin.

A picture of the little girl appeared on the screen behind him.

DANI: She would be a grown woman today, if she's alive. Maybe married, maybe with a career, maybe with children of her own. But instead she's a statistic. One of the thousands of children who disappear in this country every year. This one, though, has left a special ache in our hearts. Even after all this time, New Yorkers remember Lucy Devlin.

There was a rapid-fire progression of video clips and headlines from the past—more pictures of Lucy, the scene from the Devlins' town house, police press conferences, etcetera.

While this was happening, Brett and Dani brought the viewers up to date on the latest information about the mysterious e-mail and Anne Devlin's battle with cancer.

> BRETT: And now, for an exclusive interview with Lucy Devlin's mother, here's our Clare Carlson, who won a Pulitzer Prize for her reporting on this story when Lucy first disappeared.

There was a cut to me interviewing Anne Devlin:

> ME: Mrs. Devlin, you were recently diagnosed with lung cancer...

> ANNE DEVLIN: Yes. The doctor told me I have only a few months to live. That's why I'm here now.

> ME: Explain what you mean by that.

> ANNE DEVLIN: I'm not afraid to die. We are all put on this earth for a purpose, and then we all die. I just need to accomplish my purpose before I go. I believe my purpose was to be Lucy's mother. I need to find out the answers to what happened to her before I die.

> ME: Do you think she's still alive?

> ANNE DEVLIN: Yes, I do.

ME: Mrs. Devlin, unfortunately, statistics show that abducted children who are not found within seventy-two hours are generally slain. Even the police speculate that whoever took Lucy probably killed her soon after the kidnapping. Why do you still hold out hope after all this time?

ANNE DEVLIN: A mother knows. I feel her out there. She's still waiting for me. Somewhere.

She then told the story about the mysterious e-mail she'd gotten and the report of Lucy being seen on the back of motorcycles with members of the Warlock Warriors and other gangs in New Hampshire all those years ago.

ME: Mrs. Devlin, if you could give a message—a plea—to whoever abducted Lucy, what would you say? He or she might be watching this show right now. What would you tell them?

ANNE DEVLIN: (looking directly at the camera). I don't know why you did this. Or why you did it to my daughter. What you've done to me is the worst crime imaginable. Children are murdered, but this was worse. The uncertainty, the never knowing. I wake up every morning and the first thing I think about is Lucy. Where is she? Is she all right? Is she unhappy? If you had killed me, it would have been so much easier. This is like slow death for me. But I don't care about why you did it now. I just want my daughter back. I want to love my daughter again before I die. I want to look in her eyes, stroke her hair, and hold her close to me. If you have a shred of humanity in you, tell me where she is. Please. Please . . .

She broke down in tears at that point.

It was powerful stuff. So powerful that Brett Wolff and Dani Blaine sat there in stunned silence for a few seconds after they came back on the screen.

> "Thank you for that report, Clare," Dani finally said. "The hearts and prayers of all New Yorkers are with you, Mrs. Devlin."

*   *   *

Jack Faron came to see me in my office after the show.

"Nice job, Clare," Faron said. "I knew you could do it."

"Yeah, you never doubted me for a second, huh?"

"I've always been in your corner."

He sat down in front of my desk.

"Let's talk about the next piece on Lucy Devlin," Faron said.

"What next piece?"

"Well, there are some things in Anne Devlin's story we can check out."

I nodded. I'd been thinking the same thing.

"The motorcycle convention in New Hampshire, for instance," he said.

"Yeah, I checked. There's still a Warlock Warriors chapter here in the city. The guy who's the head of it has been around for a long time. His name is Sandy Marston. Maybe Marston knows something about what happened at that convention back then."

"So assign a reporter to talk to him."

"I'll go myself."

"You?"

"Yeah, me, Jack. I'm going to keep reporting on this story."

"But I thought this was going to be just a onetime thing for you because the Devlin woman asked for you to do the interview."

"I thought that, too. But Anne Devlin really got to me with that emotional appearance and the story about the long-ago biker convention. All my old reporting instincts kicked in. If there is more to this whole thing still out there, then I want to be the one to break it. Old habits die hard, I guess."

But, even as I was telling all this to Faron, there was a part of me thinking how maybe this wasn't such a good idea. That I should just give the Lucy Devlin story to Brett and Dani and Cassie and Janelle and the rest of them to do from here on. Sure, this story had been a big part of my career—and my life—in the past. It had made me successful and famous. But maybe it was best to just leave the past alone.

Of course, I didn't seek out the story this time. It found me. There was nothing I could do about that. But deep down I wondered if this was true. Did the Lucy Devlin story just fall into my lap again by chance after all these years?

Or were Lucy and I always fated to be together?

CHAPTER 7

THE HEADQUARTERS OF the Warlock Warriors was in Hell's Kitchen on the West Side of Manhattan. Hell's Kitchen was once a tough, gritty neighborhood, but it had become much more gentrified and trendy in recent times. The Warlock Warriors were still there, though, a remnant from the area's more violent past. When you went past the place, you always saw the motorcycles lined up in front and maybe some of the members hanging out on them.

The neighborhood residents pretty much kept their distance and the police did, too. Every once in a while, the cops would go in to bust someone on a warrant or quiet things down if they got out of hand. But mostly everyone simply looked the other way and let the Warlock Warriors go about their business. Whatever that was.

I stood in front of the building now. I hadn't brought a TV crew with me; I figured that might scare away anyone who wanted to talk to us. So, it was just me. I figured they weren't likely to chain up a woman to their motorcycles or sell someone into sexual slavery during broad daylight in the middle of Manhattan. At least I hoped that was true.

I walked up to the front door and pressed the buzzer. A burly guy opened the door. He had long curly blond hair and he was wearing a pair of tight jeans and had a t-shirt that said: "Warlocks Do It Better!"

"I'm looking for Sandy Marston," I said.

"Does he know you're coming?"

"No."

"Who are you?"

"My name is Clare Carlson. I'm with Channel 10 News."

"Why do you want to see Sandy?"

"It's about a story we're working on."

He said he'd see if Marston wanted to meet with me. When he was gone, I checked out the place. It wasn't that bad. I kind of expected motorcycles in the hall, chains hanging from the ceiling, and maybe a body or two lying around. Instead, it was amazingly sedate and normal-looking. All it needed was soft music and some magazines, and I could have been in a doctor's waiting room.

This illusion of normalcy, however, was quickly shattered when a woman walked into the room. She was big. Big tall, like more than six feet. And big all over, too. Zaftig couldn't even begin to describe her. She was about my age, but that seemed to be the only similarity. She was wearing tight black leather pants, black motorcycle boots, and a black leather vest. Her hair was green with a pink stripe through it. It hung all the way down to her waist.

"What the hell do you think you're doing here?" she asked me.

I went through my spiel again.

"My name is Clare Carlson. I'm with Channel 10 News and . . ."

"Are you chasing around after my man?"

"Would your man by any chance be Sandy Marston?" I asked.

"Damn straight! And I don't know why he'd be messing around with a skinny ass bitch like you."

Skinny ass?

"I can assure you there is nothing untoward going on between Mr. Marston and myself," I said. "I'm simply here in my capacity as TV news journalist. There's no reason for you to be upset."

"I'm going to kick your skinny ass out of here in about two seconds unless you tell me why you really came," she said to me now.

That was the second time she had called me skinny ass. There were many occasions where I might have taken that as a compliment. Somehow, I didn't think she meant it that way now.

"Well, well, we seem to be a little short on sisterly love here," a voice said, and I saw a man come into the room.

He introduced himself as Sandy Marston. Marston was in his fifties, with long brown hair wrapped in a bandanna. He was wearing jeans and motorcycle boots, too, but a flowered shirt. He looked like more of a refugee from a Grateful Dead concert than a guy in a motorcycle gang. He whispered something in the woman's ear. She glared at me one more time and then left.

"That's Big Lou," he said. "Big Lou's very protective of me. So what can I do for you?"

I told him the story about Anne Devlin. About the mysterious e-mail she'd received. About the missing girl at the bikers' convention. About the Warlock Warriors and about the other gang member she supposedly left with. About the mysterious man named Elliott.

"Let me get this straight," he said when I was finished. "You got an anonymous tip about an event that happened nearly fifteen years ago that might or might not involve the girl you're looking for. And that's it? That's all you've got? That's your whole story?"

"I always try to maintain a positive outlook," I told him.

"Well, first off, I wasn't even at that convention."

"Why not?"

"I was otherwise engaged."

"Doing what?"

"I was in jail."

"Oh."

"I stabbed a guy in the stomach that year. He almost died. The cops picked me up and I never made bail. I got convicted of manslaughter and was serving time."

"I'm sure it was probably just an innocent misunderstanding," I said.

"You know, that's the same thing I told them at the time."

"Would anyone else here have been at the convention?"

"We have a lot of turnover." He sighed. "People come and go all the time. Only a few of us, like me, stay in it for the long haul."

I nodded. This didn't seem to be going anywhere, but I had a few more questions for him.

"Did you know anyone named Elliott?"

"Elliott?"

"The guy from another gang that the e-mail said took the little girl with him on his bike."

He laughed. "You don't find too many guys named Elliott in motorcycle gangs."

"Why not?"

"It's not the kind of name you want in my business," Marston said. "Christ, if your name is Elliott, you sure don't tell anybody that. You change it or you get yourself a tough-sounding nickname. Elliott just sounds a little prissy, a little fancy, a little . . . well, you know, unmanly."

I wondered if I should point out to him that Sandy was a girl's name. I decided not to. I wasn't too afraid of Sandy Marston. But he might sic Big Lou back on me.

"How about a Patrick Devlin?" I asked. "Did you ever know him?"

Marston shook his head no.

We talked for another ten minutes or so. But he just kept saying he didn't know anything. That he wasn't at the convention. That he didn't know anything about any missing girl.

I wasn't too disappointed. I pretty much knew going in that this was going to turn out to be a dead end. That chasing this elusive new lead in the Lucy Devlin case was going to be even more hopeless than I had feared. What the hell . . . Lucy was probably long dead. And, even if she wasn't, I probably wasn't going to find anything out about her in this place.

Except for two things.

First, Marston had never actually answered my question about whether he remembered anyone named Elliott in the motorcycle gang world. He changed the subject, and he talked about the name. But he didn't say whether or not he ever knew an Elliott. It was a very clever ploy, one I'd used myself on more than one occasion. Not exactly the truth, not exactly a lie. More like a non-denial denial.

Second, why didn't Marston know Patrick Devlin? Anne Devlin said Patrick had been in the Warlock Warriors group when he was younger. Marston had been there most of his life. Wouldn't he remember him? I mean, it wasn't like they were this giant corporation with thousands of employees. These guys lived together, hung out together, drank together, and partied together. If Anne Devlin was telling the truth about her husband once being a member of the Warlock Warriors, and I had no reason to think she wasn't, then Sandy Marston was hiding something.

Of course, I had absolutely no idea of what that might be.

"Sure wish I could be of more help." Marston smiled.

He did promise to ask around for me to see if anyone else there remembered anything at all about that long-ago convention and seeing a little girl there.

I thanked him and gave him my business card.

"Call me if you find out anything," I said.

On my way out, I kept hoping I'd run into Big Lou again. Because I'd thought of the perfect comeback. The next time she called me "skinny ass," I was going to call her "fat ass." It was so simple, so right. I didn't understand why I hadn't thought of it in the first place. But there was no sign of her anywhere.

Then I looked back at the gang headquarters and saw her staring at me through a second-floor window. I stared back. Both of us stayed that way for a long time, like two kids in a playground engaged in a stare-down. Then she was gone.

I had a feeling that my business with Big Lou wasn't over.

That I'd run into her again at some point if I pursued this story.

I just didn't realize how soon that would be.

CHAPTER 8

"There's a woman here to see you," Maggie came into my office to tell me the next day.

"Who is she?"

"She said her name was Louise Carbone."

"Never heard of her."

"She said she met you yesterday at some motorcycle club headquarters. She said she's been thinking about what you said. She said she has something to tell you."

I looked out in the newsroom.

It was her, all right.

Big Lou.

She didn't look quite as threatening as the last time I'd seen her. She'd changed from the leather pants, vest, and boots to jeans, a sweatshirt, and sandals. The green hair was still there, but she wore a baseball cap that covered up a lot of it. She didn't even look quite as tall as our first encounter, which made me wonder if she might have been wearing lifts in those motorcycle boots. The truth is she seemed . . . well, almost normal.

Her demeanor was different, too. She didn't threaten to kick my skinny ass or anything when she walked into my office. She just sat down on my couch. I was drinking a cup of coffee, and she asked me if she could have some, too. I went into the kitchen area, poured another cup, and brought it back to her. Then I sat down in a chair across from her.

"I saw that little girl," she said. "The one you were talking to Sandy about."

"You were at the motorcycle convention?"

She nodded. "I'd just joined up with the Warlock Warriors. I wasn't with Sandy back then. I was this wide-eyed girl from the suburbs who thought it would be a great life to get on the back of some guy's chopper and ride around the country."

The way she said it sounded like maybe she didn't think it was such a great life anymore.

"That day," she said, sipping on the coffee, "I saw the young girl standing by herself next to one of the bikes. I thought she might be lost or in trouble or something, so I asked her if she was okay. She said she was waiting for someone. I asked her where she was from. She said New York City. She said she'd ridden up there on the back of a Harley. She was so little and so adorable that my heart went out to her. We talked for a while."

"The biker chick with the heart of gold," I said.

As soon as I did, I wished I hadn't. No point in antagonizing her at this point. It didn't seem to matter, though.

"Look, I know what you probably think of me," she said. "But I didn't spend my whole life hanging out with a motorcycle gang. My name really is Louise Carbone, and I'm from New Jersey. My mother still lives there, although I don't see her very much. I was a wild kid, and I thought it would be exciting to ride with a motorcycle gang. Eventually, I moved on. I got married, I had a kid of my own—we even had a house in Lodi, New Jersey. Only it didn't work out the way I wanted. I started drinking, doing some drugs, and that got me in trouble with the child welfare authorities. Eventually, they took away my daughter. She lives with her father now. I drifted back to New York, hung out here, and met Sandy. We've been together for a long time now. It's like my family, Sandy and the gang. I know that may sound strange to you, but they're the family I never had."

I didn't say anything sarcastic this time. Actually, what she said made a great deal of sense. I could relate to some of it. The truth was I was starting to like Big Lou.

"Anyway, I asked the little girl what her name was. She said it was Lucy. I asked her about her father and mother. She said they weren't around. She said she was with her uncle Elliott."

I nodded solemnly. It sounded good, but I still wasn't sure what I had here. All I knew for sure was that some girl—whose name might or might not have been Lucy—was at a bikers' convention a long time ago in New Hampshire, very soon after Lucy Devlin disappeared from New York City. There was no indication that the girl in New Hampshire was Lucy Devlin. That she was in any kind of trouble. She could have simply been a little girl with her uncle whose name was Elliott. Nothing more. There was also the very real possibility that both the e-mail and Big Lou's story were bullshit, that they were simply telling people what they thought they wanted to hear for some unfathomable reason.

"Did you meet Elliott?" I asked.

"Yes, when he came to get the girl."

"What did he say?"

"The same thing she said. He was her uncle. He was taking care of her because her parents were away. She loved riding on motor-cycles. So he brought her along with him. We talked a little while, and they both left. Him and the little girl. It didn't seem like that big a deal at the time."

"What about later?"

"I saw an article about the missing girl. Lucy Devlin. I thought she looked something like the girl I'd met in New Hampshire. I never did anything about it. I wasn't sure and I wasn't exactly sure what to do. Maybe I should have told someone back then. Anyway, when I heard you talking to Sandy about this yesterday, it all came back to me. I agonized about it all last night. Sandy doesn't know I'm here. He'd be furious if he found out. He doesn't believe in cooperating with the authorities or the media or anyone else in the establishment. But I always wondered what happened to that little girl. Is she dead? Where is she now? Was it really Lucy Devlin? It's something that's bothered me for a long time. I guess I finally just want to know the answers to those questions. So I decided to come over here now and tell you what I know. Before it was too late . . ."

She was wrong about that, of course. It was already too late. If she'd gone to the authorities back then at the motorcycle conference, maybe they would have gotten some answers. But she didn't. Now here she was, sitting in my office, trying to help me go down a trail for a missing girl that had grown cold a long time ago.

"Elliott didn't by any chance tell you his last name, did he?"

"No."

"Anything about himself?"

"He was extremely vague."

"You don't know any more . . ."

"Oh, I found all about him later."

"How?"

"I saw him on TV."

"When?"

"A year or so ago. That's when I found out his name."

I sat there waiting. I realized she was probably enjoying this. Enjoying having my complete attention. I let her play it out the way she wanted.

"Aren't you going to ask me who he is?" she said.

"Who is he?" I asked mechanically.

"Elliott Grayson."

I thought maybe I hadn't heard her right.

"Elliott Grayson?"

"Yes."

"*The* Elliott Grayson?"

"He's the only one I know."

Elliott Grayson was the federal attorney in Manhattan and also a candidate for the US Senate. Grayson had been in the headlines recently when he took down one of New York's biggest crime families. Before that, he made a name for himself by busting up a big drug cartel. He was good-looking, charming, a regular on the TV news shows—Channel 10 included. A few months ago, he announced he was running for the Senate. The latest polls showed him winning handily. Some people were already talking about him having a future in the White House.

"What the hell was Elliott Grayson doing at a motorcycle convention with a little girl on the back of his bike?" Big Lou asked me.

I wondered the same thing.

CHAPTER 9

I CALLED ELLIOTT Grayson's office at the US Government Building in Foley Square. I got a woman named Gwen, who said she was Grayson's special assistant.

"My name is Clare Carlson. I'm with Channel 10 News. I'd like to set up an interview with Mr. Grayson as soon as I can for a story we're doing. When could I come over?"

"What's the story about?"

"I'd rather discuss that with Mr. Grayson when I see him."

"You can tell me."

"I'm sorry, but I can't do that."

"Why not?"

"I want to do it face-to-face with Mr. Grayson himself."

"You can tell *me*," she repeated, with more emphasis this time. "I'm his special assistant."

"It's confidential."

"What does that mean?"

"Confidential is a term we use in the TV business for something we don't reveal to anyone without a double secret security clearance."

She did not laugh.

"There's an opening at three o'clock tomorrow afternoon," she said.

"I was hoping for something today."

"Three o'clock tomorrow," she said again.

Gwen was starting to get on my nerves.

"We're the highest-rated news show in town," I said, stretching the truth just a bit. "Millions of New Yorkers watch every night. This could be a great opportunity for Elliott Grayson. A chance to be seen and heard by a lot of people. I think perhaps you might want to reconsider your answer."

There was a pause, like she was checking something, then she came back on the line.

"Okay, two o'clock tomorrow."

"The power of the press isn't what it used to be."

"What do you mean?"

"That speech used to be able to buy me more than an hour."

"Do you want to see Mr. Grayson at two o'clock or not?"

I said that was fine.

I already knew a lot about Elliott Grayson. About his spectacular record of success as a federal prosecutor who had put a lot of high-profile criminals behind bars. About his run now for the Senate with all sorts of speculation on his big political future. There were plenty of stories about him that I found online and in our video files at the station. We'd been covering him big-time for a while. But what I needed to know now was what Elliott Grayson was really all about as a person as well as a politician. The kind of real, behind-the-scenes stuff that doesn't always get printed in news articles or put on the air.

I called Cliff Whitten. Whitten used to be a political columnist for the *New York Tribune*, the newspaper I worked for. But too many long liquid lunches and a few ugly confrontations in the newsroom after he'd been drinking convinced the bosses he wasn't exactly *Tribune* material. Whitten got fired, drifted to the *Daily News,* and eventually lost his job there, too, for the same reason. Now he covered local politics for a political website.

I'd been friends with him at the *Tribune*. That's all, just good friends. We'd spent many a long night drinking and having conversations about the state of the world.

I asked him now if he wanted to meet me for a drink.

"I don't drink anymore, Clare," he said. "It's been almost three years since my last drink."

"Congratulations. I guess."

"I'm on my way to the health club right now," he said. "We could meet there and talk. Or maybe you could join me for a workout."

"You've got to be kidding . . ."

The health club was on West 14th Street. When I got there, Whitten was doing pull-ups on one of the machines.

"I've abused my body for sixty years, Clare. Now I'm trying to change my lifestyle—no drinking, a healthy diet, and regular exercise. I want to see a few more elections before I die. You should try it, too."

"Do I look like I'm out of shape?"

"Everybody could stand to lose a few pounds."

"That's not the answer I wanted to hear."

I explained that I was working on a story about Grayson, and I just wanted to find out more about what made him tick. I didn't say what the story was about.

"Elliott Grayson." Whitten chuckled when I was finished. He was running on a treadmill now. "The hotshot federal prosecutor. Grayson figures maybe he can do what Rudy Giuliani never quite pulled off—go from crime-busting US Attorney to the Senate and maybe even to the White House one day. And you know what? He might just pull it off."

"What's the status of the election right now?"

"You've got Grayson and Teddy Weller vying for the Democratic nomination. You couldn't find two candidates at more opposite ends of the political spectrum.

"Weller is old school. He's been a congressman for years. Before that, he was Brooklyn Borough President and then in the State Assembly. He's got so many markers and chits out in the city and state for all the political favors he's done that he ought to get enough votes just from those people alone. On the issues, he's practically out of the stone ages. Against welfare, against sex education in the schools, against city funding going to abortion clinics, pro-death penalty—he's a Democrat in name only.

"Grayson, on the other hand, is the new hope for the liberals in New York City. Kind of a combination of John Lindsay and Robert F. Kennedy for the twenty-first century. He's got that same kind of charm, that same mass appeal. Grayson walks through impoverished neighborhoods in Harlem or the South Bronx in his shirtsleeves, just like Kennedy and Lindsay once did, and the people love him. He's made a lot of big promises for things that he'd do if elected. Funding for food programs, better schools, court reform, etcetera. He's also very big on fighting crime. He points to his experience as a law enforcement official, and he says he can make the streets safer than they've ever been. A lot of people believe him."

"So who's going to win?"

"Well, Grayson's got a big lead in the polls. Everyone is predicting a bright political future for him on the national stage."

"And you figure he's a sure thing to win?"

"Nothing's a sure thing in politics, Clare. You know that. Grayson looks unstoppable now. But there's still a long way to go. Anything could tilt it back to Weller before the primary election in September. A big endorsement, a misspoken word in a campaign speech, a scandal. I guess that's what Teddy Weller is hoping for. Some kind of a big scandal or other pitfall for Grayson. It's pretty much his only hope at this point."

"What about the general election in November?"

Whitten shrugged. "The Republican candidate is Les Goodman. A longtime legislator from upstate. Not much talk about him right now since he has the GOP nomination sewed up. Goodman could surprise people for the general election in November, I suppose. But right now, it's all about Weller and Grayson. Most people figure Grayson's got a clear path to the Senate and a bright political future on the national stage after that."

After he was finished with the treadmill, Whitten moved to the swimming pool. He began leisurely swimming laps in the lane closest to the side. He was doing a sidestroke, which left him able to talk to me as he swam. I walked alongside, carrying a towel for him and shouting out questions.

"You've met Grayson, right?" I asked.

"Sure."

"Do you like him?"

Whitten didn't answer right away.

"Is there some problem with him?"

"Look, Clare, the truth is everything about the guy seems on the up and up. I mean he's a hard worker, he's smart, he's successful, and he talks a helluva game. It's just . . ."

"What?"

"Well, I have this feeling about him. Like there's something missing. Or maybe something I simply don't know about him."

"A dark side?"

"I'm not saying that."

"Then what?"

"I just have the feeling he's the kind of guy that would do anything to get what he wants. His goals might be laudable. But not the way he goes about achieving them. I guess it's a matter of the ends justifying the means for him. And that scares me."

When he was finished swimming his laps, he pulled himself out of the pool. I handed him the towel.

"How far do you think Grayson would go to get elected to the Senate?" I asked.

"Let me tell you a story. A few years ago, when Elliott Grayson was a prosecutor in the New York office, there was this family that lived next door to a mob boss named Jackie Moreno. Moreno was a bad guy. He claimed he ran a waste disposal company, but he was really a murderer, a drug pusher, an extortionist—you name it, this guy was guilty. But he was smart, too, and always able to beat the rap. People figured he was paying off cops and judges, but no one could ever prove it.

"Anyway, one day Moreno's neighbor just disappears. He's a guy named William Granger, and he's as straight as Moreno is crooked. Runs his own accounting firm, he and his wife are active members of the local church, he's a great father to their three kids . . . all in all, just an upstanding citizen. Only he got in this fight with Moreno. It was over something stupid, like somebody's trash can was in the wrong spot or one of the kids was playing on the other's lawn or whatever. But it escalated to the point where they started exchanging blows, right there in Granger's driveway.

"It turned out Granger was a pretty good fighter, and he tagged Moreno with a haymaker that knocked him on his ass in front of the whole neighborhood. This was very humiliating for Moreno, who always acted like a tough guy. He screamed at Granger in front of maybe a dozen people that he was a dead man.

"The next night, Granger never came home from work. His abandoned car was found a few blocks away. A witness said she saw him being dragged from his car and thrown in the trunk of a Cadillac. She got the license plate number, which turned out to belong to Moreno's company. He was arrested, and it seemed like an open and shut case for Grayson, who was the prosecutor. I mean, Moreno threatened the victim and one of his cars was seen kidnapping him.

"Only the jury came back with a not guilty verdict. It turns out—even though they could never prove it—that Moreno bought off members of the jury. After he was acquitted, he had a big victory celebration at his house. Next door, poor Granger's wife and kids had to listen to him and his friends partying over the fact that he got away with murder. The wife goes to Grayson in tears. She asked him how such a horrible injustice could happen. He said he sympathized with her pain and anguish, but there was nothing legally that could be done.

"Except a funny thing happened afterward. Moreno got stopped in a routine traffic patrol by federal officers doing terror checks. They didn't find any terror materials in his car, but they did seize a large amount of heroin. Moreno insisted it wasn't his and claimed the federal officers planted it. He got convicted this time and sentenced to five to fifteen years in Sing Sing for drug trafficking. Two weeks after he got there, someone stabbed him to death in the prison rec room. No one ever found out who did it.

"I was interviewing Grayson one day and I asked him about the Moreno story. I said that some people believed it was payback for the William Granger murder. That the federal officers stopped Moreno on Grayson's orders, put the drugs in his car, and fixed it so he would definitely go to prison this time. Grayson just laughed, but he never denied it. He could have, but he didn't. That's when I realized what he was doing. He wanted me to believe the story was true. He wanted everyone to believe he was capable of doing something like that. Moreno was a bad guy. Now Moreno was gone. Grayson got rid of him."

"The ends justified the means," I said.

"Exactly."

I wasn't sure how this fit into the Lucy Devlin case. But what if Grayson had something to hide? Some secret that might prevent him from being elected to the Senate? How far would he go to prevent that secret from ever being revealed?

There was another possibility, too.

"What about his opponent, this Weller guy?" I asked Whitten. "How far would he go to be elected?"

"Teddy Weller—to paraphrase infamous Charles Colson of Watergate fame—would shove his grandmother in front of a bus if he thought it would help him to get elected."

"You said he needed a miracle—some kind of huge scandal to derail Grayson—to win the primary. Do you think he might deliberately smear Grayson and try to plant some kind of incriminating evidence against him, even if he knew it wasn't true?"

"In a heartbeat."

"So, basically," I said, "you got two guys who would go to any lengths to win?"

"I think that sums up the situation pretty well."

"Beautiful."

"Clare, that's what makes politics so much fun to cover."

CHAPTER 10

MAGGIE LANG SAID she needed to talk to me urgently when I got back to the station.

"I assigned someone to check out the records for the motorcycle thing in Mountainboro," she said when we met in my office. "I thought there might be a lead for a good follow-up story to your Anne Devlin interview. I didn't find anything too interesting there. No real trouble. Just the usual—a few busts for drugs, disturbing the peace, that sort of thing. But then we kept going, and we did find something that had happened in Mountainboro. A few years ago, a guy who owned some land not far from where the motorcycle gangs met sold it to a developer who wanted to build a mall there. They started digging and that's when it happened."

"They found a body buried there?" I said.

It seemed like a logical guess.

"Six of them."

"Men? Women?"

"Six children. Three boys, three girls. Ages ran from six to thirteen."

"Could any of them have been . . ."

"Lucy Devlin? No. They identified all the remains through dental charts and missing persons records and stuff like that. There was a big federal task force involved. The feds coordinated the whole thing. It was a big deal for a while."

"Was there ever any suggestion there might be more bodies?"

"There was a massive search at the time. They dug up much of the area—everything they could get to, anyway. If there were any more bodies around there, no one ever found them."

"Did the investigators think the killer—or killers—murdered all six children at one time? Or maybe that it was a burial ground for a series of killings over a period of time?"

"Hard to say. The remains were too old to ascertain any kind of time of death. But the victims all seemed to have died of different kinds of injuries. Stabbing, beating, strangulation. Which suggests it wasn't just one killer, but a series of them. Or else someone who liked to vary their pattern from victim to victim."

"Maybe it was someone who lived in the area, who kept burying the bodies there every time he killed."

"Or someone who killed them somewhere, then dumped them all in this spot to avoid suspicion. For whatever it's worth, none of the victims had any local ties. No obvious reason they would have been killed in that area."

"And no one was ever caught?"

"That's right, the murders are all still unsolved."

She handed me a list with six names on it. Along with their ages, hometowns, and apparent cause of death.

As I read through them, I felt the adrenaline of a big story surging through me again. I make my living these days worrying mostly about summer diet specials and ratings sweeps weeks and audience demographics. But I was still a journalist at heart. I always tried to balance the fluff of TV news with the importance of real reporting. That's what I constantly tell the people who work for me. Just because you're in TV journalism, that doesn't mean you can't be a serious journalist, I say.

"Something's going on here," I said.

I didn't know that for a fact, of course. But every instinct I had as a newswoman told me Lucy Devlin was suddenly a big story again. After all these years, events had somehow been set in motion. Long-buried secrets were coming to the surface. Some people—like Anne Devlin, Big Lou, and whoever sent the e-mail—seemed to want it to happen. Others, like Patrick Devlin and maybe Elliott Grayson, may have had secrets to hide that they didn't want to come out. Me, I was somewhere in the middle. I wanted to know the answers, but I was afraid what some of them might be. You see, I had my own secrets, too.

* * *

After Maggie left, I sat down at my computer and Googled "Mountainboro" and "six bodies" and "missing children" and "task force" and a few other key words. I knew Maggie and her reporting team had already done that—but I still like to do my own reporting. A lot of hits came back from my search. The discovery of the bodies had been a big deal at the time in the New England press, which covered the story heavily.

The best thing about reporting is you never know exactly where it's going to take you. I mean, you think you know where a story is headed, and then you discover something completely unexpected.

That's what happened here.

I was reading an article from the *Boston Globe* about the discovery of the six children's bodies. It told how a contractor had seen a bone when he was digging in the area, then discovered the first skeletal remains. The local cops came in, saw the extent of the crime, and pretty soon the feds had set up a special task force and taken over the investigation. Like Maggie had said, the feds ran the entire operation.

Nothing much I didn't already know there.

Except that the newspaper article gave the name of the federal law enforcement official who handled the whole thing.

The head of the special task force.

His name wouldn't have had any special significance in connection with this story to Maggie and the reporters who'd done all the research.

Of course, they hadn't talked to Big Lou—and I hadn't told anyone else yet at the station about our conversation.

But I had, and the name—the federal official who oversaw the investigation into the discovery of the six children's bodies in Mountainboro, New Hampshire—practically jumped off the screen at me.

It was Elliott Grayson.

CHAPTER 11

THERE WAS A big picture of Elliott Grayson staring at me when I walked into the US Attorney's office near Foley Square. It was a campaign poster hanging over his assistant's desk. He looked good—handsome, charismatic, big friendly smile on his face. The words underneath were: "Tired of the same old excuses? Maybe it's time to find a new face." Below that, it said: "Vote Elliott Grayson for Senator."

"Nice teeth," I told Grayson's assistant.

"Excuse me?" she said, looking up from a computer screen she was staring at. The nameplate on her desk said Gwen Thompson. This must be the woman that I'd talked to on the phone.

"Your boss has nice teeth. That's important. I never trust a politician who has bad teeth. John Kennedy had great teeth. So did Bill Clinton. Barack Obama, too. Richard Nixon had terrible teeth. All the worst leaders in history have had bad oral hygiene. Adolf Hitler? Boy, you want to talk about bad breath! On the other hand, George Washington is the father of our country, and he had wooden teeth. So it doesn't always work. But, all things considered, I like big, healthy choppers in the person I vote for."

Gwen Thompson didn't say anything. She just stared at me with an impatient look on her face—and then finally asked what I wanted. I told her I was there to see Elliott Grayson for the

interview I'd scheduled. She said he'd be available in a few minutes. Then she went back to staring at her computer screen.

While I was waiting, I checked her out some more. Plain-
looking—mousy brown hair, unflattering glasses, and wearing a
loose-fitting dress that hid her figure. I decided she was a lonely
spinster who was devoted to her job and to Elliott Grayson. Hell,
she was probably in love with Grayson and fantasizing about him
all the time. Of course, she could also be a man-hating psycho
who was going to come in here one day and open up on Elliott
Grayson with an Uzi. Hey, you never know.

I'd brought a film crew with me. My plan was to pretend I was
there to tape a segment on Grayson's election campaign for the
Senate. I'd throw him a few softball questions and let him do his
campaign rhetoric for the camera. Once his guard was down,
I'd surprise him with questions about the motorcycle gang and
Lucy Devlin.

Gwen said Grayson was ready to see me and the film crew now,
and she ushered us into his office. It was a corner office with a
nice view of Lower Manhattan. There was a big old-fashioned
desk, with a plaque on it that said it was the same desk Thomas
Dewey used as a crime-busting New York district attorney before
he ran for President in the 1940s. There were pictures on the wall
of Grayson with all sorts of famous people.

Grayson himself was even more impressive than the office. He
was about my age, midforties—tall, good-looking, with wavy
brown hair and a nice body that looked like he worked out regularly. He walked over to me, stuck out his hand, and flashed me a
big smile. Just like the smile on his campaign poster outside.

"You're here to talk to me about my campaign?" he said.

"I want to know everything."

"You're really interested in politics?"

"I am the ultimate political junkie."

"Funny, but you don't look like the political type to me."

"Believe me, I can hardly wait to see how you do on Election Day in November."

"It's September."

"Whatever . . ."

We sat down and started going through the stock questions. I asked him about stuff like terrorism, health care, and federal budget cuts. While we talked, the Channel 10 film crew taped the whole thing. So far, everything was going according to plan.

Except for one thing.

I thought I caught him checking out my legs while I was asking him a question. Probably my imagination. But, just to make sure, I deliberately crossed and uncrossed my legs again before my next question. Same thing happened. This time I was sure I'd seen him sneaking a peek.

I smiled at him, and he smiled back. He knew I'd caught him looking, but he didn't care. My God, Elliott Grayson was flirting with me. I wasn't prepared for that. I did my best to plow ahead with the questioning as if nothing had happened.

Finally, after talking about political issues and his campaign strategy for ten or fifteen minutes, I decided it was time to switch gears and cleverly spring my trap.

"Mr. Grayson," I said suddenly, "were you ever a member of a motorcycle gang?"

"Of course," he replied without any hesitation.

"Excuse me?"

"I belonged to a motorcycle gang when I was younger. I loved motorcycles, and it just seemed like a cool thing to do. I only stayed for a short time. Then I began a career in law enforcement. I've never made any secrets of my motorcycle gang past. I was a little wild as a youth. I think it's good for politicians to admit they've lost their way sometimes, but eventually got back on the right path. That's why I've talked about it at times in my speeches and campaign literature. But I'm sure you know all that because of the research you did before you came here, right?"

"Absolutely," I lied.

Damn! Why hadn't I read anything about that? Probably because I was so intent on finding out something bad about Elliott Grayson, I hadn't followed the most basic rule of reporting: Keep digging.

"Do you remember attending a motorcycle convention back in those days in a place called Mountainboro, New Hampshire?" I asked.

"Sure, that happened every year back then. Hells Angels, Outlaws, Pagans, other motorcycle groups from around the country. It was kind of like a bikers' summit conference. I went to one of them. I've talked about that in interviews and speeches, too. Because that gathering was a real turning point for me. It wasn't long after that when I left the gang I was riding with back then."

This wasn't going exactly the way I had hoped. I needed to ask Grayson a question that he didn't know the answer to.

"Did you meet Lucy Devlin there?"

"Who?"

He wasn't looking at my legs anymore.

"Lucy Devlin. She disappeared here in New York City on her way to school, a few weeks before that motorcycle conference."

"Sure, I'm obviously familiar with the case. It's still an open file in our books."

"Did you see my TV interview with Lucy's mother recently?"

"Yes, I watched it."

"She said she got an e-mail from someone who claimed they saw a little girl that might have been Lucy on the back of a motorcycle with someone named Elliott there."

"And you think that Elliott was me?"

"Someone else identified you to me later as definitely being there. Said you had a little girl on the back of your motorcycle. And that this girl looked like Lucy Devlin. So, was Lucy Devlin with you?"

"Of course not."

"Were you with any little girl?"

"No."

"Then why would someone say you were?"

"Look, I have a very high profile in this job. I've put a lot of people away, made a lot of people mad at me. Now I'm running for the Senate. There are opponents of mine out there who don't like that either. It would make sense that someone's trying to smear me, to hurt me so I don't get elected. Right?"

He was right. That would make sense.

"A few years ago, the bodies of six children were found in a mass grave in that same small town of Mountainboro," I said. "You went back there again and supervised that investigation."

"I know."

"You know what?"

"I know I was there."

"Don't you think that's a pretty remarkable coincidence?"

"What's a coincidence?"

"You attended a biker gathering there. Someone saw a little girl who looked like Lucy Devlin with you. Later, the bodies of six missing children just like Lucy turn up in the same town, and you wind up being the guy who's in charge of the entire law enforcement operation. What do you make of that, Mr. Grayson?"

"I don't know, Clare. What do you make of it?"

He was smiling at me. He seemed more amused than upset by my questions.

"Well, I . . . I just think it all seems a little unusual."

"First, I never was with Lucy Devlin in Mountainboro or anywhere else. Second, none of those six bodies in the grave were Lucy Devlin or had anything to do with her case—so I'm not really sure what she has to do with any of this. Third, the biker convention I went to in Mountainboro was not the same year that Lucy Devlin disappeared, no matter what someone told you. By the time of the Lucy Devlin case, I was long gone from that world. In fact, I had already started working in law enforcement for the US Justice Department. You could have checked this all out before you showed up here."

Grayson looked at me intently now, like he was trying to make up his mind about something. Maybe it was whether to call security immediately and have me thrown out of his office.

"Let me ask you a question," he finally said. "I've done a lot of interrogating of people in my time. So I feel like I am some sort of an expert in this technique. What I don't understand is what you hoped to accomplish here with me. What did you think was going to happen? That you were just going to waltz in here and ask me a lot of softball questions about politics, then somehow get me to reveal some deep dark secret about my past? Like I was some kind of crazed biker bad guy or something? Is that what this was all about? I'm just curious. I'm really trying to get a handle on where you're coming from here."

"That was sort of the plan," I said softly.

"Not much of a plan."

There didn't seem to be much else to say. I stood up and started to signal to the film crew that the interview was over. They left and I stayed around for a minute to say good-bye to Grayson. I was pretty embarrassed by the way the whole thing had worked out. And I sure wasn't expecting what happened next.

"We should talk again sometime," Grayson said.

"Who?"

"You and me."

"About what?"

"Anything you want. Maybe we could even meet for coffee or a drink one night."

I'm very rarely speechless. But this was one of those times.

"Sure," I finally said.

He smiled. "I'll call you."

CHAPTER 12

"ELLIOTT GRAYSON ASKED you out?" my friend Janet Wood asked me.

"Sort of."

"Well, did he or didn't he?"

"I'm not sure."

"How can you not be sure?"

"You had to be there," I said.

Janet Wood is my closest confidante, the person I go to for advice about both my professional and personal problems. She's a successful lawyer with a big Manhattan firm, who handled all three of my divorce cases—which, as she loves to point out, is almost a full-time legal career. She's also my best friend, maybe the only real friend I have outside the newsroom. She actually started as a journalist, too. We met at the *Tribune*. But when newspapers began to go out of business, she went to law school instead of the unemployment line like so many other reporters. Janet is pretty damn smart. I trust her implicitly and I tell her everything. Well, almost everything.

We were sitting in a Starbucks near the Channel 10 offices. Janet was drinking black coffee, I had a large café mocha.

"So what exactly did Grayson say?" Janet asked.

"He asked me if I wanted to talk some more . . ."

"That could mean anything."

". . . over coffee or a drink or something one night."

"Coffee? A drink? Meeting at night? Yeah, that sounds like a date."

"I thought so, too."

She picked up her coffee and took a sip. She drank coffee like she did everything else—precise, well-thought out, always in control. Janet was married to a successful Wall Street broker. They had two adorable young daughters and they lived in a three-bedroom co-op apartment on the Hudson River. Her life seemed so perfect in every way that I sometimes wondered what her sex life was like. I couldn't even imagine her in bed with her husband, Bob. Some people are just too wholesome to think about stuff like that. On the other hand, once the bedroom door was closed, Janet and Bob might break out the whips and chains and kinky videos. Hell, you never know about people.

"Do you want to go out with him?" Janet asked.

"I'm not sure."

"Is he married?"

"No."

"A point in his favor."

"He does date a lot of famous starlets and models though, according to the gossip columns."

"No law against that."

"He could be a kidnapper, if you believe Big Lou and the e-mail Anne Devlin got," I pointed out.

"That might be problematic," she said.

"My instincts are telling me that a relationship with this guy—no matter how good-looking and successful he is—will be trouble."

"Your instincts with men haven't exactly always been infallible in the past," Janet pointed out.

"Fair point."

I picked up my own coffee, drank some, and sat there thinking some more about the plusses and minuses of plunging into a romantic relationship with Elliott Grayson. The plusses were he was good-looking, charming, and probably going to be a US Senator. The minuses were he could be a child kidnapper—or even a killer.

"What are you going to do?" Janet asked.

"Wait and see if he calls me."

"Or you could call him."

"The eternal dating dilemma," I said.

* * *

The interview with Grayson ran on the six-o'clock news that night. The edited version, of course.

Nothing about Lucy Devlin, because there was nothing there to report. So it just included the stuff about the Senate campaign. Him talking about the issues and the election and his record as a prosecutor. It was all very routine, very pedestrian.

Jack Faron came into my office after the newscast and asked me about the Lucy Devlin story. I'd told him about all the potential Elliott Grayson connections before I did the interview.

"Grayson said he never was with Lucy and doesn't know anything new about the case," I told him.

"Of course. What did you think he was going to say?"

I shrugged.

"I might talk to him one more time though."

"What for?"

"It was his idea. I figure maybe he wants to get me on his side for the campaign. I'll talk to him about that, but I'll keep pushing on the Lucy Devlin front, too. I'm still intrigued by the coincidence that Mountainboro, New Hampshire—where the e-mailer claimed to have seen Lucy—was the same place where Grayson dug up those six kids' bodies a few years later. I'll keep hunting for any other information about that motorcycle gathering and the children they found buried up there."

"Probably time to assign this to someone else."

"I said I'd do it myself."

"Clare—"

"It's my damn story!" I snapped at him. "And I'm not giving it up to anyone else here. I started this story, and I'm going to finish it."

Faron had a concerned look on his face.

"Why does this story mean so much to you, Clare?" Faron asked me. "Oh, I know all about your Pulitzer Prize and everything, your special relationship with Anne Devlin and how your name has always been associated with the Lucy Devlin story. But it just seems like there's more to it than that. I've never seen you react to a story like this, Clare. This one just seems so personal to you."

There were a lot of printouts and other material about the Lucy Devlin case spread out on my desk. One of them had a picture of Lucy.

"Look, I know it's a rule for a journalist never to get personally involved in a story," I said to Faron. "I really understand that you always have to keep a wall up between you and the people that you cover. You need to get into their lives, but don't ever let them get into yours. Otherwise, this job will eat you up alive. That's a rule I learned a long time ago—and I've taught it to a lot of young reporters since I came here."

I looked down at the picture of Lucy Devlin on my desk now. The wholesome little eleven-year-old girl with the big smile on her face. Thinking she had her whole life in front of her and all the time in the world to enjoy it. Without a clue of whatever terrible things were going to happen to her.

"But here's the other thing about that rule: It's all bullshit. Sooner or later, a story comes along that's so big and so powerful for you that it sucks you in emotionally and it becomes personal."

"Is that what happened to you with Lucy Devlin?" he asked.

I nodded.

"I got personally involved in this story a long time ago, Jack. And I guess I still am."

CHAPTER 13

THE NAMES OF the six young bodies found near where the motorcycle convention had been held in Mountainboro were:

Joseph Manielli
Emily Neiman
William O'Shaughnessy
Tamara Greene
Donald Chang
Becky Gale

Three girls, three boys. One of them was black, one Asian, one Jewish, one Irish, one Italian, and one a combination of several ethnic backgrounds. Whoever killed them was not motivated by race or religion, that was clear. This was an equal opportunity killer.

I gathered background material on the cases from online and other places—and then spent a lot of time going through all of it. The pictures were the toughest to take. Headshots of all of them looking cute and adorable before something terrible happened and they disappeared into that lonely grave.

Tamara Greene was the youngest at six, Donald Chang the oldest at thirteen. The rest were various ages falling in between the two. I'd always assumed that someone who preyed on young children had a fixation on a particular age. Or sex. A six-year-old girl was sure a lot different than a thirteen-year-old boy. This could mean there was more than one killer. Or that there was a series of killings, at different times and different places by different people, with the bodies all being dumped together for some reason. Or it was a single killer who played by his own rules.

There was no geographic pattern that I could discern. Becky Gale was from New Jersey; Tamara Greene from Ohio; Joseph Manielli from Pennsylvania; William O'Shaughnessy from Florida; Emily Neiman from Texas; and Donald Chang from Southern California. I plotted them all on a map and then drew lines between each location, looking for some kind of clue. There was nothing. Whoever did this would have had to crisscross the country to find his victims.

The children had all gone missing long before the bodies were found. All within a few years of the Lucy Devlin disappearance. Just like with Lucy, there had been reports of sightings after that, but never any confirmed accounts.

The bodies were too far decomposed to determine an official cause of death. But the medical examiner determined that all of the children had been beaten—and some appeared to have been strangled or stabbed. In any case, the IDs were eventually established by investigators who painstakingly cross-checked against nationwide missing kids' reports, and the parents received the sad news that the search for their children had ended.

Over the years, a few suspects had been questioned about some of the individual cases, but no one was ever arrested. All of the cases were still open.

One of the newspaper articles was about Elliott Grayson, the man who'd been in charge of the digging operation and subsequent investigation. It was a glowing profile, describing him as a hard-nosed but compassionate law enforcement official who agonized over the fate of the children he'd uncovered. There's no question the case had been a career maker for him. Six months after that, he was promoted to a big job in the New York office. He later became Deputy US Attorney, then moved into the top spot a few years later. Since then, he'd gone after drug lords, mob figures, and corporate scammers with such success that it had elevated him to political stardom.

Six bodies had been found at the site in New Hampshire. That didn't mean there weren't more. Authorities said they'd checked, but they couldn't dig up the whole town. Even more distressing was the idea that there could be a series of these burial grounds across the country, which no one had ever found. What if there were tens or hundreds more bodies who'd been killed by the same person?

* * *

I knew a guy in the FBI. His name was Gary Belton.

When I say I knew Belton, I mean in the biblical sense. We'd met on a story a few years ago when I was in between marriages— and I had slept with him a number of times. We had a great time together. Good sex and good conversation, too. We talked about a lot of things in bed and out of bed.

Unfortunately, the one thing Belton didn't talk about was the fact that he was married. When I found out, I told him I didn't want to sleep with him anymore. He took this news very badly, which I assumed was a compliment to me—sexually speaking. Anyway, I hadn't talked to him since then.

"What do you want?" he asked when I got him on the phone.

"I need some information."

"And why would I give you information?"

"Because we're old friends?"

"Okay, how friendly do you want to be?"

"What does that mean?"

"Maybe we could get together again one night."

"Like old times?"

"Sure, what do you think, friend?"

"Will you be bringing your wife this time?"

"I'm not married anymore."

"Really?"

"Yep, I'm a single man now."

"You wouldn't be just saying that to get me into bed with you?"

"Honest, Barbara and I got divorced right after I stopped seeing you."

"Maybe I should call her up and offer my condolences."

"Don't do that!"

"Why not?"

There was a long pause.

"Okay, I'm still married." He sighed.

"I knew that," I said.

I told him about the graves in New Hampshire and the six kids. I asked him if he could check to see if any similar clustering of bodies had been found anywhere in the country. He hemmed and hawed a bit, but eventually agreed. He also gave me some other facts and figures that startled me.

"More than eight hundred thousand children go missing every year," he said. "Most of them are found in a day or two, but some aren't. A lot of them eventually turn up, of course. But the rest just disappear off the face of the earth. Maybe three hundred children a year fall into that category—they just walk out of the door one day and never return. You have to figure that many of them are dead. The parents keep on hoping for a miracle, of course. What else can they do? But they know, as well as we do, what the odds are. Once a kid's gone for any length of time, he's as good as dead. Or worse. Even if you find that child, it won't be the same child that you remember."

"Let's say one person killed all six of the kids in New Hampshire," I said. "What are the odds that he's killed others, too?"

"Well, six is a big number. I mean someone could kill once and never do it again. But if he killed six times . . . let's just say I don't think he would have stopped. No, there's more bodies out there somewhere. Unless he's dead or he's in jail, that is. If he isn't, the toll is higher than six. There's one other thing, too . . ."

"He's still killing," I said.

"Absolutely."

After I hung up with Belton, I looked again at the pictures of the six dead children found in New Hampshire.

Joey Manielli, Becky Gale, Donald Chang, Emily Neiman, William O'Shaughnessy, and Tamara Greene.

All six of them were smiling in the photos.

All six of them looked happy.

None of them seemed to have any hint that they had so little time left in their short lives.

Just like Lucy Devlin.

CHAPTER 14

THERE WAS A story meeting the next day in Jack Faron's office. Me, Maggie, Brett, Dani.

Cassie and Janelle were there. A handful of other editors and writers and on-air reporters, too. The goal was to come up with some enterprise ideas to cover in the upcoming weeks leading up to summer.

"How about an end of school series?" Brett asked. "Prom fashions, tips on studying for finals, advice on getting summer jobs—that sort of thing."

"We could do a shape up for the beach special," Dani said. "For all the viewers who promised to lose weight for the New Year, but never did. Now we tell them how to diet and exercise and get rid of some of those excess pounds before Memorial Day."

"Let's do something on day trips people can take right now before their summer vacations," Cassie suggested. "Amusement parks, local beaches, camping trips. Short jaunts when things aren't that crowded yet."

This was all what I liked to call the "ratings bait" stuff we do in TV news. High interest, short attention span required, quick hits on things like weight loss, fashion advice, vacation tips. This was the bread and butter of TV news—especially during the big ratings sweeps periods.

We weren't breaking any major news here, exposing any kind of secret wrongdoing, making a contribution to fighting climate control, or battling air pollution or anything else to better the world and the human race. It was just entertainment, plain and simple.

But, every once in a while, there is a chance to do a meaningful story on television amid all this fluff.

That's what I wanted to do now.

"Let's talk about Lucy Devlin," I said.

Brett shrugged. "We've already interviewed the mother," he said. "You could try the father again, but he wouldn't talk to you last time. Your Elliott Grayson tip didn't go anywhere, which wasn't exactly a surprise. I'm not sure where else there is to go with it, Clare."

"What about all the other missing kids out there?" I said. "Lucy's just one of thousands of them who disappear every year. Let's look at a few of them. Some of the others out there just like Lucy Devlin. Who are they, what happened to them, what was the effect on their families and friends and classmates? We could even do a series. It might be very powerful television."

"Okay," he said. "That could work."

"I agree," Maggie said. "We take a hard look at the six bodies that were found up in New Hampshire. The ones in that little town where someone thought they once saw Lucy Devlin and where Grayson supervised the digging up of the mass grave. That way we could still keep him as part of the story, too, since he is running for the Senate. Tell the viewers how he found out the tragic fate of these six other tragic Lucy Devlin–like children. All the emotion Anne Devlin and everyone felt over little Lucy . . . well, all six of these families must have undergone the same thing. All we have to do is tell their story. Plus, we can still keep Lucy as the peg for it all. That way we can include her, and keep that story going, too."

Faron nodded. "That's not bad," he said.

"Not bad?" I asked.

"Okay, it's pretty damn good."

It was a victory for real journalism amid the clutter of the TV news landscape. But only a small victory. After that, we went back to discussing the normal business of what goes on behind the scenes of a TV news show. We had recently changed the set a bit—part of my "keep them moving" strategy that had worked so well for us in the ratings thus far. Instead of the traditional look of just two anchors sitting behind a desk to read the news, the plan now was to have them move over to a living room setting— complete with a big couch and some comfortable chairs—to interview people and discuss some of the events of the day. Also, a TV consulting firm we hired to make suggestions about the show thought it made the anchors seem more personal and more human and more likeable.

The problem was we were now going to be seeing a lot more of Brett and Dani than ever before, and again, not just from the waist up like traditional TV anchor people.

"We need to figure out the right length of skirt Dani should wear," Faron said at one point. "The skirts need to be short enough to keep the viewers interested, but not too short to get the religious groups and parents organizations and God knows who else mad at us for X-rated TV."

"Are we really having a discussion here about the length of Dani's skirt?" someone asked.

"This could have a big effect on our ratings," Faron pointed out.

"How about we just put her in hot pants and blow the roof off the Nielson meters?" I said.

"I'm looking for some serious suggestions here, Clare."

"Okay, how about we put Brett in hot pants then?"

"Oh, God," Dani said, "I can just hear the sound of TV sets being clicked off all over New York City."

"Laugh if you want," Brett said, "but you're just jealous because I'm going to be a bigger sex symbol than you."

It was finally decided that Dani's skirt should be well above the knee without showing too much of her thigh. I just let the rest of them figure it all out. Sure, I was the news editor, but I wasn't in the mood for this kind of discussion right now. I wanted to concentrate on the real news. The news about Lucy Devlin.

* * *

My phone was ringing when I got back to my own office. It was Gwen, Elliott Grayson's assistant.

"Mr. Grayson would like to have another meeting with you later this week," she said.

He's having his assistant make the appointment for him? That sure didn't sound like a personal date.

"He suggests meeting you for a drink and/or possible dinner tomorrow night, if you're free for that," Gwen said.

On the other hand, a drink and dinner did sound very personal.

"I'd love to," I said.

"Let me check Mr. Grayson's schedule, and I will get back to you or someone in your office with more specific information about the appointment," she said. "Is that satisfactory, Ms. Carlson?"

Damn. Could this woman be any more officious?

"Sure," I said. "Just have your people talk to my people—and we'll make this sucker happen."

After I hung up, I clicked on my computer and Googled Elliott Grayson's name. I read through some more material about him. I wanted to be prepared this time before I met him again. Most of the stuff was the same PR crap I'd read before. Elliott Grayson was a dogged crime fighter, a rising young star, he had a big political future . . . blah, blah, blah. The list of Elliott Grayson items was a long one. Just for the hell of it, I started cross-referencing it online in the search engine with some other names. I tried Lucy Devlin. Anne Devlin. The cops who handled the Devlin case. The Warlock Warriors. Finally, I tried Patrick Devlin. There was one listing for both men. It was from a political website called ElectGraysonforSenate.com. There was a picture of Elliott Grayson and Patrick Devlin shaking hands at a fund-raiser dinner. The caption said: "Elliott Grayson thanks Patrick Devlin, head of the Boston-based Devlin Construction Corp., for his generous contribution to the Senate campaign."

Elliott Grayson and Patrick Devlin knew each other.

Another coincidence.

Just like it had been a coincidence Grayson was the one who dug up the six kids' bodies in Mountainboro.

Sure were a lot of coincidences in this case.

CHAPTER 15

NOTHING IS EVER what it seems.

When I'd looked at the picture of Joey Manielli—one of the six dead children found in the grave—I envisioned another Lucy Devlin. An adorable kid from an all-American family whose lives would never recover from the terrible tragedy of losing a child that way. But the reality turned out to be a lot different.

The Manielli family lived in a trailer park outside Allentown, Pennsylvania. That was about a two-hour drive from New York City. I went the next morning in a Channel 10 van with a film crew.

Janis Manielli, Joey's mother, was sitting on a lawn chair in front of the trailer when we got there, drinking from a can of beer. She was wearing a loose-fitting housecoat that couldn't hide the fact she was seriously overweight.

It was barely eleven a.m., but the beer she was drinking was probably not her first can of the morning. I surmised that by the empty cans scattered around her chair. Also by the way she slurred her words as she spoke. Then there was the belching. The first one I thought was just an accident. I expected her to excuse herself, but she didn't. After a while, I realized it was a pattern as natural to her as breathing. She'd take a big swig of beer, talk for a while, and then let another belch rip.

"That kid was always trouble," she said now about her dead son. "Missing school, running away, pissing off me and his father. A real pain in the ass. I mean I tried to be a good mother, but you know"—she belched loudly— "there's only so much you can do."

"How old was he?" I asked.

"Twelve."

"It's kind of hard to imagine him being that much of a trouble-maker when he was only twelve."

"Sometimes kids are just no good."

She reached under the lawn chair and pulled out another beer. There was a case of them there. She did not offer any to me or my film crew. More for her that way.

"Tell me about Joey," I said.

"What's to tell?" She shrugged. "He's dead."

"Do you know what happened?"

"The police said someone abducted him. Or maybe he went willingly. Then they killed him."

"Did you call the police right away once you realized he was missing?"

"Nah, we waited for about a week or so."

"Why?"

"Just figured he'd run away. Did that a couple of times before. Once he even stole a car and made it all the way to Delaware. The cops arrested him, and we had to go down to the station house to pick him up. Damn kid's only twelve, and he's already stealing cars. Most of the time when he ran away, he came back when he got hungry or tired enough. Then his father would whip his butt, and that would be it until the next time. Only this time he never came back."

"What made you eventually decide to call the police?"

"The welfare lady."

"What do you mean?"

"The welfare lady came out here one day to check on us. Since we couldn't find Joey, she said we wouldn't get paid for him. I told her he'd run away. She said I should report it to the police as an official missing persons case. That way we could still get our money. So that's what I did."

"Right," I said casually, as if her answer was the most logical one in the world.

"Anyway, the cops never found out anything about Joey for a long time. After a while, we just sort of forgot about him. Then one day these federal agents showed up at the door with the local police. They said they'd found his body in New Hampshire somewhere with a bunch of other kids. They think some pervert killed him."

She casually took another swig of her beer and belched loudly, as if she she'd just finished talking about losing the family dog.

After a while, we just sort of forgot about him?

"What do you remember about the last time you saw Joey?" I asked.

"I don't know . . . it was a long time ago."

"What did he say?"

"Something like . . . 'Ma, I'm going down to the highway.'"

"The highway?"

"He liked to go down to the highway that passes by about a half mile from here."

"What did he do there?"

"He watched the trucks."

"That's all?"

"Like I said, he was a weird kid."

"Did he have any friends that he might have confided in?"

"I don't remember."

"You don't remember if he had any friends?"

"I really didn't pay that much attention."

"If there's anyone at all you can think of . . ."

She shook her head no. "I never noticed who he was with."

The door of the trailer slammed and a big man wearing a sleeveless t-shirt and cutoff shorts came out. Ralph Manielli, Joey's father. He had several days' worth of stubble on his face and scratched his crotch as he looked first at us, then at his wife.

"Are these the TV people who were supposed to come here today?" he asked her.

"No, asshole, this is the Avon lady taking a picture of me. Of course it's the TV people asking me about Joey. Who the hell do you think it would be anyway?"

"Why didn't you wake me up?"

"I tried."

"I don't remember."

"That's because you were out drinking all night with those drunken friends of yours."

Ralph Manielli didn't deny the accusation. Instead he looked down at the beer cans under her chair.

"Is that my beer?"

"It's my beer, too."

"How come you're drinking it this early in the morning?"

"Nothing better to do."

"Why don't you go inside and clean up our place for once in your life, you lazy bitch?" His voice angry now. "I'm tired of living in a pigsty."

"Clean it yourself," she said, opening another can of the beer. "Hell, you've got time. I mean it's not like you've got a job or anything."

Manielli moved menacingly toward her with his fists clenched. For a second, I thought he was going to hit her. I wasn't sure what to do if that happened and exchanged worried glances with the members of my film crew. But he thought better of it and stopped.

"You better stay away from me," his wife said. "You remember what the sheriff said the last time you beat me. One more time, and you're going to jail. I'll call the cops and swear out a complaint if you lay a hand on me."

"Ain't going to jail again," he muttered, as he reached down and took one of the beers. "Ain't worth it for the likes of you."

He didn't know much more about what happened to Joey than his wife did. He remembered giving him a beating a few days before he disappeared for something or other, he couldn't remember exactly what it was. Then it was all kind of a blur until the authorities told them they'd found the body.

"He was always a bad kid," Manielli said. "He did everything wrong. It doesn't surprise me that he wound up getting himself killed that way."

After we left, I asked the guy driving the van to stop by the highway for a minute. The highway where Joey Manielli had gone that last day before he disappeared.

Sitting there, watching the traffic pass by, I wondered what it must have been like for little Joey. Living in a place like this. Getting beaten up regularly by his father—and probably his mother, too. Growing up without knowing what it felt like to be loved. He was only twelve years old, but maybe he imagined that there must be a better world out there somewhere.

So he came down here to the highway and looked at the trucks and dreamed of being on one of them and driving far away from here. Maybe someone stopped and took advantage of this. Maybe he even got into the truck or the car with them voluntarily. *Nothing could be worse than the world I live in now*, he might have thought to himself as he made the fateful decision.

But he was wrong.

He was an unhappy, confused little twelve-year-old boy who dreamed about a better life somewhere else.

One way or another, that dream turned into a nightmare.

CHAPTER 16

BECKY GALE HAD lived in Princeton, New Jersey. That was less than a hundred miles away from Joey Manielli and the trailer park in Allentown, but it seemed like a million miles' difference between the two places.

Princeton was everything an Ivy League college town should be—quiet tree-lined streets, quaint shops, students spread out reading on the campus green. The Gales' house was on a cul-de-sac about a half mile from the heart of town. There were two cars in the driveway and a swimming pool in the back. From the front porch, you could see woods, a nearby lake, and some of the buildings on the Princeton campus.

Victoria Gale, Becky's mother, was no Janis Manielli either. She answered the door wearing a fashionable pantsuit, all made up and with her hair carefully combed. Inside, the house was immaculate and—by my standards—expensively furnished. There was a big picture of Jesus Christ on the coffee table and a painting of Jesus on the cross hanging from the wall. I assumed the Gales must be a religious family. I wondered idly if that had happened before or after their daughter was murdered. Mrs. Gale offered me some iced tea and what appeared to be freshly baked cookies. I sipped on the tea and ate a cookie while the crew set up for the interview around me.

"Have you lived here for a long time, Mrs. Gale?" I asked.

"Yes, it's a wonderful area."

"Does your husband work for the college?"

"Oh, no." She laughed. "We'd never been able to afford this house if he had. Professors and academics don't get rich, I'm afraid. My husband was a financial investor. He worked for Dow Jones for a while, then went out on his own. Started his own company. He went to Princeton University, though. That's how we first moved here after we were married."

"Where is he now?"

"Oh, Paul died several years ago."

"I'm sorry. I didn't know. All the articles at the time they identified your daughter's body talked about the two of you . . ."

"It was a blessing really when he went. He had bone cancer. A nasty disease. He was in a lot of pain at the end." She looked over at the picture of Jesus on the coffee table in front of us. "I was grateful to the Lord for taking him to heaven."

She said it almost by rote, like it was a refrain that she had uttered many times before. She picked up her tea, took a sip, and smiled at me.

I smiled back.

"Did you have any other children besides Becky?" I asked.

"Yes, Becky had a sister. Samantha. She lives in New York now. Becky was a year older. Actually, Becky's birthday would be coming up now if . . ."

Her voice trailed off slowly and she looked again at the Jesus picture as if it could somehow give her comfort.

"I'm sorry for your loss, Mrs. Gale," I said, not knowing what else to tell her.

"God has a plan for us all," she said. "We just have to be strong and trust Him and keep our faith in the Almighty."

The camera was ready now. I did the interview with Mrs. Gale about her daughter Becky. She told me how Becky had gone off to have a piano lesson on that fateful day. When she didn't come home, the Gales called the police. The piano teacher said he never saw her. He was interrogated relentlessly by the cops, but eventually passed a lie detector test. They tracked her route from the Gale house to the piano teacher's place, no more than a quarter of a mile. No one saw anything. No one heard anything. No one knew anything. Becky Gale simply walked out of her house one day and then disappeared. Just like Lucy Devlin.

"We always held out hope," she said. "My husband used to say that one day we would find her and she'd be all right. But she wasn't, of course. The police came here a few years ago and told us about finding her body. They said she had been . . ."

Her voice broke now and she began to cry. She sobbed for a few minutes. The cameras got it all. It was great TV, but I felt uncomfortable. It was as if this woman had let her guard down and let me get a glimpse of her that she didn't show the world very often.

She pulled herself together then. She asked me if I had any other questions. There didn't seem to be much else to say. We already had the money shot of her crying, so I just shut the cameras down.

While the crew was packing up their gear, I tried to make some small talk with Mrs. Gale to fill the time.

"It's hard to imagine something so terrible happening in a wonderful place like this," I said, looking at the pristine neighborhood outside her living room window.

"Sometimes evil comes from where you least expect," she said.

Suddenly Mrs. Gale began to cry again.

Talking about her daughter during the interview had obviously brought a lot of long-buried emotions to the surface again.

"Sometimes I just don't understand," she said. "This was a good house. A God-fearing house. Paul and I and the girls went to church every Sunday. We read the Bible regularly to them. We always taught them right from wrong. But now Paul is gone. And Becky too. I'm all alone."

"What about your other daughter?" I asked.

"Samantha?"

"Yes, you said she lived in New York. Do you see her often?"

Mrs. Gale shook her head sadly. "Samantha and I haven't talked in years."

"Why is that?" I asked.

"I had such high hopes for my daughters. They were both so bright, they loved to read, they did well in school. I wanted them to go to college at Princeton one day, just like their father. But then suddenly Becky was gone and after that . . . well, Samantha was never the same. Her grades fell off, she started to run with the wrong crowd, and she even tried to run away a few times. As soon as she was old enough, she did move out and went to New York City. She never comes back here. She won't return my phone calls. She sends back my letters unopened. I've lost her, too. Just like I lost Becky."

I thought again about the way Patrick and Anne Devlin's marriage had fallen apart after Lucy disappeared. The loss of a child frequently has far-reaching repercussions that we don't realize until much later. The family can never be the same. It leaves behind a wound that time can ease a bit, but never truly heal.

"I know God has a reason for putting me through all of this," she said, looking one more time at the picture on the wall. "He has a reason for everything. There must be a purpose, an explanation for what has happened. I have to believe that. I have to have faith in His eternal wisdom. I have to accept that there is a reason for everything that takes place in His kingdom. Don't you agree?"

I wasn't sure what to say to her.

Because I didn't see any reason for any of this.

No reason at all.

I left Victoria Gale there all alone in the big empty house with her memories.

*   *   *

I went online and made a lot of phone calls when I got back to New York to track down information about the other four kids in that New Hampshire grave from their families and teachers and friends around the country.

Donald Chang had gone to an arcade near the Santa Monica pier in California and was last seen playing one of the machines there. Someone thought they spotted him talking to an older man, but no one ever confirmed that. He never came home that night. Like Anne Devlin, his parents had spent years putting up posters and chasing down false leads until they finally got the news that his body had been uncovered.

Tamara Greene was on a school outing when she disappeared. She lived in Elyria, Ohio, just outside of Cleveland. Her class had taken a school bus into Cleveland for a tour of the historical museum there. The teacher remembered her going into the museum with the rest of the class. But, when they reassembled by the bus a few hours later, she was gone. A massive search turned up no evidence about what happened to her. Her parents later filed a lawsuit against the local school board for negligence in her disappearance.

William O'Shaughnessy went missing on a Florida beach not far from his house. He'd bicycled over there with a group of friends on a hot summer day. At first, everyone assumed he must have gone into the water and drowned. But his bicycle was missing, too, and he was positively identified by a vendor who sold him an ice cream cone later that day. The vendor said the O'Shaughnessy boy was with a man who acted as if he were his father. But the father had been at work all day, and the identity of the mystery man was never resolved. A few years ago, William O'Shaughnessy's father had gone into the garage, turned on the ignition of his car, and committed suicide by carbon monoxide poisoning. People said he'd never gotten over the loss of his son.

Emily Neiman disappeared from a Houston mall while her mother was trying on a skirt in one of the shops. The mother was only inside the dressing room for a minute or two, but there was no sign of Emily in the chair where she'd left her. The family hired private detectives, put up posters all over the Houston area, and got volunteers to conduct massive searches for their daughter— all to no avail. "I'll never give up hope," the mother said in interviews. "Never, no matter how long it takes. I know she's out there somewhere and she wants to come home." There was an article in the Houston paper a few years later about how the mother had left Emily's bedroom and possessions untouched ever since then, waiting for her to return one day. That waiting ended when her body was discovered with the others in New Hampshire.

By the time I was finished with the calls, I had plenty of facts on all six kids. Plenty of stuff to do the soft feature piece I'd promised Faron for our newscast. But that was all I had.

I couldn't figure out any connection between the six deaths— how they all wound up in that single grave in rural New Hampshire.

I couldn't figure out any connection between them and Lucy Devlin's disappearance either.

And I couldn't figure out what any of this could possibly have to do with Elliott Grayson.

CHAPTER 17

THE TOWNHOUSE WHERE the Devlins had lived was between Third Avenue and a quiet little street called Irving Place. There were trees and bushes out front and a walkway with a metal gate that took you up to the front door. It was a peaceful, pleasant-looking neighborhood. Not the type of place you'd expect to have been the scene for one of New York City's most infamous crimes.

I'd gone back to it just to get the feel of that day when Lucy Devlin walked out the door on her way to school and was never seen again. Looking for some sort of inspiration, I suppose. I wanted to see the house again and trigger whatever memories it might still hold after all these years.

The person living there now was named Liz Girabaldi. I knew that because I'd checked the listing from the office.

I stood there staring at the house for a long time. The sun was shining, but there was a chill in the air. The weather forecast said the temperature was going to go below freezing tonight, and we might even get snow. Springtime in New York is always like that—Mother Nature teases you with a few nice days, then throws some more winter at you. I thought about how nice it would be if I were someplace warm like Southern California right now. I thought about how nice it would be if I were in Miami Beach or the Bahamas. I thought about how nice it would be if I were anywhere else instead of standing in front of Lucy Devlin's old building.

I pushed open the metal gate, walked up the steps, and knocked on the front door. A woman who looked to be in her late twenties answered. She had frizzy blond hair, and she was wearing blue jeans and a white blouse, which were covered with a plastic smock. The smock had splotches of paint on it. She was carrying a small paintbrush in her hand. Probably an artist, I decided.

"Liz Girabaldi?"

"Yes."

I told her who I was.

"I have a strange favor to ask. I'd like to come inside for a few minutes and look around your house. I know this probably doesn't make any sense to you, but I'm . . ."

"This is about Lucy Devlin, right?"

"You know?"

"Sure. I didn't know when I bought the place. The real estate agent conveniently neglected to tell me before I closed the deal. But pretty soon people started coming around, just like you today, because this is almost like a tourist attraction. Home of the little girl who vanished. To be honest, I've actually come to believe it's a good thing. I mean it probably will raise the property value for this place if I want to sell it. Anyway, you might as well come in and take the tour."

I followed her down a hallway and into the living room. The place looked different, of course, with new furniture and a new color of paint on the walls and even a new fireplace I didn't remember being there before. But the basics were still the same. A living room and kitchen and small study that Patrick Devlin used for his office on the first floor. The bedrooms were upstairs, one for the Devlins and the other for Lucy.

I thought about the last time I'd been inside the Devlins' house. It had probably been that day I made the tearful vow to Anne Devlin that I'd never forget about the search for her daughter, no matter what. I tried to imagine Lucy in this house. As a little girl, playing amid a loving family. Did she have any premonition of something bad happening that last day? Or was she blissfully unaware until the end of the evil that existed in the world?

I walked upstairs to the bedrooms. I went into the one that used to belong to Lucy first. Liz Girabaldi had converted it to an artist's studio. But when I closed my eyes, I saw Lucy in there—playing video games, watching TV and doing her homework. I walked around the room with a purposeful air, as if I knew what I was looking for. But, of course, I didn't. There was nothing there for me.

The main bedroom was different, too. I remembered the Devlins had it filled with pictures of them as a family. Anne and Patrick with Lucy at Disneyworld or at the beach or just playing with a dog in the neighborhood.

Now the walls were covered with art, mostly pictures of landscapes and street scenes. I assume they were Liz Girabaldi's. The only picture was one of Girabaldi and another woman with their arms around each other. I also noticed there were two end tables, one at each side of the bed. The first one had a book about art theory lying on it, the other a Sandra Brown novel. I'd noticed two sets of everything in the bathroom, too. Probably Liz Girabaldi lived with someone. Maybe the woman in the picture. Maybe they were a lesbian couple.

Not that it mattered, but I couldn't help but be aware of stuff like that. I thought of them making love in this same room where Patrick and Anne Devlin had once slept. Anne had said Lucy had talked about her father wanting to have sex right before she disappeared. I tried to block that thought out of my mind, but the image was too strong. I got out of the bedroom in a hurry and went back downstairs.

I opened the back door onto the yard behind the town house. It was surrounded by a big wooden fence that always made it seem like a bucolic spot secluded away from the hustle and bustle of New York City. I remembered that fifteen years ago when I'd been here, Anne Devlin had an overflowing garden in this yard that she painstakingly maintained. Now the garden was gone, and it was just a backyard. Liz Girabaldi must not be into gardening. Or maybe Anne gave up on the garden herself before they sold the house once her daughter was gone. A lot of stuff changes in fifteen years.

"Find what you were looking for?" Liz Girabaldi asked.

"I'm not even sure what that was."

"Did you know the little girl that lived here?"

"I covered the story."

"And now you're covering it again."

"In a way, it never really ended for me."

She asked me if I wanted any coffee. I said sure. I didn't really want coffee, but I wanted to spend a few more minutes in this house where Lucy Devlin had once lived.

"You're an artist?" I asked after we sat down.

"That's right."

"You make a living doing that?"

"Not yet, but I'm hopeful."

I looked around the apartment. I pretended like I was interested in her paintings, but the truth is I don't know a damn thing about art.

"Not that it's any of my business, but how do you afford a Manhattan town house like this as a struggling artist?"

"My father paid for it."

"Why?"

"He believes in me as an artist."

"So, you get to paint pretty pictures all day and your father pays the bills?"

"Something like that."

"Nice work if you can get it."

"Well, I guess we can't all do something as socially significant as working for a television show."

"Good point." I smiled.

She took a big sip of her coffee. There was something she wanted to say.

"I think about her sometimes," she said. "That little girl who lived in this house. It's like I can almost sense her presence. Or at least I think I can sense her there. It's an eerie feeling, but nice, too. Not a scary ghost, more like a friendly one. Do you think there's any possibility that she's still alive?"

"No . . . yes . . . I'm not sure."

"If she were alive, I wonder what she'd do. What if she decided to come home? I mean, the last home she remembers as a little girl would be this one, right? Where would she go? I mean, I might open up my door one day, just like I did to you today, and Lucy Devlin could be standing there."

"If that happens," I said to Liz Girabaldi, "be sure you call me first."

* * *

I was supposed to meet Elliott Grayson for our drinks date that night. I had a little time to kill before that.

So, after I left Liz Girabaldi at the town house, I walked toward Third Avenue where Anne Devlin had put her eleven-year-old daughter on a school bus. Taking the same route that Lucy and her mother did on that fateful morning. I tried to pretend I was her, looking at the trees and the cars and the street as I walked. Were those the last images Lucy ever had?

By the time I got to Third Avenue, the last place anyone saw her alive, I realized I was shaking.

Not out of emotion, but because the temperature had really dropped while I was inside that house. The snow was definitely coming. People around me were bundled up in fur coats and scarves.

It was cold.

Very cold.

Just like the trail for Lucy Devlin.

CHAPTER 18

THE SNOW HAD begun to fall by the time I left to meet Grayson for our date—or whatever the hell it was. It started as a light dusting, but when I got to the bar, the streets were already covered in white. I was wearing a coat, but it was a thin spring one—and I was completely unprepared for snow. I also had absolutely no idea what I was going to say to Grayson when I got there. All in all, I was not exactly ready for prime time here.

The bar he'd picked was one of the trendy spots in SoHo. The kind of place where the prices are so high that the only people who can afford to go there are on big expense accounts. On top of that, it was almost impossible to get into. There was always a line of people outside, and the wait could last for hours.

I didn't have to wait, though. Grayson had left someone at the door to let me in. I was whisked past the masses outside and led into the bar area. Grayson was waiting for me there, surrounded by a group of advisers and onlookers. He moved away from them when he saw me coming, leading me to a corner table where we could be alone.

I ordered a gin and tonic. He was drinking bourbon straight up.

"Some weather," he said.

"Unbelievable weather," I agreed.

"Snow in April. I mean, it's supposed to be April showers bring May flowers."

"I just wore a new spring outfit yesterday."

"Did you ever see weather like this?"

"I think I remember walking in the snow one April day a long time ago."

"No kidding?"

"Actually, it might have been in March."

"Okay."

"And it might not have been real snow . . . maybe just sleet or a frozen rain."

"Right."

"As a matter of fact, I might just be remembering something I saw in a movie once."

I'd pretty much run out of things to say about the weather at this point.

"I watched your piece about me on TV," Grayson said. "It was good. Although I must say that the actual interview in my office that day was even more . . . well, interesting."

There was something I wanted to know.

"I think—and correct me if I'm wrong—that you were checking me out during that interview."

"What are you talking about?"

"You were looking at my legs."

"I was not looking at your legs."

"Oh, you were looking at my legs."

"Can you prove that?" He smiled.

"Actually, I can—the whole thing is on video."

"Are you telling me that you went back to that video and watched it just to see if I was indeed looking at your legs, as you somehow suspected I was?"

"Yes," I admitted.

"What did the video show?"

"It was kind of inconclusive."

"I rest my case." He laughed. "Look, your legs are extremely attractive. Very nice legs. You should be damn proud of those legs, Clare. But I've seen a lot of good-looking legs in my time. I mean, as great as your legs are, they're not keeping me up at night or anything. Okay?"

"Okay. Glad we got that cleared up."

I decided it was time to try and cleverly segue into another topic.

"Let's talk about you and Patrick Devlin," I said.

"Lucy Devlin's father?"

"Yes."

"You're still hung up on this Lucy Devlin thing?"

"Do you know Patrick Devlin?"

I realized I'd posed the question the wrong way. I'd done it as if I knew he knew Patrick Devlin. So he knew I already knew something. If he denied it, I had him. But he wasn't going to deny it.

"Sure, I know Patrick Devlin," he said.

"How?"

"We met a long time ago when we were both younger."

"When you were both in motorcycle gangs?"

"That's right."

"Did you know him well back then?"

"Just casually. We were in different gangs, different places. We didn't exactly hang out together that often."

"Have you seen him recently?"

"Yes, he contributed money to my Senate campaign. He lives in Boston now, but he still does some construction projects here in New York City. He believes in some of the things my campaign stands for and also, I suppose, he wants to be on the winning side once I get elected. His contribution is on file with campaign election officials for anyone to see. What is this all about anyway?"

The waiter brought my gin and tonic to the table. I took a sip.

"Why don't we do this the easy way?" he said. "How about you just tell me what you're looking for, and I'll do my best to help you. That's one of the reasons I asked you to meet me here tonight. So we could straighten this all out."

"One of the reasons?"

"One of the reasons," he repeated.

I told Grayson pretty much everything I'd discovered over the past few days. Except for the part about Big Lou being the source who had named him, of course. When I was finished, I took a big gulp of my drink and waited to see what he was going to say. I was hoping he might confess to something—anything—but I wasn't exactly counting on it.

"If you don't mind me saying so, I think you're going about this all wrong," he said. "I mean, there are a lot of holes in your story. First, you get a hold of this anonymous e-mail that claims Lucy might have been at this motorcycle convention with a man named Elliott. Another source—you won't say who—just happens to remember now that they saw her with me. Even though all this happened years and years ago, and no one ever mentioned a word of it until now. Doesn't that seem a little strange to you?"

I had to admit that I'd thought the same thing.

"And the grave with the six kids up in New Hampshire really has nothing to do with Lucy Devlin. You've got absolutely no connection, as I see it, except for the fact that they both—the supposed sighting of a little girl who might have been Lucy Devlin and the discovery of the six bodies—happened in the same general area."

I couldn't argue with that either.

"As I told you in my office, Clare, there's a lot at stake in this election. For me and for the other side. There are people out there who would do anything to smear me by making up some kind of bizarre connection to this case. My point is that I believe someone is using you. And using the memory of that poor missing little girl."

"Assuming that were true—and I'm not saying I agree with you—how would I go about finding that out?"

"If I were you, I'd go back and check out everything you found out from the beginning."

"Check out what?"

"Everyone you talked to."

"Like who?"

"Well, you won't like my answer. But you didn't really talk to that many people. Not to the person who sent the e-mail. Neither did Lucy's mother. Everything else you have is pretty much out there—the Mountainboro conference, me riding with a motorcycle gang a long time ago, the fact that Patrick Devlin was once in a motorcycle gang, too, and that he recently contributed to my campaign. Which only leaves you one person you know who might be feeding you bogus information for some reason."

"My source."

"Your source," he said.

Big Lou.

We talked for a while about what I'd found out in talking to the families of the six dead children from New Hampshire. I told him about meeting Ralph and Janis Manielli and Victoria Gale. About the different impacts tragedies like this seemed to have on families. How the Manielli family barely gave a thought to Joey, while Victoria Gale's life had been shattered. Even her relationship with her surviving daughter was irreparably changed by what had happened.

"I don't understand that," I said when I'd finished telling him about Samantha Gale's break with her mother.

"Who knows?" he said. "Maybe you'd react like that, too, if it was your brother or sister who just walked out the door one day and never came back."

"I'm an only child."

He nodded.

"What about you?" I asked.

"I had a sister, but she died."

"I'm sorry."

"It was a long time ago." He shrugged.

An aide came over and whispered something in Grayson's ear. He explained to me that he had to leave in a few minutes for a campaign appearance. This was a busy guy.

"There's one more thing I wanted to say to you," Grayson said. "As you probably know, I have a lot of power, a lot of clout. I like to take care of my friends, and punish the people who are against me. I have the ability to do that. If I get elected to the Senate, I'll have even more power and more clout. Do you know what I'm saying here, Clare?"

"Are you threatening me? Trying to scare me away from pursuing this story? Because I don't respond well to threats. They just make me mad."

"My God, Clare, I was about to offer you a job."

"A job?"

"Yes, with my campaign. I like you. You're smart, you're tough, you're not afraid of anything. I could use someone like you on my team."

"I already have a job with Channel 10."

"Forget about TV. If I get elected to the Senate, you get to come along for the ride. Like I said, lots of power and lots of clout and lots of influence. That sounds much more rewarding than working for a TV station, doesn't it? Are you interested?"

I shook my head no.

"Bribery doesn't work on me either," I said.

The aide signaled Grayson his car was ready. I stood up. He stood up. I figured that was a signal our meeting was officially over.

"I have one more question for you," I said to him. "You told me that trying to straighten things out between us over this Lucy Devlin business was one of the reasons you wanted to see me tonight. I'm curious. What was the other reason?"

He leaned forward and put his mouth right next to my ear. "I really did like your legs," he whispered.

Then he kissed me softly on the cheek and left.

I watched him walk out the door with his entourage. Then I sat back down and finished my gin and tonic in one big swig.

Nope, threats and bribery don't work on me.

But flattery . . . well, that's another story.

CHAPTER 19

GRAYSON WAS RIGHT. There was something wrong with my source. Something wrong about Big Lou's story.

I'd sensed it even before he brought it up, but I had tried to put it out of my mind. Now I wanted some answers.

Big Lou wasn't at the Warlock Warriors headquarters in Hell's Kitchen. Neither was Sandy Marston. I asked one of the people there when they were expected back. Whenever they feel like showing up, was the reply. It took a while, but I finally found out that they had gotten on their motorcycles and hadn't been seen since then. Right after Big Lou came to my office to tell her story.

They could be far away by now, of course. Roaming the country on their motorcycles like something out of *Easy Rider*. If they were, I had no chance to track them down. I had to hope they went to a specific destination. Someplace I could figure out, find them, and go talk.

Sandy Marston was a hard person to get a handle on. He'd lived at the group's headquarters most of his life. Big Lou, on the other hand, had a family and roots. Louise Carbone, she had said her name was. "I got married, I had a kid—we had a house in Lodi, New Jersey," she told me that day in my office. "But then I got in trouble, and they took my daughter away from me." I somehow convinced one of the Warlock Warriors to give me the address of Big Lou's husband in Lodi.

Lodi is a hardscrabble, working-class community about fifteen miles from New York City. I drove over the George Washington Bridge, turned off onto Route 80, which took me to Lodi, and then followed Main Street to the address where Big Lou had once lived. It was a small but neat little house, with a well-groomed front yard and a pickup truck in the driveway. A group of young children were playing on the sidewalk next door. I tried to picture Big Lou here, living like a suburban mother. I couldn't see it.

Her husband wasn't what I expected. I figured he'd be a Neanderthal type, but he turned out to be a smallish, soft-spoken, middle-aged man with glasses who looked like he could be a schoolteacher. He told me his name was Dave Weber—Louise had stopped using their last name a long time ago—and he operated a hardware store in Lodi. Weber listened calmly while I told him I was looking for his ex-wife.

"What did she do now?" he asked.

"I just have some questions about an interview we did. Have you seen her recently?"

He nodded. "She was here. She roared up my driveway on that motorcycle of hers. Her and that boyfriend, Marston."

"What did she want?"

"Money, what else?"

"She asked you for money?"

"They said they were going away. They said they needed to get their hands on some money. Louise had a savings account—well, that is we had a savings account when we were married. But the court froze it after her last trouble with the law. She can't touch it. I can't either. I have to go through paperwork just for a few dollars for living expenses. I told her this. They were upset, but there was nothing anybody could do. So they left."

"Did they say where they were going?"

"No."

"And all they came for was the money?"

"Well, Louise wanted to see Maureen."

I remembered Louise had told me about having a child.

"Maureen's her daughter?"

"My daughter, really. Louise, she never took care of her. Maureen's a grown-up teenager now—almost ready to graduate from high school—and I'm pretty much the only parent she's ever had. Louise was always out partying somewhere or in jail or in some rehab. She had a lot of problems with alcohol and drugs. That's why the authorities gave me full custody. Louise isn't even supposed to see her. I told her and Marston that."

"What happened then?"

"I thought there was going to be trouble. Marston's a big guy, you know. I was all set to call the police. But then Louise just started to cry. I don't ever remember her crying in all the time we were together."

"What was she crying about?"

"She said she just wanted to say good-bye to Maureen. She said she was going away for a long time and she didn't know when she'd be back. She wanted to hug Maureen before she left."

"Did you let her see Maureen?"

"I tried, but it was no good."

"What do you mean?"

"Maureen wouldn't come out of the house. She wanted nothing to do with Louise. She's got a lot of anger against her mother for leaving us the way she did. Anyway, when it became clear that Maureen wouldn't see her, Louise got really upset. Marston put his arm around her, and then the two of them got on their motorcycles and drove off. That was the last I saw of them."

I thought about what he was telling me. Had the story about Lucy Devlin triggered some long-lost maternal urge in Big Lou that made her come here and try to see her own daughter again? It seemed like a reasonable assumption.

"Do you have any idea at all where they might have gone after they left here?"

"Well, you might try her mother's house."

"Where's that?"

"Wayne. About ten minutes down Route 80 from here."

"Why would she go there?" I asked, remembering how she told me her mother had disowned her.

"Why does Louise do anything?"

"Money?"

Weber nodded. "She needed money," he said. "I just assumed that after I said no, she'd try her mother."

*   *   *

Big Lou's mother lived in a section of Wayne called Packanack Lake. It was an actual lake, surrounded by houses. The Carbone house was on the north side of the lake. There was a small pier attached, with a rowboat and a sailboat. It all looked very bucolic and wholesome. How did Big Lou start off living in a place like this and wind up with a motorcycle gang?

Irene Carbone—a gray-haired woman in her midsixties and almost as big as Big Lou—told me that her daughter and Sandy Marston had been there.

"I was surprised," she said. "I haven't seen Louise in maybe five years. Ever since she had her last bout of trouble with the law. I told her then I was finished with her. She knew I meant it this time. So when she showed up, I knew she must be in real trouble."

"What kind of trouble?"

"She didn't say."

"Then how do you know she's in trouble?"

"They were scared. You could see it in their eyes. They were afraid of something. Marston, he kept looking around . . . like he was afraid someone was following them. The two of them were running, no question about it. That's why they needed the money."

"You gave them money?"

"Whatever I had in the house. A few thousand dollars."

"Why? I thought you'd disowned them."

She shrugged. "Louise was so upset. Not just about needing the money. Apparently, she'd tried to see her daughter, but Maureen wouldn't speak to her. That really shook her up. I felt sorry for her. I vowed I'd never help her again. But I'm still her mother and she's my daughter. Just like with her and Maureen, the bond's a tough one to break sometimes."

"Did they say where they were headed?"

"Just that they were going out west."

"San Francisco? Los Angeles?"

"Probably somewhere else."

"What do you mean?"

"At another point, they said they were headed south."

"Which one is right?"

"I'm not sure they knew where they were headed. Or, if they did, they didn't want to tell anyone. Not even me."

I thanked her for her time and said she'd been very helpful. It hadn't been that helpful. I was at a dead end; I had no idea where to go next. But I figured she'd given me everything she could.

"All I did was tell you the truth." She shrugged. "Just like I did with the others."

A warning bell went off in my head. "What others?" I asked.

"The two men who came here before you asking questions about Louise."

"Were they cops?"

"Yes, but not from around here. They showed me identification from the US Justice Department."

"Feds," I muttered.

"I've had cops here looking for Louise a lot of times over the years. Local cops, state troopers, probations officers. But never anyone from the Justice Department. Why are they looking for Louise?"

I didn't know the answer to that question either.

But I bet I knew who did.

Elliott Grayson.

CHAPTER 20

ELLIOT GRAYSON KEPT popping up everywhere I looked. Some of it might be coincidence, but not all. And the timing with the Senate election bothered me. Why was all this happening now, just before the Democratic primary?

I decided to use the Barbie Twins to try to get some answers about him. Cassie O'Neal and Janelle Wright, Channel 10's own pair of fluff girls. They were smart enough to find out any relevant information, even if they weren't smart enough to know exactly the whole scope of the story. I wanted both of them to spend the next few days attempting to infiltrate the Grayson and Weller campaigns. I expected some reservations because neither of them cared much about politics. But I was ready for that.

"I just wanted you to know that I'm assigning Cassie to the Teddy Weller campaign for the next few days," I told Janelle Wright.

"What does this have to do with me?" she asked.

"Absolutely nothing."

"Good."

"It wouldn't be the right kind of assignment for you."

"I don't do politics."

"Nor should you."

"That's right."

"Which is why I assigned Cassie to the story."

"Better her than me."

"I just wanted to make sure you heard it from me, not from her or anyone else. I didn't want your feelings hurt. No reason for that. There's plenty of other things we can find for you to do."

I was counting on her ego here. Janelle and Cassie looked alike, sounded alike, and even walked alike. They were virtually interchangeable in the world of TV news. But they didn't see it like that. Each one thought she was the real deal, and the other was just a bimbo for window dressing at the station. Sure enough, Janelle was almost to the door when she turned around and came back to my desk.

"Why should my feelings be hurt?" she asked.

"Well, this could turn into a big story."

"Then why not give it to me?"

"Like you said, you weren't right for it."

"And Cassie is?"

"She seemed very excited about it."

"Of course she is. She thinks she's going to score with a big exclusive here."

"Yes, that is possible."

"I want to do the story, Clare."

"But I've already given it to Cassie."

"Tell her you made a mistake. Tell her you changed your mind. Tell her whatever you want. But I want this assignment."

"Okay." I shrugged. "I'll see what I can do."

A short time later, I was doing the same routine with Cassie O'Neal.

"Janelle is a no-talent bimbo," she said.

"I wouldn't put it quite that way. But I do think you bring greater skills to the table than she does."

"Then why give her this Grayson campaign assignment?"

"You mean you want to do it?"

"You're damn right I do!"

"If you insist," I said.

* * *

Maggie wanted to know why I was suddenly so interested in doing a behind-the-scenes investigation of a Senate race.

And, more importantly, why I hadn't told her about it first.

"You heard about Cassie and Janelle, huh?" I said.

"I am the assignment editor, Clare."

"And you're upset that I didn't let you do the assigning on this story?"

"It would have been nice to know about it."

I nodded. Maggie was right, of course. I would have reacted the same way if I'd been in her position. But, just because I understood where she was coming from, that didn't make it any easier to answer her question.

"I just wanted to set it in motion in a hurry," I said. "This is a big Senate race, a major political story. I wanted Channel 10 to begin taking the lead in covering serious political stories like this. Instead of a lot of the other stuff we're putting on the air at the moment."

"Gee, I kinda remember someone telling me to stay away as much as possible from the serious political coverage. That our viewers really didn't care about serious politics and it was a real ratings killer. I think the exact quote was, 'Every time we put a political story on the air, people reach for their remote and change the channel.'"

"Who told you that?"

"You did."

"Oh."

"You want to tell me what's going on here?"

I sighed.

"I don't really care about the inside story from the election camps, like I told Cassie and Janelle," I said.

"Surprise, surprise."

"But I needed to play it like that so that there appeared to be a reason for assigning them to spend time with the two candidates' camps."

"Is this still all about Lucy Devlin?" Maggie asked.

"Sort of," I said.

I told her everything I knew. Well, pretty much everything. About Marston and Big Lou and the Justice Department showing up at her mother's place and all the rest. I didn't tell her about my encounter with Elliott Grayson at the bar when he kissed me on the cheek and told me he liked my legs. I was afraid those little details might somehow detract from the image of the serious journalist pursuing this story.

"I wasn't sure what else to do or where to go, Maggie. So, I decided to throw up a bit of a Hail Mary desperation play here in the hope that something just might come out of it. Sure, it's a long shot. But it's the only shot I had to make some sense out of all this. I've checked out everything else."

"Not everything."

"What do you mean?"

"Sandy Marston."

I stared at her.

"You know a lot about Elliott Grayson," Maggie said. "You know a lot about Louise Carbone—including meeting her ex-husband and her mother. But how much do we really know about Sandy Marston?"

CHAPTER 21

IT'S AN OLD adage in the news business: "Check everything out."

That's a basic rule for any journalist. A very simple rule. Never take anything for granted. Never believe anyone without corroboration. Never assume anything. It was a damn good rule, and most of the time I tried my best to follow that journalistic rule. But every once in a while, I got sloppy.

Sandy Marston had told me he was in prison during the period when Lucy Devlin disappeared and a little girl who may or may not have been Lucy was seen at the motorcycle convention in Mountainboro, New Hampshire.

But was that really true?

I looked up the number for the New York State Department of Corrections and called it. After navigating through a maze of bureaucratic misdirection, I was finally put through to a supervisor named Gloria Del Rio, who said she would look up information on Marston for me.

I asked her about his bust for stabbing the guy that he told me about. Then I waited while she went through his file. She found what I was looking for. Sandy Marston had received a one- to three-year sentence for it. He'd spent eight months in jail before being released on parole. His release came in January of the year Lucy Devlin disappeared. She'd gone missing in April. That meant Marston had lied. He was out at the time of that and also for the motorcycle convention a few days later in New Hampshire.

"Are you one hundred percent sure about that release date?" I asked.

"Absolutely."

"No chance he could have been held in jail for another few months?"

"Nope. I have his parole report here, too. He began reporting to his parole officer on January 10. Showed up every week like clockwork for a while. I guess he didn't want to go back to jail."

"Did he get in any trouble with the law again after that?"

"Yes, he got arrested again in September of that year."

"So, he was free for maybe nine months?"

"That's right."

Sometimes it's a good idea to just keep asking questions. Even if you're not sure what you're asking them for. That's what happened here.

"What did he get arrested for in September?" I asked, even though I really had no reason to think it mattered.

"Attempted child molestation," Gloria Del Rio said.

"Child molestation," I said slowly.

"Yeah, from what I can see here, he was busted for trying to pick up a little girl off the street."

"When did this supposedly happen?"

"In April."

She gave me the date. It was a few days before Lucy Devlin disappeared.

"Tell me about it."

"A twelve-year-old girl was on her way to school on the West Side, not far from the Warlock Warriors headquarters. Marston pulled up alongside her on his cycle. He tried to talk to her. She kept walking, and he kept harassing her. Then he tried to drag her onto the cycle with him. A passerby saw the struggle, she started screaming, and the girl ran away. Marston took off. The girl's mother didn't want to report it because she was afraid of more trauma for her daughter. But then, some six months later, she got an attack of conscience for some reason and went to the police. The girl picked Marston out of a book of police mug shots, and the cops arrested him later."

"Any chance you could give me the name of the girl or her mother?" I asked.

"C'mon, you know better than that. It's a sex crime file."

"Confidentiality, huh?"

"It's not even in the report. I wish I could help."

"You have, Gloria," I said. "Believe me, you have."

Just days before Lucy disappeared, Sandy Marston had tried to abduct a little girl off a street near the Warlock Warriors headquarters. It didn't require a long stretch of imagination to theorize that Marston—after being thwarted trying for the first girl—did it again a few days later. This time with Lucy Devlin.

It all made a certain kind of sense.

And now Marston was on the run.

Big Lou, too.

I asked Del Rio to check out Louise Carbone. Her record was pretty much like everyone had said. In and out of jail a few times. Lost custody of her daughter to her husband because of substance abuse and her criminal record. She was free, too, during the Lucy disappearance and the Mountainboro convention. But she'd already told me about being there, so that didn't really matter.

Del Rio went through her rap sheet in detail for me. The worst offense was when she spent some time in prison for aggravated assault. She'd cut up a woman in a bar with an open beer bottle because she thought the woman was flirting with her boyfriend. The boyfriend wasn't identified, but I figured it probably was Marston.

I thought about my own encounter with her that first day at the place in Hell's Kitchen. I didn't take her seriously at the time. Maybe I should have.

Is that what happened with Lucy Devlin? Marston picks her up off the street because he's attracted to little girls. Big Lou finds out, loses it in a fit of jealousy, and attacks the girl. Maybe even kills her.

It was possible, I suppose, but I couldn't really see it. For one thing, she'd told me she wasn't even with Marston back then when Lucy disappeared. Besides, I'd liked her that day she came to talk to me in my office. I didn't want to believe that she might be capable of something like that.

On the other hand, I remembered her fury when she thought I was interested in Sandy Marston.

Which one was the real Big Lou?

Or maybe both of them were.

CHAPTER 22

CASSIE O'NEAL AND Janelle Wright had both taped their respective pieces on Elliott Grayson and Teddy Weller for a segment I called: "Campaign Confidential: The Inside Scoop on the Senate Race."

I watched both now.

Janelle's piece portrayed a consummate and veteran politician, Teddy Weller, who was somehow convinced he'd whip this upstart newcomer when all was said and done. She talked about the old-school Democrats backing him, the large amount of fund-raising he had done, and the political chits he was calling in from all the favors he'd done for people over the years. He'd waited a long time for his shot at this, paid his dues in the political area, and he truly believed he was the man who should—and ultimately would—be elected to the Senate.

Cassie, on the other hand, reported on the dedication and energy and almost cultlike adoration Grayson got from his followers, many of them young and active in a political campaign for the first time. "Elliott Grayson is a fresh face, a fresh name, and a fresh point of view to many people tired of politics as usual," she said. "The question is whether or not there are enough of them to get Grayson elected. Elliott Grayson is betting there are, and a lot of political experts agree with him. This is Cassie O'Neal reporting from inside the Grayson campaign."

Of course, it was what they didn't say on the air that I was most interested in. I went back to both Cassie and Janelle after the broadcast and tried to find out anything that might give me a clue or a lead.

"The word in the Weller camp is that some big scandal is about to blow up on Grayson," Janelle told me. "No one's sure exactly what it is or how it's going to come out, but they're all buzzing about it over there. The feeling is there's something out there that's going to hurt Grayson bad enough to cost him the election."

If Weller was saying that, that could mean he was the one who started it by sending the original Lucy Devlin e-mail. On the other hand, maybe they just heard rumors about it and didn't have any involvement beyond that.

The main thing going on behind the scenes of the Grayson campaign seemed to be sex.

"The word is that our boy Elliott is an even more ambitious swordsman with the ladies than he is a politician," Cassie said. "He supposedly has cut quite a swath through many of the pretty young things working for him. He might even be sleeping with a few Weller staffers, too. This guy is the new Bill Clinton, all right, in more ways than one."

The way she said it made me wonder if she had slept with him, too.

"And no, I'm not on that list," she said, as if she were reading my mind. "I did flirt with him a bit. Just to see if he responded the way everyone said he did to good-looking women. I figured it would be good for the story if I could get him to come on to me and maybe even try to get me into bed."

"And?"

"He wasn't interested."

"That's surprising."

"Yeah, I could hardly believe it. But he didn't want to talk about me at all. There was only one thing he wanted to ask me about."

"What?"

"You."

"Me?"

"Yes, all Grayson wanted from me was to find out more about you."

Maybe it was time to go talk to him again.

* * *

I stuck my head into Faron's office afterward.

"Can I ask your opinion on something, Jack?" I said to him.

"Sure," he said.

I plopped down in front of his desk.

"It's a hypothetical situation," I told him. "Hypothetically speaking, let's say there's this woman journalist covering a story, and the guy she's reporting on starts flirting with her and seems interested in her. Can you think of a situation in which it might be journalistically justifiable, in terms of journalism ethics, for this woman to pursue such a relationship?"

"Hypothetically speaking, who is the guy?"

"Elliott Grayson."

"And the journalist . . ."

"Hypothetically, that would be me."

"You?"

"Yeah, why so surprised?"

"Why would Grayson be interested in you?"

"I really don't think that's the point of this discussion . . ."

"I mean the guy's got everything. Good looks, charm, power, and a big political profile. He's going to the Senate, for chrissakes. He could have any woman in the city that he wanted."

"Okay, he's a terrific guy."

"And he's really interested in you?"

"Again, I think we're getting away from the subject at hand . . ."

"Wow! You and Elliott Grayson. Who would have figured that?"

"Yeah, well . . ."

"How far has this relationship between the two of you actually gone?" he asked.

"What do you mean?"

"Have you slept with Grayson?"

"No."

"Do you plan to sleep with him?"

"I don't really feel comfortable answering these kinds of personal questions with my boss."

"Hey, you brought the topic up."

I sighed.

"I have no immediate plans to sleep with Elliott Grayson."

"So, exactly how intimate have the two of you gotten then?"

"Intimate?"

"Has he gotten to second base? Third base?"

"Jeez, Jack, all I want to know is whether or not I'm violating any of the station's ethics standards for journalists by going out with the guy."

Faron thought about that for a second. I was hoping he'd say I was. Say that I shouldn't have any kind of personal relationship with Grayson. Say that my job might be in jeopardy if I did. It would make things so much easier that way.

"If you were still in newspapers, this would be a big deal," he said. "There's a very specific standard there between what you do professionally and your personal life. At a newspaper, the answer would be: No, you can't do that. If you did, and anyone found out about your personal relationship with someone you're covering, it would jeopardize your credentials as a journalist. Newspapers take this kind of thing very seriously."

"So, I should break it off with Grayson right now?"

He shook his head no.

"This isn't newspapers, Clare. This is television. Different rules. To be honest, no one really cares about that sort of stuff here. Whatever you want to do in your personal life, go ahead and do. Just don't tell me any more about it. I don't want to know who you are—or aren't—sleeping with."

Damn.

I was kinda hoping Jack Faron might make this easy for me.

But it looked like whether or not to get personal with Elliott Grayson was a decision I was going to have to make myself.

CHAPTER 23

"Why are you looking for Louise Carbone and Sandy Marston?" I asked Elliott Grayson.

"Who are they?"

"Two bikers from the Warlock Warriors motorcycle gang."

"And I'm supposed to be looking for them?"

"Yes."

"Who told you that?"

"Louise Carbone's mother. She said two feds showed up at her door asking about her daughter and Marston. They worked for the Justice Department. You work for the Justice Department. So how about you drop the 'Golly, gee—I have no idea what you're talking about' approach and tell me what's going on here."

I was sitting in Grayson's office. The scene of my previous interview with him. There were no TV cameras in the room this time. Just the two of us.

"I don't have to tell you anything, you know," he said.

"I understand that."

"So, why should I?"

"Because I have relevant information I will share with you."

"What kind of information?"

"Louise Carbone was my source who claimed she'd seen you and Lucy Devlin together after Lucy disappeared."

He nodded slightly. I couldn't tell if he was surprised or not.

"I read the e-mail sent to Anne Devlin about Lucy being with some motorcycle guy named Elliott in Mountainboro, New Hampshire, and then Louise Carbone said that Elliott was actually you," I told him. "After that, I found out about how you used to ride with a motorcycle gang and how you'd also been in charge of digging up all of the bodies in Mountainboro years later. I put two and two together, and it didn't come out to four. I rushed to a judgment that wasn't supported by the facts. I jumped to some conclusions I shouldn't have about you. I've subsequently found out some new information that makes me believe Sandy Marston—and possibly Louise Carbone, too—could have been the ones responsible for Lucy Devlin's disappearance."

I told him about Marston's arrest record for trying to grab a little girl off the street just days before Lucy Devlin disappeared. About how Marston lied to me about his whereabouts during the time Lucy went missing.

"Sandy Marston wasn't arrested for the attempted abduction of the first girl until months later. I think it's very possible he tried again, this time with Lucy Devlin. At the very least he seems like a damn good suspect. If someone had known about the first attempt that failed, they might have solved the Devlin case right then. But, by the time the charges were filed, no one ever put the pieces together.

"Anyway, Marston, I think, got Louise Carbone to feed me the claims of your involvement to set you up for some reason. Maybe to throw suspicion off them once I started asking questions about the case again. Whatever they were trying to pull off, it seems to have gone bad. They're gone. They're on the run somewhere."

Grayson didn't say anything when I was finished. Instead, he just reached over to his computer and clicked on an audio recording.

"I want you to hear this," he said. "It's a voice mail of a phone call I received here recently."

A woman's voice said: "Elliott Grayson, I know what you did. I know about Lucy Devlin. I know about the other children. I will go public with this information and make it available to your political opponents unless you pay me $250,000. I think $250,000 is a cheap price to pay to avoid seeing your chance to be Senator go up in flames, don't you? I'll be in contact with you in the next twenty-four hours to work out the details. Just make sure the money's ready then, or I'll tell everybody what I know. Have a nice day."

I recognized the woman's voice.

It was Louise Carbone.

"She was pretty stupid about it," Grayson said after the voice mail ended. "She made the call from her own phone and the number popped up on our call identification system here. It was easy to identify it as her number at the Warlock Warriors place. We went over there to talk to her, but she and Marston must have slipped away before we got there. Later, we found the mother's address in New Jersey, but we missed them there, too. Marston obviously put the Carbone woman up to it. Maybe they sent that original e-mail to the Devlin woman or maybe they just came up with this wacky idea to take advantage of it once you went to them. In any case, we have nationwide arrest warrants out for them on charges of extortion. From what you've just told me, it sounds like that when we do find Marston and the Carbone woman, we should take a hard look at them in the Lucy Devlin case, too. It definitely sounds like Marston could have had something to do with the Devlin girl's disappearance."

"What about the other six bodies you found in New Hampshire?"

"What about them?"

"How do they fit in?"

"They don't."

"But Louise Carbone talked about the 'other children' besides Lucy in that message. What did she mean?"

"Who knows? Maybe she found out about the New Hampshire bodies just like you did because I got so much publicity for that case. Maybe she was talking about some other children altogether. Or maybe she was just out of her mind on crack or speed or whatever else she's using these days. Louise Carbone has a long history of drug abuse, you realize. She and Marston are not exactly sane, rational people."

"You definitely don't think there's any connection between the six dead kids in New Hampshire and Lucy Devlin?"

"We haven't been able to find one single piece of evidence to support that theory."

"Me neither," I admitted.

"Those six murders are not part of our Lucy Devlin investigation," Grayson said.

It all made sense, but there was one thing that was still bothering me.

"How come no one ever talked to Marston about Lucy Devlin before this?" I asked.

"What do you mean?"

"Well, it wasn't that hard for me to find out the information about him being suspected of child molestation in the past and how he'd tried to pick up that other little girl just a few days before Lucy. How come none of the investigators at the time ever checked him out or looked at him hard as a suspect? They must have been going through the files looking for people with records like that."

Grayson shrugged. "Law enforcement isn't perfect. Sometimes we just miss things. The important thing is that we get the bad guy in the end. Sooner or later, we usually do that."

"In this case, much later," I said.

There was something more pressing on my mind right now, though.

"I've got one favor to ask in return for telling you all this," I told him.

"Go ahead."

"Don't tell any of the rest of the press about this yet. Let me break it on the Channel 10 news tonight. You can call a press conference tomorrow. Tell everyone then that I got a leak somehow, you're furious about it—whatever you want to say to cover your ass. But it has to be my story."

"Done," he said.

"Just like that?"

"Sure. All you have to do is one favor for me in return. Have dinner with me some night."

"I really don't think that's a good idea."

"Why not?"

"You and me having any kind of personal relationship, which I think is what we're talking about here, it just seems . . . well, unethical."

"Is that a no?"

"I didn't say that."

"A yes, then?"

"Maybe," I told Grayson.

"Well, then, Clare." He laughed. "We're making progress."

* * *

I went back to the Channel 10 offices and started to put together a piece for the 6 p.m. newscast.

I wrote my own copy, got some of the production people to
pull up file footage from the Lucy Devlin case and put in calls
to a lot of people, including Lucy's mother, for comment. Then
I briefed Brett and Dani on what was going to happen. After all
this was done, I taped a fifteen-second promo. That's the blurb
you see while you're watching Ellen or Dr. Phil that tells you
what's coming up on the news.

The one I did said:

> STARTLING NEW DEVELOPMENTS IN A SENSA-
> TIONAL NEW YORK CITY MISSING PERSONS CASE:
> Two suspects are now being hunted for questioning in
> connection with the long-ago disappearance of Lucy Devlin.
> Exclusive details at six. Stay right here for Channel 10 News.

I spent the rest of the afternoon working on the story. I tried to
concentrate on Lucy Devlin and Anne Devlin and Sandy Marston
and Louise Carbone and make some sense out of it all. Finally, at
6 p.m. the red light went on and the intro for the evening newscast began to roll. Brett and Dani went right to my story from the
top. They set me up and then cut to me in the studio.

I looked into the camera and began to talk:

> ME: In a stunning development, Channel 10 News
> has learned that arrest warrants were issued today for
> two suspects in connection with the fifteen-year-old
> disappearance of Lucy Devlin. Federal authorities are
> searching nationwide for Sandy Marston, fifty-one,
> and Louise Carbone, forty-six, both members of the
> Warlock Warriors motorcycle gang. The two are accused

of attempted extortion. But authorities believe they may also have information about the Devlin disappearance and may actually have been involved in it. US Attorney Elliott Grayson revealed few details publicly. Nevertheless, Channel 10 News has learned law enforcement officials are confident that a break in the case, one of New York City's most baffling crimes, is near . . .

I loved the feeling of breaking a big exclusive like this. It was a feeling I hadn't had for a long time. It was never the same as an editor. I never felt as close to the news as I did as a reporter.

Lucy Devlin had been the biggest story I ever covered in my career.

Now it was a big story for me all over again.

I knew that it was a sad story and that it had caused so much anguish for Anne Devlin and her husband and lots of other people.

But, for me, at that moment in time . . .

Well, it felt good.

God help me, it felt good.

CHAPTER 24

"YOU WANT TO go where?" Jack Faron asked me.

"Mountainboro, New Hampshire."

"Why?"

"To follow the trail of the six dead children."

"I thought that's what you just did."

"Yes, I followed the trail around the country."

"So then why go to New Hampshire?"

"Because that's where the trail leads me."

"But the kids are all dead. What are you going to find out in New Hampshire?"

"I won't know that until I get there."

Faron seemed dubious.

"When I'm finished there, I'm going to go to Boston."

"What's in Boston?"

"Patrick Devlin, Lucy's father."

"I thought he refused to talk to you."

"He did."

"So why go there?"

"Maybe I can get him to change his mind. I knew him pretty well fifteen years ago when I was covering the Lucy story. Just like I knew Anne Devlin. Meeting face-to-face is always better than trying to convince someone to talk over the telephone. That's right out of the Journalism 101 manual, Jack. You know that as well as I do."

Faron shook his head. He still didn't like it, but I knew I had enough clout to convince him. I was the news editor, and he had entrusted me to run the Channel 10 newsroom. In the end, he had to give me the power to pursue this story the way I wanted to do it. Not that he was happy about it though.

"Why can't you just put the story you have about the six families on the air and be done with it? Everything always has to be so complicated with you."

"Simple is not necessarily a good thing."

"If this were Cassie or Janelle, this story would be on the air already."

"My point exactly."

* * *

I spent the rest of the day being a news director again.

I had one big problem already. The breaking news story of the day was a subway crash in Brooklyn. One person had been killed and more than two dozen injured when a rush-hour train smashed into the back of another train at the Hoyt-Schermerhorn station. Cassie O'Neal had been assigned to cover the story. Now I knew there was no way that Cassie would ever be able to pronounce *Schermerhorn* correctly on a live feed. My solution was for her to simply stand under the Hoyt-Schermerhorn sign in the station and say dramatically: "This subway station looked like any other subway station in the city this morning, until tragedy struck at 8:02 a.m. . . ."

The other issue of the day was a feud between Steve Stratton, our sports anchor, and Wendy Jeffers, who did the weather. Wendy had closed her report the night before by saying that an impending rainstorm was probably going to wipe out the New York Yankees game in the Bronx in a few hours. Stratton had planned to lead his sports segment with an update on the weather conditions for the game. Since it was being rained out, he had nothing else to say about it. So, there was this moment of the most dreaded thing in TV news ... dead air. Afterward, the two of them got into a shouting match about encroaching on each other's territory. Territorial boundaries are a big thing in TV news. I told Wendy she should avoid sports and the next time just say that the rain was going to make a mess out of the commuter rush hour. I told Stratton that he should find some sports news that didn't involve meteorological updates. It was a Solomon-like decision, and they both went away happy. At least for that day.

The lead story on the newscast was going to be a feature on "Flirting in the Office: The Hot New Way to Find Romance." It just seemed more interesting than the subway crash. We interviewed men and women who'd found love where they worked. Amazingly enough, all the people we talked to were young, good-looking, and sexy. There was also a feature on finding the right suntan lotion for the beach, the best ice cream cones in town, and some celebrity stuff. For the actual news, we had the subway crash and we did an update on the Senate race and some other political stuff.

* * *

That night at home, as I packed for the trip to New Hampshire, I took out the scrapbook of all the Lucy Devlin stories I'd done.

I paged through them like I'd done so many times before. The first big story about Lucy's disappearance; the long ordeal of Anne and Patrick Devlin as they waited, hoped, and prayed for some word about Lucy; the city's obsession over the fate of the missing adorable little eleven-year-old girl; and finally, the article that the *New York Tribune* had run about me winning the Pulitzer for my coverage of the Lucy Devlin story.

There was a picture of me standing in the *Tribune* newsroom holding the Pulitzer certificate with the editor, Bill Paulson, and the paper's managing editor, Ted Whitby. Paulson and Whitby were dead now. So was the *Tribune*.

Me, I was still around chasing the same damn story.

Somehow Lucy Devlin had come full circle and found me again after all these years.

CHAPTER 25

THE POLICE CHIEF of Mountainboro, New Hampshire, was a man named Oscar Robles. He'd been the police chief there for twenty-five years, and he was the first law enforcement official on the scene when the six bodies had been found.

I interviewed Robles in his office. I'd brought along my best video guy at Channel 10, Scott Haussman, to shoot this and any other interviews I did in New Hampshire. Haussman was a whiz with a camera and also with the pre-broadcast production and editing—a video geek who could work magic with the stuff we put on the air. But even he was going to have a problem with Robles. The guy was old, cranky, impatient, and clearly did not want to spend much time talking with me.

"I'm a busy man today," Robles said. "I've got to go on patrol by myself, because my one deputy—who's part-time at that—called in sick. And the only police car we have has a dirty carburetor, which means I need to get it serviced at the filling station. I don't really have a lot of time to discuss something that happened years ago."

"It might be connected to another missing child case in New York City," I said. "Lucy Devlin. I'm trying to find out as much as I can about these six here to see if there's any possible link."

Robles shrugged. "All we did up here was find the bodies," he said. "The minute that happened, the feds moved in with a task force. It turned out they had a big missing children operation already going and this was the kind of thing they were looking for. Call the feds and talk to them. This is a dead end. Whatever you're looking for isn't here."

"The crime scene's still here," I pointed out. "The place where the bodies were found."

"It's a shopping mall now."

"A shopping mall?"

"Yes, that's what they were getting ready to build when they found the bodies. After the graves were dug up and the investigation was over, they went back to work. Finished it a few years ago. It's a helluva shopping mall. Thirty-six stores, a movie theater, lots of parking. It's the biggest shopping mall in the area."

"Let's go see it."

"What do you think you're going to find there?"

"Hey, you never know . . ."

Robles told me what he could about the missing bodies. I think he did it because he realized that was the only way he was going to get rid of me.

"It was the biggest thing that ever happened around here," he said. "Most of the crimes I deal with are disturbing the peace, speeding, one of the local kids who has too much to drink—that sort of thing. We never had a murder here, not in all the years I was on the job.

"When the call came in from the contracting company about finding a body, it was pretty hard to believe. I figured it was just going to be some animal bones. I kept thinking that way on the whole drive over. I mean, there were no reports of violence or anyone missing in the area. So, who could it be? I just figured I was going to find a dog or a coyote.

"Of course, it wasn't an animal. The body was clearly human. Definitely a child. By the time I got there, they'd already found the second one. That's when I knew this was really bad. I called in a bunch of people to help with the digging. By that night, we'd found all six bodies. At that point, of course, we kept expecting more. Dug for days in the whole area around the site, but those six were all we ever found.

"I wasn't prepared for anything like that. We didn't have a crime lab or anything. So, I called the state police first. Then after that they called in the feds. Pretty soon a federal task force was here and they completely cordoned off the entire area. They handled it from there."

"Do you remember the man heading up the federal task force?"

"A young guy. Very businesslike, very determined, very ambitious—that was my take on him."

"His name was Elliott Grayson. He's running for the US Senate now."

"I figured he was going to wind up being somebody."

"You don't remember anything unusual at all?"

"How would I know? Like I told you before, the feds shut down the whole area as soon as they got there. They could have been having an orgy in there for all I know. I just backed off and did my job. I'm only a small-town cop. This was way beyond me. This guy Grayson you mentioned was the big shot."

We talked for a while more, but the bottom line was he really didn't have much. He'd been the first law enforcement officer on the scene. He'd been there when they dug up the bodies. He'd started the preliminary investigation. But then he'd been shunted aside by Grayson and the feds.

"Anything else at all you remember that might be significant?" I asked.

"Significant?"

"Out of the ordinary. Something that just didn't seem right or make sense to you at the time."

He thought about that for a second.

"Well, there was one thing. I don't know if it's what you're talking about, but the bodies weren't all together."

"What do you mean?"

"We found five of the bodies in the same spot, almost on top of each other. The other one wasn't as deep. It was near the top of the soil. That was the first one that was found. I don't know what the feds made of it, but it only meant one thing to me."

"That body was buried at a different time than the others."

"Right."

"Do you remember which child it was?"

"It was one of the girls. The one from Jersey, I think."

Becky Gale.

Six children were found in a grave. All from different parts of the country and different backgrounds. None of them were from this area. But they all wound up buried in the same place. Only five of them were apparently buried at the same time. The sixth—Becky Gale—came later.

But what did it all mean?

*　*　*

Robles took me after that to see the shopping mall where the bodies had been found during the excavation for the mall's construction. It had a Gap, a Banana Republic, a Home Depot, and lots of restaurants and snack bars. Looking at the place, it didn't seem possible this had been the scene of a mass burial a few years before. I tried to imagine a killer digging the hole in the middle of it all. It seemed incongruous.

"Satisfied?" he asked me after we'd been walking around the mall for a little while. "I told you there was nothing here."

I said there was one more place that I wanted to see. The site of the long-ago motorcycle convention where both the person who sent Anne Devlin the e-mail and Louise Carbone had claimed they'd seen a little girl that they thought was Lucy.

"Why?" he asked.

"It might have really been Lucy Devlin on the back of that motorcycle."

"Lucy Devlin wasn't in that grave. Her body was never found."

"I still think it's all connected somehow. The motorcycle convention. The six bodies. Lucy Devlin. Maybe a lot more missing children, too. Let's go see where the motorcycle convention was held."

"Not me. I gotta go back to work."

Robles drove Haussman and me back to my motel where I'd left my rental car. Before heading back to the police station, he gave us directions to get to the farm fields where the motorcycle gathering had been held. He also gave me his phone number. He asked me if I had a cell phone. I said I did. He told me to call him if I got into any trouble.

"Why do you think I might get into trouble?" I asked.

"Hey, you never know," he said.

CHAPTER 26

THE SITE OF the motorcycle convention was about two miles outside of town. You had to drive down a remote road to get there, well off the main highway. Maybe that was the appeal of the place to the bikers. They didn't have to worry about cops or anybody else butting into their business.

Haussman and I drove to the spot from Robles' directions. When we got there, I stopped the car and got out. I stood there looking at the fields rolling off into the distance. There was a lake on the horizon. It was kind of beautiful, actually. Lucy Devlin might have stood on this same spot a long time ago. Haussman started shooting some stuff of the scene for B-roll copy to go along with the Robles interview about what might or might not have happened here.

While he was doing this, a pickup truck came down a dirt road from the direction of the lake. It stopped when it got to us. An old man leaned out the window.

"Are you people lost?" he asked.

"No, we're fine."

"What are you doing out here in the middle of nowhere? You sure don't look like you're from around here. And, if you're tourists, this is a long way from any of the local attractions you probably really want to visit."

"I just wanted to see this place," I said. "I understand motorcycle guys used to hang out here."

"Still do. This is a big hangout for bikers. Lots of them live up here. Then their friends come and it gets even worse. They hold these big gatherings here, but that's only once a year or so. The real problem is the day-to-day stuff. All of them hang out at this bar called the Rusty Spike. Sometimes they cause trouble. We've all just gotten pretty used to it up here, I guess."

"Where's the Rusty Spike?" I asked.

"About another mile and a half down this road." He pointed in the opposite direction from town.

* * *

Even if I hadn't known the Rusty Spike was a biker bar, I think I might have figured it out when we got to the place. A half dozen motorcycles were parked outside. I pulled up in front and sat there with Haussman for a minute, trying to decide what to do. I thought about calling Robles at the number he'd left me and asking him to go inside with me. I mean he had a gun, in case things went badly. Of course, I did have Haussman with me. Scott was a terrific guy—smart, hardworking, an absolute whiz with video cameras, computers, and a lot of other technological stuff. Unfortunately, he was also five foot six, barely 155 pounds, wore big thick glasses, and had a high squeaky voice. I told him to bring his camera and we would try to interview some of the people inside. He didn't look happy, but followed me inside.

It was early afternoon, and the only people in the Rusty Spike were the kind of people who hang out in a bar at that time of day. A couple of bikers were shooting pool in the back, another was playing a pinball machine against the wall, and one guy was nursing a beer at the bar. They all turned around and looked at me. One of the bikers shooting pool poked the other one, said something to him—and they both laughed uproariously. So did the guy at the pinball machine. The one sitting at the bar didn't laugh at all. He just kept staring at me with these dead eyes that showed no emotion whatsoever. I was more worried about him than any of the others.

There was a big man working behind the bar. Haussman and I walked over to him and sat down at a stool, as far away from the guy at the other end as we could.

I decided to do what I needed to do and then get the hell out of there as quickly as possible. I told the bartender how I was a TV journalist from New York, Haussman was my video guy, and we were working on a story here. He said his name was Dan Adcock and he owned the Rusty Spike. He also said he wouldn't answer any of my questions unless I bought something. I ordered an Amstel. Haussman asked for a Diet Coke. I kinda wished he'd ordered a bourbon or something to at least pretend he was a tough guy. But then I remembered he didn't drink.

"Do you happen to remember—or remember hearing about—a motorcycle group convention that was held up here about fifteen years ago? A lot of cycle gangs from around the country would have attended . . ."

"Sure, they're here every year."

"They still meet?"

"About a mile down the road in that field by the lake. What's so special about this one time?"

"There might have been a lost little girl there."

"And you're just looking for her now?"

"It's a complicated story."

He shrugged. I had a feeling he didn't care whether it was complicated or not. He wasn't that interested.

I took three pictures out of my purse. I showed him the first one.

"Did you ever see this guy up here?" I asked.

He glanced down at the picture of Sandy Marston and recognized him immediately.

"Sure, that's Sandy. He used to come up here a lot."

"Do you happen to know if he might have been at the motorcycle convention held here fifteen years ago?"

"I wouldn't remember something like that. Like I told you, there's bikers coming in and out of there all the time."

I nodded and showed him the second picture. Elliott Grayson.

"Did you ever see him before?"

"He looks familiar."

"From up here?"

"Nah, I think I saw him on TV. Isn't he somebody famous?"

"He's running for the US Senate."

"Okay."

"But he's never been in this bar?"

"No." He laughed. "He's never been in this bar."

I showed him the third picture now. This one was Patrick Devlin, the other person I now knew had once belonged to a motorcycle gang.

"Hey, that's Patty," he said.

"You know him?"

"Sure, he's been here."

"Do you know if he was at the biker rally fifteen years ago?"

"I have no idea."

"Well, when do you remember seeing him?"

"Last week. He came in here and sat down at the bar and ordered a couple of beers. He said he was just passing through on some business. We talked about old times, people we knew, and then he left. Why? What's Patty got to do with anything?"

Last week?

What the hell was Patrick Devlin doing in Mountainboro last week?

How did he fit into all this?

While Adcock was talking to me about Patrick Delvin, I heard something else that bothered me. Or rather, it's what I didn't hear. The sound of pool being played had stopped. I looked over at the table, and the two bikers weren't there anymore. I turned around and saw them headed toward me. One of them was a big fat guy. The other one was short, but looked lean and tough.

"Hey, how about you and us have a little party?" the fat one said to me.

"Actually, I'm just about to leave," I said, as if the request was the most normal thing anyone could say. "Maybe some other time."

"Nah, you get rid of your little girlfriend here," he said, gesturing over to Haussman. "Then you and me and Dave can have us some fun. Show you what a real man looks like instead of this sissy boy you're with."

I looked around the place. The guy at the end of the bar hadn't moved; he was still staring at us. The pinball player kept at his game and paid no attention. Adcock was watching the whole thing from behind the bar with a bemused expression on his face.

Finally, Adcock said something.

"All right, Cliff, put it back in your pants. You and Dave, get the hell out of here. I don't want that kind of crap in my bar. If there's any trouble here, the cops will close me down. I can't lose that money. It isn't worth it for a piece of ass, not in my bar."

The message seemed to be that he didn't care what they did to us, but don't do it in his place. That was okay with me at the moment. The two bikers gave me one last leer and then they walked out the front door.

I watched them go, then looked over at Haussman. He had a shell-shocked expression on his face. I don't think he'd ever been in a situation like this before. I had, but that didn't make it any easier or less scary. I leaned over to him and whispered, "Let's give it a few minutes in hopes those two will be gone by the time we get outside. Then we run to the car, get in, and burn rubber all the way back to town."

Haussman nodded eagerly. That was fine with him.

But when we finally ventured outside, both of them—Cliff and Dave, in all their manhood splendor—were standing next to our rental car. The tires of the car had been slashed, the windshield broken, and the hood was now open with parts of the engine scattered on the ground.

"Looks like you've had a bit of car trouble," the fat one said. "You're not going anywhere for a while, honey. I guess we'll have time for that party, after all."

They started moving toward us. I knew we were in big trouble. We were out in the middle of a remote area with these two Neanderthals. Haussman did his best to put up a fight, but he was no match for them. He tried to get to the car, but they knocked the video camera out of his hand to the ground, then pinned him against the car. One of them punched him and he fell to the ground.

I reached in my purse for my cell phone. If I could dial Robles' number before they got to us, we might have a chance. At least they'd know the police were coming. I started to punch in the number. But then someone knocked the cell phone out of my hand and grabbed me from behind.

I turned around and found myself face-to-face with the dead-eyed guy from the bar. He was one of them. He'd followed me outside.

Suddenly, a gunshot went off and everyone froze.

At first, I thought one of them might be shooting at me. But they all seemed as stunned as I was. I figured then it was Adcock the bartender deciding to come to my rescue. But it turned out to be better than that. It was Oscar Robles.

He stood there with his gun out.

"Let her go," he said. "Let them both go."

Everyone backed off.

"All of you, on the ground with your hands behind your back," he barked at the three bikers.

They quickly followed his orders. A few minutes later, police cars began showing up. Soon after that, the three of them were being handcuffed and taken away to jail.

"How'd you know to show up?" I asked Robles as they were being led away.

"I followed you from your motel."

"I thought you said you had to go back to work."

"Like I said, I decided you'd probably just get into some trouble."

I was both mad and glad at the same time.

"That's not very flattering," I said. "I know how to take care of myself."

"Yeah, it looked like you were doing just great until I showed up."

"What do you want me to say?"

"You might say 'thank you.'"

He was right, of course.

"Thank you," I told him.

"You're welcome."

Before leaving, Robles asked me some more questions about the case—the story I was working on.

He seemed interested now. I'm not sure why. Maybe it was because of the altercation I had with the bikers at the bar trying to pursue it. Or maybe it was just a lawman's curiosity. I got the feeling that Oscar Robles just might be a lot better law enforcement official than I thought at first. I was starting to like him. I tend to do that when people save me from a gang of motorcycle freaks.

Anyway, I told Robles everything I knew.

"None of it makes any sense," I said. "But I think it would if I could figure out how to put all the individual pieces together. It's like a giant puzzle. It completely baffles you for a long time until you find the right piece of the puzzle. Once that happens, the rest of it all falls into place. I'm still looking for that part of the puzzle that can help me figure out what happened to Lucy."

"I guess you're headed to Boston next."

"How'd you know that?"

"That's where the father, Patrick Devlin, lives now, right?"

"He's a missing part of the puzzle," I said.

CHAPTER 27

PATRICK DEVLIN MADE it clear right up front that he wanted no
part of me or this story.

I'd tracked him down at a construction project he was super-
vising, an office complex in Plymouth—outside of Boston. I was
by myself this time. I'd sent Haussman back to New York. He was
pretty shaken up and a bit bruised physically from his confrontation with the bikers. Besides, I didn't figure Patrick Devlin was
going to be willing to go on the air with me. I just wanted to talk
to him. Face-to-face. I'd known him a long time ago, and I needed
to see firsthand what kind of a monster he had become. A monster who didn't even care about his missing daughter anymore.

"What the hell are you doing here?" he snapped when I made a
surprise appearance on the doorstep of his business.

"We need to talk about Lucy and some other stuff."

"How'd you find me?"

"Your office told me where you were."

"They're not supposed to do that," Devlin said. "Not to a goddamned TV reporter."

"Well, I didn't actually tell them I was a TV reporter."

"What did you say?"

"That I was the secretary for the gravel company delivering a
load to this project, and the driver had lost the directions and the

cement would start settling if I couldn't help him get to the site in a hurry."

"You lied!"

"Technically, yes."

"I told you on the phone I didn't want to talk about Lucy."

"Hence, my personal appearance here."

"What's so important that you need to know from me?"

"Let's start with why you don't even want to talk about your own daughter anymore."

Devlin looked pained by the question. His shoulders slumped and he looked down at the ground, like he wanted to avoid my gaze. He seemed a lot older and more vulnerable than I remembered. When I knew him fifteen years ago—at the time I'd covered Lucy's disappearance—he was a kind of cocky, macho, muscular type of guy. Now he had gray hair, a lot of the muscle had turned to fat, and much of the bravado was gone, too. The years and the unanswered questions had taken their toll on him, too, just like his ex-wife.

"Let's you and me take a walk," Devlin said.

"Where?"

"Over there."

He pointed to a temporary shed that had been built on the site. It was surrounded by construction equipment—bulldozers, steam shovels, cement mixers. I suddenly remembered that the bodies of the six children in New Hampshire had been found by a contracting crew. I wondered if there was any possibility they were connected to Patrick Devlin's company. It was a long shot, but still worth checking when I got back to New York.

"Why do you want us to go inside there?" I asked.

"More privacy."

"You're not going to bury me in cement or anything, are you?"

"What?"

"Hey, I've watched the *Sopranos, Goodfellas* . . ."

"I think I owe you some answers," he said.

We walked over to the shed and went inside. It was small and cramped, the air was stuffy, and you could hear the noise from construction equipment outside. Devlin seemed more comfortable though.

"When Lucy disappeared, I thought my life had ended, too," he said. "I didn't know how to deal with the grief and the pain and the guilt. Could I have done something to prevent this? Should I have protected her more? All of it was eating me up inside. For a while, Anne and I tried to make it work between us, but there was too much to deal with.

"She reacted to it by trying to keep everything the same as it had always been. She acted as if Lucy was going to walk in the door on her own one day like nothing had happened. She kept Lucy's room just the way she'd left it, refused to get rid of any of her belongings, she even kept Lucy's favorite foods stocked in the cupboard and refrigerator. Finally, when it became clear Lucy wasn't coming home, she turned her life into a crusade to find her. Traveling the country, looking for tips or leads or clues. It became the only thing she cared about anymore. I thought it was sick, and I told her that. Eventually, we split up.

"Me, I took the opposite approach. The only way for me to get over my grief about Lucy was to put her behind me. I started my life all over again. I moved to Boston, I started a new company here. I rebuilt my business from the ground up and made it a successful one all over again. I remarried, I had a family, everything changed for me—after a while Lucy just became a bad memory. That's why I can't deal with this anymore. There's too many memories. I need to move on and not dwell on the past. Maybe that makes me the bad guy in the eyes of you and a lot of other people. But that's the only way I can survive. Otherwise, the grief would destroy me. Just look what it's done to Anne."

He was talking to me, but at the same time I think he was talking to himself. Trying to rationalize the things he had done and—even more importantly—the things he hadn't done. I waited until he finished before I said anything.

"Did you used to be in a motorcycle gang?" I asked.

"Sure, a long time ago."

"What gang?"

"The Warlock Warriors."

"In New York?"

"That's right."

"Did you know Sandy Marston?"

"Yes, he was the head of the chapter."

"How come he didn't know you?"

"What do you mean?"

"I asked him once if he knew you. He said he didn't. Why would he say that?"

"I don't know. If he had something to do with Lucy's disappearance—like they're now saying—maybe he was trying to hide something. I wish I had the answers for a lot of things, but I don't."

"Did you guys keep in touch after you left the gang?"

"Me and Sandy Marston? No, we didn't keep in touch."

"How about you and Elliott Grayson? He's the US Attorney for Manhattan now. He's also running for the Senate."

"I know who he is."

"He was in a motorcycle gang, too."

"I know."

"Is that how you met him?"

"Sure, we hooked up a few times at some biker events. Both of us knew that life wasn't for us and we wanted to get out, so maybe we kinda bonded a bit over that. We kept in touch from time to time over the years. I donated some money to his Senate campaign a few months ago because I wanted to help him win. Elliott's a good man."

"Did you know that he was the lead investigator on a federal task force that helped dig up the bodies of six children in Mountainboro, New Hampshire, a few years ago?"

"Okay."

"That's the same place where the e-mail to your wife said Lucy had been spotted on the back of a motorcycle a few days after she disappeared. The e-mail said the guy with her was named Elliott. Someone else identified him to me as Elliott Grayson."

Devlin shrugged. "I don't know what any of this has to do with me . . ."

"Have you ever been to Mountainboro?" I asked.

"Not that I remember."

"Are you sure about that?"

"Maybe once or twice a long time ago."

"You were there last week. The bartender of the Rusty Spike positively identified you from a picture I showed him."

"He's lying."

"Now why would he lie about that?"

Devlin started to answer me, but then stopped. He seemed agitated. He stood up, clenched his fists, and began moving toward me. I thought for a second he might hit me. Instead, he walked over to a small filing cabinet behind me. He took out a sheet of paper and put it down in front of me.

"What's this?"

"Read it."

It was a copy of an e-mail. Just like the one Anne Devlin had gotten. Only this one was addressed to him. It talked about Mountainboro. The guy named Elliott on the motorcycle. How the writer talked to the little girl with him and thought it might be Lucy.

"I got this the same time Anne did, I guess. Anne, she made a big deal of it—bringing it to you and going on television and all. Me, I just tried to pretend I'd never seen it. But then one day, I decided to drive out there and just poke around. You're right. I went to that town and that bar when I was in the Warlock Warriors. I stopped in for a beer, just for old times' sakes. I'm still not sure why I went there at all. I guess I was just curious from the e-mail. I didn't find out anything, but I tried."

"I thought you said you'd put Lucy completely out of your mind."

"It doesn't always work that way."

"That's the only time you've been to Mountainboro since your Warlock Warrior days?"

"Right. Look, I've got to get back to work. Any other questions?"

There was one more thing I needed to talk to him about. It was the toughest thing. That's why I'd left it until last. But it had been bothering me ever since my conversation with Anne Devlin.

"Anne said that Lucy had told her something right before she disappeared that made Anne suspect you of doing something horrible to your daughter. Anne said she never told that to anyone before, but it's always bothered her. At first, I thought she was just confused or jumping to some kind of crazy conclusion because of all the stress she's been under. But now I'm not so sure. Maybe Anne was right."

"Right about what?"

"She suspects there was something going on between you and Lucy."

"What are you saying?"

"Were you having sexual relations with your own daughter, Patrick?"

I'm not sure what I expected him to say or do. But I wasn't prepared for the way he reacted. He stood up again with his fists clenched and a look of rage on his face. He pounded on the table in front of him and then kicked a metal trash can against the wall so hard I thought the metal structure was shaking.

"She thinks that? She thinks I did that to Lucy? That bitch, that goddamn bitch!"

He strode over to the door, flung it open, and called out to someone. Two security guards appeared very quickly.

"Get her out of here and off my property," he said, angrily pointing a finger at me.

The guards each took one of my arms and led me off the construction site and out onto the street.

"What happened back there?" one of them asked me.

"I'm a TV reporter; I was conducting an interview."

"So why was Mr. Devlin so mad at you?"

"I guess he didn't like my last question."

CHAPTER 28

ANNOUNCER: It's the Channel 10 News at six. With Brett Wolff and Dani Blaine on the anchor desk, Steve Stratton doing sports, and Wendy Jeffers with the Channel 10 Accu-weather for the tri-state area.

Channel 10 is the news station that's ALWAYS on the move. When you want your news fast, you want it quick, you want it now . . . turn to Channel 10.

And now, here's Brett and Dani . . .

BRETT: Good evening. Three people are dead tonight after a shooting in the Bronx.

DANI: A big oil spill on the Long Island Expressway has turned the rush hour into crawl hour.

BRETT: There's a new poll out on the Democratic primary in the Senate race. Is the race getting tighter or is one of the candidates pulling ahead? We'll tell you all the latest political developments.

DANI: But first . . . it's not too early to start thinking about the best—and the safest—way to get a tan at the beach this year. Summer is just around the corner, and we've got some expert tips on how you can look good after a day in the sun—and still make sure you stay healthy.

My story didn't even make the first twenty minutes of the newscast. I couldn't justify putting it at the top of the show, even if I did think it was more important than traffic jams or holiday preparations. The problem was I didn't really have a lot I could put on the air. What I had was a lot of tantalizing leads without any hard facts to back them up. Even in TV news, you have to have at least a few facts.

What I wound up with was a soft feature about six children who'd been murdered and mysteriously buried together in a small New Hampshire town. I ran my interview with Oscar Robles. I showed footage of the area where the bodies had been uncovered. I talked again about the six missing children found dead there. I concluded it all like this:

> ME: Mountainboro, New Hampshire. Someone claimed Lucy Devlin had been spotted there just after her abduction. Years later, the bodies of six other children were found in a grave in this bucolic little New England town. Was there any connection? And what really did happen to Lucy Devlin— and these six children buried here? In the end, we're left with lots of questions, and precious few answers.

The camera went back to Brett and Dani, who looked slightly confused.

> DANI: Thank you, Clare, for that . . . uh, report.

> BRETT: And now onto a brighter side of the news.

> DANI: Cats may have nine lives, but you don't want to spend nine of yours looking for the right pet.

> BRETT: We'll be back with some tips on how to find a feline friend that's just . . . well, Purr-fect.

They both laughed uproariously.

* * *

I'd debated about using any of the video I had from the altercation with the bikers at the Rusty Spike. Haussman had managed to get some footage from both inside the bar and outside—including the moment the camera was knocked out of his hands. But in the end, I decided that—no matter how dramatic the incident was— it really had nothing to do with the story. Sure, the bartender had told me about Patrick Devlin visiting there recently. But Devlin had given me a reasonable explanation for that, so it had no real significance.

The story of my incident at the biker bar with Haussman quickly became the biggest topic talked about in the newsroom, though.

"What's the latest version?" I asked Maggie at one point.

"They say you got jumped on by ten guys and tied down to a pool table. You somehow got loose, grabbed a pool cue and a bicycle chain, and then fought them off. You broke the pool cue over one guy's head and almost put another one's eye out swinging the bicycle chain. Then this whole SWAT team of like a hundred cops swooped down and hauled them off to jail."

"That's a tad exaggerated."

"What really happened?"

"There were three of them. They threatened me and Scott inside the bar, then attacked him and grabbed me when we went outside. We would have been in trouble, but a cop showed up and saved us."

"Still pretty cool," Maggie said.

"It sounds a lot cooler talking about it than it was at the time. It was actually pretty scary."

She was right though.

It did sound pretty cool.

And a helluva lot more interesting than anything I was able to go with that evening on the air.

* * *

"How do you think that went?" I asked Jack Faron after the newscast.

"It was a bit weak."

"I couldn't use most of my best stuff."

"Maybe you shouldn't have used any of it."

"What are you trying to say?"

"The story's over, Clare."

He was right, of course. If someone else had done the report I'd just done, I wouldn't have even put it on the air. There was no real news value to it. I did it because I'd spent all this time going to New Hampshire and because it mattered to me. I was letting my personal feelings and prejudices take precedence over my news judgment. That wasn't a very good thing to do when you were the news director.

"I've given you a lot of leeway on this story," Faron said. "I knew it was important to you because of your history with the Devlin family and the story. And we got some good stuff out of it. But now I think it's just time to move on."

"Sandy Marston is still on the loose. When they catch him and his girlfriend Louise, there could be some big news out of that."

"So, when that happens, we'll put it on the air. Okay?"

"You're saying you want me to drop the whole thing for now?"

"I need you back as my news director, Clare."

CHAPTER 29

"I've hit a wall with this story," I told Janet Wood. "I've gone everywhere I can think of, I've talked to everyone who might know something about Lucy or any of the six bodies in New Hampshire ... and I still don't have any answers to what really happened to Lucy or any of the others."

"Maybe there are no answers," Janet said.

"What does that mean?"

"That's something you told me a couple of times, Clare. Sometimes you just have to cut your losses and walk away from a story. You know that as well as I do. In the end, sometimes you simply have to walk away."

We were sitting at the bar of the Water Club in Manhattan, which overlooks the East River. I'd asked Janet to meet me there after the meeting in Jack Faron's office. I just needed to talk to someone. I swiveled around on my barstool now and looked out the glass window surrounding the restaurant. You could see the water outside and the lights of Brooklyn and Queens in the distance.

"I like this place," I said. "Do you want to know why?"

"No bikers at the bar?"

I smiled.

"My first year in New York, when I started working for the *Tribune,* I won an award from the Newspaper Women's Association as the best new reporter in the city. There was a big presentation ceremony here. I stood up, made a little speech, and everyone patted me on the back and told me what a great future I had. I can remember it like it was yesterday. Coming to this place and accepting that award. I was still young then, and the future seemed so damn bright to me back then."

"Hey, let's not get so maudlin, Clare—I'd say things have worked out pretty well for you."

"You think?"

"Sure. You had a terrific run as a newspaper reporter, then went on TV. Now you're a big executive on a New York City station. Not a lot of women have done as much as you, even in this day and age. You've come a long way, Clare."

"Professionally speaking."

"What else is there?"

"My personal life."

"Oh, that . . ."

"Not so good on that front, huh?"

"There's probably some room for improvement," Janet said diplomatically.

I signaled the bartender for another drink. I was drinking Amstel Light, mostly because I can drink a lot of beer without getting drunk. Janet was drinking a daiquiri.

"Three marriages, three divorces," I said. "Three strikes and out. Okay, I just have to admit to myself that I'm not very good with marriage, huh? The funny thing is, though, I always thought I would have had the perfect marriage when I got married the first time. That we'd have perfect babies and live happily ever after. Felt that way about the second and third times I got married, too, believe it or not. Until they fell apart just like my first marriage. Hell, I should have known better. Should have learned that it didn't work that way from my own parents when I was growing up."

"They didn't have a good marriage?"

I'd never talked about my childhood much before, not even with Janet. But I'd had a few drinks, and it was on my mind after everything that had happened.

"My parents were married for like forty years," I said. "Never cheated on each other, never split up, never even spent a night apart during that entire time. On the surface, their marriage seemed fine—everyone thought they were a happy couple. The reality was it was a big lie. At least for my mother.

"My father never let her do anything. He ran the house like a tyrant, and she took it. He never hit her or anything like that. He abused her in a worse way. She had no life. She'd married him when she was nineteen, and that's what young girls did then. She never had a chance to express herself or find out anything about herself. My father wouldn't let her drive a car, go out with friends, even go to the movies without him. At home, she had to watch the same TV shows as he did.

"One day, when I was sixteen or seventeen and in high school, she came into my room. I could tell she'd been crying. She suddenly told me that the only reason she stayed with him was me. She didn't want me to come from a broken home, that was very important to her. Then she told me that once I was old enough, I needed to move far from home and get away from him. Go to college, live and work in a different city . . . whatever it took. She said she wanted me to have a real life, and not wind up like her.

"A few years later, I experienced my father's wrath firsthand. I did something wrong—something he couldn't find it in his heart to forgive me for. We had a big falling out. I didn't speak to him for a couple of years after that. Even at the end, when he was dying, I always thought he was still mad at me. Mad because he couldn't control me, the way he'd controlled my mother.

"So," I said, looking down at my Amstel, "I guess you could say I'm not exactly a big fan of the institution of marriage."

Janet picked up her daiquiri and took a sip. She drank like she did everything else. Precise, well-thought out, always in complete control. I'd never seen Janet drunk. Or out of control at all. Not even a little bit high. She was always so perfect in everything she did.

"Not all marriages are like that," Janet said.

"Right, some are worse."

"And some are good."

"Name one."

"Okay, mine."

"That doesn't count. You're goddamned perfect, Janet. Everything else about you is perfect, so your marriage must be, too."

Janet shook her head. "My marriage isn't perfect, Clare. There's a lot of things wrong with it. It's not a fairy tale. You don't just live happily ever after. But it's sure better than the alternative."

"Which is?"

"Being alone like you."

I didn't have an answer for that one.

"I'm curious about something," Janet said. "What did you do that was so bad your father never forgave you?"

"It's not important."

"You don't want to talk about it?"

"Some other time."

I'd told her too much already.

She asked me about Elliott Grayson. I told her about our meeting at the bar in SoHo, how he had kissed me on the cheek at the end, made the comment that he whispered into my ear about liking my legs—and how he continued to make it clear he was interested in pursuing a more intimate relationship with me than just reporter/politician.

"How do you feel about that?"

"Ambivalent."

"What are you going to do?"

"I don't know."

"Good to see you have a definite plan of action."

"Look, he called me a few times while I was away. He wants to get together again. I'm supposed to get back to him with an answer soon. My only problem is I have no idea what my answer is going to be."

"Why not go out with him?"

"Just like that?"

"Sure, see what happens."

"You don't think it exhibits a certain lack of journalistic integrity on my part?"

"You said your boss was okay with it."

"Yeah, but I figured you would disapprove."

"Hey, Elliott Grayson is quite a catch."

"That's what everybody keeps telling me."

CHAPTER 30

"I'M REALLY GLAD you decided to see me tonight," Grayson said.

"Me, too."

"For a while there, I wasn't sure you were going to show up."

"It was touch and go," I admitted.

We were sitting in Grayson's apartment. It was in a high-rise on the Upper East Side, in the East 80s near the East River. Nice apartment, nice location. Of course, he could be living in Washington, DC, pretty soon if the election turned out right for him.

We'd come upstairs after having dinner at the Palm Restaurant in Midtown Manhattan, where I discovered his picture was on the wall along with the other politicians and celebrities that ate there. I was impressed. Afterward, we went to a small café for drinks and dessert. Then he asked me if I wanted to come to his place for some coffee or something to finish the night.

Now, I knew that he wasn't really talking about coffee. He knew that he wasn't talking about coffee. He knew that I knew he wasn't talking about coffee. When a man asks you at the end of a date if you want to come up to his apartment for coffee, he's really talking about sex. The word coffee is simply a substitute for sex. This is one of the unwritten rules of dating. I knew very well that going up to Elliott Grayson's apartment for coffee was tantamount to signing a letter of intent that I'd already made up my mind to sleep with the guy.

And so there I was.

Sitting in his living room now.

Drinking coffee, making small talk, and waiting for Elliott Grayson to make his move.

"There's something I need to say here before whatever is going to happen between us happens," I said.

"Sure."

"I realize now that I may have misjudged you."

"Really?" he said with feigned astonishment.

"I do make mistakes."

"I'm sure you do."

"Then why act so surprised?"

"I just didn't think you admitted them."

"Yeah, well . . ."

"Is that why you decided to come back to my place with me tonight?"

"Let me say this my way."

"Sorry. Go ahead with your apology."

"It's not exactly an apology."

"It sure sounds like an apology."

"Actually, it's more like a clarification."

"Okay."

"Maybe an apologetic clarification."

"Whatever you say."

I took a deep breath and plunged ahead.

"I really did suspect in the beginning that you had something to do with Lucy Devlin's disappearance. And with those six dead kids in New Hampshire, too. I know it sounds crazy, but I convinced myself that you were hiding something and that the two cases were definitely connected. Maybe you were just too inviting a target. Big-shot prosecutor, big-time Senate candidate—I thought about what a good story it would be if you turned out to be the bad guy here. Somewhere along the line, I lost sight of the actual facts in this story—which I don't normally do. I'm sorry."

"See, that was an apology."

"You're right, it's an apology."

He smiled.

"So, I'm no longer a suspect in your mind for the disappearance of Lucy Devlin?"

"No."

"Or those six dead children in New Hampshire?"

"No."

"You don't suspect me of criminal activity of any kind?"

"No, I wouldn't be here if I did."

Grayson made an exaggerated gesture of wiping sweat from his brow. "Whew, that's a big relief!" he said.

I looked around the room. There was a picture on the end table next to me of him as a young boy. An older man and woman were in the picture with him.

"Your parents?" I asked.

"Yes."

"Are they still alive?"

"No, they're both dead now," he said.

"Mine, too."

I took a sip of my coffee and looked again at the picture.

"How come there's no Mrs. Grayson for you now?"

"Never found the right woman, I guess."

"Not yet."

That's when he leaned over and kissed me full on the lips. It was a clumsy move and, frankly, a little disappointing from such an important guy. I mean, it reminded me of a guy I dated in high school coming at me in the back seat of the car at the neighborhood drive-in. I guess all guys—young and old, rich and poor, experienced or not—all tend to revert to the same basic instincts at that particular moment.

"I love your lips," he said as he kissed me.

"Hmmm."

Another kiss. This one gentler, but somehow more passionate.

"I love your eyes," he whispered in my ear.

More kisses. This was definitely moving to a new plateau.

"I love your hair," he was saying now.

"You're in luck," I told him. "I'm running a special this week. You get all of them in one package."

He kept kissing me.

"Do you know what I think we should do?" he asked.

"Debate the issue of public school versus private school spending for the average taxpayer?" I asked as he nibbled on my ear.

"I think we should go into the bedroom and make love."

I sighed.

"There could be a problem with that," I said.

"What's the problem?"

"Oh, there's these pesky rules about a newswoman sleeping with someone she's covering on a story."

"What kind of rules?"

"Journalistic rules."

"What happens if you break them?"

"That's kind of a gray area."

He kissed me again, this time on the neck. I felt a tingle of excitement surge through me.

"Of course, they may not actually be rules," I said.

"Good."

Another kiss on the lips, this time deeper and more passionate.

"More like guidelines, really."

"I see."

"My boss thinks they probably don't even apply to you and me in this situation."

"Your boss sounds like a very perceptive man."

"Anyway, who's going to know?"

"I won't tell."

"It'll be our secret."

We made out for a while more on the couch. Slowly at first, then more and more aggressively when I didn't stop him.

It's funny how things work out. Under the right circumstances, Grayson and I might have really worked together. That night could have been the beginning of a long, serious relationship. But instead something happened that changed everything.

It was right after we got into the bedroom. He had taken his clothes off and was helping me out of mine.

"I guess we have Lucy Devlin to thank for this, huh?"

"What do you mean?" I asked.

"Well, if she hadn't gotten herself kidnapped that day, you and I might not be here now. Wherever she is—dead or alive—we should thank little Lucy. We're going to have sex because of her."

I pulled away from him.

"What's wrong?" he asked.

"That's a terrible thing to say."

"C'mon, I'm just kidding."

"Kidding about something like that?"

"Clare, don't make a big deal out of it."

"Yeah, well, try telling that to her mother."

He tried to kiss me again, but I pulled away. I didn't want to touch him. I suddenly couldn't stand the sight of this man.

Without even thinking about what I was doing, I stood up and started to put my clothes back on.

Grayson looked confused.

"What are you doing?"

"Leaving."

"But I thought you wanted to be here with me."

"That's before you made the Lucy Devlin crack."

"You're really overreacting."

"I don't think so."

"Okay, let's just forget about it and start all over again."

"How about you go ahead without me?"

I wasn't sure why I reacted exactly the way I did. I knew it was just a casual, offhand remark. Sure, it was in bad taste. But I said stuff like that all the time. Everyone does in a newsroom, and I've done a lot worse.

But there was something about the way he'd brought Lucy Devlin into the bedroom with us that really got to me.

Something that made me believe I could never be intimate with this man.

So, I got dressed, walked out the door of Elliott Grayson's apartment, and never looked back.

CHAPTER 31

ONE DAY NOT long after that, I got a call from a hospital in Manhattan. They said Anne Devlin had taken a sudden turn for the worse in her battle against cancer and been admitted to the hospital. They said she was asking to see me.

When I got to the hospital, there was no one else in her room. Anne was hooked to a breathing apparatus and tubes that fed her and equipment that monitored her vital body signs.

A nurse walked by in the hallway where I stood looking in the room. She was middle-aged, stocky, and had a name tag that said her name was Joyce.

"How long has she been here?" I asked.

"They brought her in yesterday," the nurse named Joyce said.

"Does her family know?"

"She said she has no family."

"She had a husband."

Joyce shook her head. "We called him. He said he had no relationship with her anymore."

"And there's no one else? Brothers? Sisters? Friends?"

"She said you were the only one she had to call."

To me, the worst thing in the world is to die alone. Without any family or friends or loved ones to grieve for you. I've sometimes been terrified that I'll end up like that. Like Anne Devlin, I had no family. Sometimes late at night, I've lain in bed and wondered what would become of me when I got old. Lying in a hospital bed somewhere, with only doctors and nurses around me. Just like Anne. The only person she could think of to call was a reporter who'd covered the tragic disappearance of her daughter years before.

I took a deep breath. I really didn't want to go into that hospital room. I've been around people dying before, and it's never an easy thing. I know people who will tell you that there's something almost beautiful about the experience. All of the pain disappears, there's a look of serenity on the dead person's face at the end, that they've found peace at last. Maybe so, but I've seen the other side, too.

I remember my father dying in the hospital. He had cancer, too, and it had spread all throughout his body. Lying there, wracked with pain and loaded with drugs, yelling at me about all the ways that I'd let him down as his daughter. My mother had died a year before, and he was angry about everything that had happened to him. Angry at the cancer that was eating away at him. Angry at my mother for leaving him. Angry at me because I was the only person left for him to be mad at, I guess. But he didn't want to let go of life. Instead, he just kept railing on about God and himself and my mother and me until his very last heartbeat. When he was finally dead, I wasn't sure if I was happy that he was finally gone or sad about the real truths left unsaid between us. Probably a bit of both.

I've watched people die on the job, too. Murder victims. Accident scenes. Hospital emergency rooms. I've never seen one go easy. I remember one guy they pulled out of his car after a high-speed, head-on collision with a tractor trailer truck. He had massive internal bleeding, critical head injuries, and damage to almost every vital organ. He lay there on the side of the road for nearly twenty minutes, with paramedics futilely doing what little they could for him. Why didn't he just die, I thought to myself that day. Finally, he did. But, like my father, the poor guy struggled to the end. Death might be inevitable, but all of us try to run from it as long as we can.

I thought about all these things now as I approached Anne Devlin in her hospital bed. She became aware of me as I got closer. She turned her head slightly toward me and tried to smile.

"How are you doing?" I asked.

"What do you think?" she whispered.

"It could be worse."

"How?"

"You're still here."

"That doctor told me not long ago I had only a few months to live. I was pretty upset about that at the time. Now, well, I'd settle for those months. So many things have been happening about Lucy. I just want to last long enough to . . ."

"You'll have plenty of time to see how things come out," I said soothingly, even though I wasn't sure if it was true.

"That means everything to me," she said. "If I could just see her once more before my time is over."

She knew about all the stuff I'd reported, of course. The search for Marston and Big Lou. The connection between Marston and the other little girl nearby a few days before Lucy disappeared. The authorities' identification of him now as a potential suspect in the case.

"Do you think he's the one who took her?" she asked.

"The police and the feds think he might be."

"Will they catch him?"

"Sooner or later."

"And then he'll tell them the truth about Lucy?"

That was the big question, of course.

"I think this is the best chance we've ever had to find out what really happened to her," I said.

It was the only thing I could think of to say.

"She's alive," Anne said.

"That's always been a possibility."

"She's alive," she repeated with grim determination.

I wasn't sure if she was trying to convince me or herself that it was true.

The problem was it was a waiting game now for the answers. The case seemed to be coming to a head, one way or another. Hopefully, the truth would be known before too long. In the best-case scenario, all we had to do was wait until Marston and Big Lou were caught, then find out what they had to say about Lucy. But even if that happened, it would take time. I couldn't tell that to Anne Delvin. Because she was just about all out of time.

"I think Lucy's alive somewhere and we'll find her very soon," I said, figuring I owed her at least some small comfort.

"Me, too," she said.

I stayed with her through the night. She kept drifting in and out of sleep. When she was awake, she talked mostly about Lucy. Things they had done together. Good-time memories. But eventually she would come back to the terrible day that she went missing.

"Why did he take her?" she cried out at one point.

"I don't know."

"He has to pay for it. They all have to pay for it. They took my daughter, goddamnit! You can't let them go free, Clare. You've got to make them tell you where she is!"

But then the anger would turn to grief.

"I'm sorry," she sobbed to me. "I'm so sorry."

"There's nothing to be sorry about."

"I was her mother. I should have protected her. I didn't do that. This is all my fault."

I looked down at her in the hospital bed and thought about how I'd wound up here. A long time ago, I'd made a promise to Anne Devlin that I'd help her find out what happened to her missing daughter, Lucy. That Lucy would never be forgotten. I knew now that I would have to keep that promise, even more than ever before.

I squeezed Anne's hand tightly, trying to let her know that I was still there for her.

She squeezed back.

I held her hand until the early morning hours, when the first rays of sunlight began streaming in through the window next to her bed and she'd made it to another day.

CHAPTER 32

THEY FOUND SANDY Marston and Louise Carbone a few days later hiding out in a remote farmhouse in Idaho.

The two of them had kept a low profile during most of their time on the run. After leaving New York, they headed west through Ohio, Indiana, and Illinois, then north through areas of Nebraska and Montana. By the time the nationwide alert went out to law enforcement officials around the country for their arrest, Marston and Big Lou were pretty much flying under the radar in an area where not many people were going to spot them.

When they got to Idaho, they came across an abandoned farmhouse and decided to hole up there for a while. They stayed hidden for a few days—and probably could have lasted months—without arousing any suspicion.

But then Marston made a mistake.

One night he got on his motorcycle and rode into a town ten miles away. They needed food and other supplies. If he'd left after that, no one probably would have paid much attention to him. There were lots of motorcycle guys passing through that part of Idaho.

Instead, he stopped for a beer at a roadside bar on the way out of town. Some guy at the bar made a derogatory remark about his motorcycle or the length of his hair or maybe both. Words were exchanged, followed by fists. Then Marston pulled out a knife and stabbed the local in the chest. He bled to death on the floor of the bar. Marston ran outside, jumped on his cycle, and roared away with a posse of Idaho police cars soon in hot pursuit.

He had a head start, and he might have been able to get away if he just kept going. But he made a U-turn and headed back to the farmhouse instead. I never understood if he did that because he wanted to get back to Big Lou or he was just stupid. In any case, the police followed him back to the house and surrounded the place. Gunfire came from the house, and everyone hunkered down for a standoff.

At some point the cops realized who they had surrounded inside. Federal agents soon descended on the area in huge numbers, with SWAT teams and all the latest weapons and technological equipment. Elliott Grayson flew out to Idaho to direct the operation himself.

It put him on every nightly newscast and—some political observers predicted—probably was going to insure his election as Senator. If Teddy Weller had tried to set up the rumors about Grayson and Lucy Devlin to make him look bad, it had backfired on him now and looked as if it might cost him any chance he might have had to still win the election.

I was there on the scene in Idaho, too. Channel 10 flew in a team of reporters—Brett and Dani even anchored the news on a remote from outside the siege at the farmhouse—since we had been the first to break the story. I did a lot of the on-camera reporting as well as directing our news operation.

Because of the danger and volatility of the situation, the press was kept back from the siege area itself. We got regular updates from a federal spokesman. But mostly we were just showing a lot of shots of Idaho countryside and speculating about what was going to happen. We were all wrong, of course. No one predicted that it would end up quite the way it did.

The actual details of what transpired that final day were never quite clear. But the official version said it happened this way:

The feds tried to talk Sandy Marston and Louise Carbone out of the house without anyone getting hurt. There were loudspeakers set up, telephone calls into the house, and even a note tied to a rock that was thrown through a window. Marston's response was to take pot shots at the agents huddled behind their cars and barricades. Finally, Grayson ran out of patience and decided to bring it all to a head.

The idea was to fire a single tear gas canister into the house to flush them out. It should have worked. The only problem was there was a fireplace in the house. Marston or Big Lou had lit a fire there at one point during the night. The tear gas canister crashed through a window and landed in the fire. It exploded, quickly setting the entire house on fire. This wasn't like Waco, where the entire building blew up. But the fire and smoke was enough to make Marston flee the house before the law enforcement people outside were ready.

He ran out the front door, holding a gun in his hand. Someone shouted for him to drop it. Instead, he opened fire. He kept running toward the line of federal agents, shooting as he moved. They returned the fire, and he died in a hail of bullets.

Louise Carbone was right behind him. Maybe if Marston hadn't opened fire the way he did, what happened next could have been avoided. But you had to put yourself in the place of the federal agents. One of the people inside the house had just tried to kill them, running toward them with a gun. Now here came the second one. She had something in her hand, too. It was hard to tell what it was amid all the smoke and confusion, but they assumed it was a weapon, too. They yelled at her to stop and drop what she was carrying. When she didn't, one of the agents fired a single shot. He said later he just wanted to hit her in the leg and wound her. But he aimed high, and the bullet crashed into her chest. She died right there on the ground outside the farmhouse, a few feet from Sandy Marston.

The object in her hand turned out not to be a gun.

It was a picture.

She was clutching it to her heart when she was hit.

The picture was of a young girl.

Maureen Carbone.

Big Lou's daughter.

CHAPTER 33

THE PRESS CONFERENCE could have gone either way.

On the one hand, Elliott Grayson and his people had accidentally set the farmhouse on fire and then shot to death both suspects, leaving many questions unanswered. And one of the dead suspects turned out to be unarmed, holding only a picture of her daughter.

On the other hand, it was hard to arouse much sympathy for Sandy Marston and Louise Carbone.

He was a member of a motorcycle gang who was now a suspect in one of the most famous missing child cases of all time. He'd stabbed to death a man in a bar for no real reason. He and Big Lou had fired on law enforcement authorities repeatedly, charged their lines, and probably deserved what they got.

That was the way it sorted out in the end.

One of the reasons for that was the impressive performance Grayson put on during the press conference after the shootout.

"Why did you shoot to kill?" one reporter asked.

"We had a suspect who had fired at federal officers and police and was still firing at them at the end. I was trying to save the lives of my men and other innocent people."

"What about the woman?"

"She was inside that house, too. There was gunfire coming from more than one place. She was shooting, too, we know that for a fact. She charged a line of federal officers who knew this. Everyone acted appropriately under the circumstances."

"You don't think the officer who fired the fatal shot into the unarmed woman, Louise Carbone, should face any type of disciplinary action?"

"No, I'm putting him in for a commendation medal."

"What is the message you think this incident sends out to people?"

"That the world is a better place today because the likes of Sandy Marston and Louise Carbone are no longer in it. Especially for the children."

Grayson was good, no question about it. I was impressed, and I was sure lots of people were going to be, too. This was the kind of thing that could get him elected, I thought to myself as I watched him deftly handing all the questions from the press that day.

He had not spoken to me since that night in his apartment. A couple of times, he caught my eye during the press conference. But he looked away. That was fine with me. I'd had a decision to make, and I made it. I had my reasons. They might not make sense to anyone else, but I had to live with myself. I didn't think I could do that and be with Elliott Grayson.

He saved the biggest news of his press conference until the very end.

"There's one more development," Grayson said. "I wasn't sure whether or not to make this public right away, but I think everyone has a right to know. Sandy Marston left a note. He talked about Lucy Devlin and about how he abducted her and what he did to her."

I stifled a gasp. It was all coming together now.

"Marston apparently realized he was going to die, and so he confessed in the note that he forced her onto his motorcycle and took her back to the Warlock Warriors headquarters. Then he raped her repeatedly. When he fell asleep, she tried to run away. He caught her and, during the struggle, threw her against a wall. She hit her head, and she died."

There was a stunned reaction from the reporters.

"Are you sure the note was from Marston?" someone finally asked.

"Yes."

"What if he just made that story up?"

"Why would he do that?"

"Some sort of sick last joke."

"Marston didn't make it up."

"How do you know that?"

"He told us where he buried Lucy Devlin's body."

* * *

The site was a wooded area in Dutchess County, some one hundred miles north of the city. There was a cabin and a lake on the property, and the Warlock Warriors had sometimes gone up there when things got too hot in the city. After he killed Lucy, Marston said in the note, he decided that was where he'd get rid of the body. He stole a car, took her up there late at night and dug a grave deep in the woods. He put Lucy's body in it, filled it up again, and then went off to get drunk.

The search in Dutchess County for the body quickly became a media event in itself. Outside contractors were brought in, and soon the area was filled with bulldozers, steam shovels, tractor trailers, and all sorts of other excavation equipment.

The note from Marston hadn't said exactly where he buried the body. So, there was a lot of area to cover. On top of that, the land had grown over extensively with trees and shrubs and weeds over the years since then. Any obvious signs of Lucy Devlin's grave were long gone.

They dug for days. It became a staple of every TV news show, including us at Channel 10. Video of the digging, the excavation equipment, the workers...and a solemn newscaster reporting that there was still no sign of poor little Lucy Devlin.

Grayson was there every day, directing the whole operation. I thought about how he'd done the same thing in New Hampshire a few years earlier where they found the other six children. I wondered about the similarities and if maybe Sandy Marston could have had something to do with those deaths, too. Or maybe he wasn't involved in any of it. I kept hoping against hope this was all a big ruse. That Sandy Marston made it all up about Lucy Devlin just to yank our chains one last time—even in death.

Then, on the tenth day, they found her.

There was no indication that she was even recognizable after all those years in the ground. But they found her skull had been crushed, just like Marston said. That appeared to be the cause of death. There were also injuries to other parts of her body, where someone apparently had beaten her before she was killed. I thought about the cute little girl—the one who loved school, who loved animals, who loved life—that I'd seen in all the pictures.

I didn't want the story to end this way.

Even then, after Grayson and his agents found the body, I suppose I still harbored some kind of deep-down fantasy that this wasn't Lucy.

That it was all a mistake.

That it was really some other child Marston had killed.

But there was no mistake.

The announcement came later that they had confirmed the identity of the little girl's body found in the grave.

It was Lucy Devlin.

CHAPTER 34

"So, Lucy Devlin's dead," Janet said. "Sandy Marston confessed to the abduction and murder in the note, and we know he was telling the truth because he knew where the body was. Now he's dead, too."

"End of story," I said.

"What about the other six bodies in New Hampshire?"

"There's no real evidence—at least that I can find—of any connection between them and Lucy Devlin."

"Marston never mentioned them in his confession note?"

"Nope."

"So that's it, right? It's over."

"It's over," I said.

"And you're unhappy about that?"

"I'm fine."

"No, you're not."

We were sitting in the living room of my apartment. Janet had shown up at the door a little earlier carrying a six-pack of beer and a large pizza with extra cheese, mushrooms, onions, and sausage. She said she thought I might need some company and some cheering up. Sure sounded like a good plan to me.

Janet picked up a knife and fork now and cut off a small piece of pizza. She put it delicately in her mouth. Not a speck of tomato sauce on her face or hands. I don't understand people who eat pizza like that.

"I think the reason you're unhappy," Janet said between chews of her pizza, "is that you always believed Lucy Devlin was still alive. And that one day you would find her. Now you know you were wrong. Hence, the feeling of disappointment and sadness and unhappiness even though you just helped break a very big story. Am I right or am I right?"

"That's a bit of an overstatement."

"You didn't hold out hope she was alive until the very end?"

"Of course, I had hope. But I knew the facts, too, Janet. I've covered missing person cases before. When a child is abducted, the chances of finding him or her is good in the first few hours, maybe even the first day or so. After that, the odds go down dramatically. I know it was a pleasant dream to think of Lucy alive, all grown up and living happily ever after somewhere. But that's all it was: a dream. I knew she was probably—hell, almost certainly—dead."

"Did you know you have a tell?" Janet asked.

"What are you talking about?"

"When you lie, you run your fingers through your hair."

"No, I don't."

I suddenly realized I was running my hand through my hair as I said it.

"See, you did it again."

"You think I'm lying?"

"I know you're lying."

I looked down at the pizza. I'd eaten three pieces already. I had the fourth in my hand. Pizza always looks so good when you first get it. Then, after you've eaten a few pieces, it doesn't look so good anymore. Right now it was making me nauseous. I put the pizza slice down.

"I hoped she was alive," I said. "I convinced myself she was. Part of this was for Anne Devlin, but part of it was for me."

"It's just a story, Clare. There'll be other stories."

"She was friggin' eleven years old."

"There's a lot of bad people out there like Sandy Marston."

"That's the other thing that bothers me."

"What?"

"I met him. I didn't think he was that bad a guy. Okay, he killed or hurt a couple of people. But that was in fights, and they were no pillars of society either. I guess I just didn't see him as being the kind of guy who could kill Lucy Devlin."

"Maybe the woman did it."

"Louise Carbone?"

"Yes. You said she was insanely jealous of other women around Marston. If he was interested in a little girl like Lucy Devlin, it could have been enough to set her off. She might have killed Lucy, then he just helped get rid of the body."

"I thought of that, too," I said.

"It makes sense."

"Except for one thing."

"What's that?"

"I liked her."

I thought about Big Lou sitting in my office that day. Telling me about wanting to start a new life. About her daughter and her family and her ex-husband. I remembered, too, the way she was holding the picture of Maureen, her daughter, when she died.

"There's one other problem I have, too," I told Janet. "If Louise did it—or even if Marston was the killer—why did she come to me and tell this whole story about Elliott Grayson? Why did she try this extortion ploy with Grayson? What was she trying to accomplish? I mean, wouldn't she and Marston have wanted it to just all go away? Instead, they turned it into a big story again. A story that wound up getting them killed in the end."

"Who knows?" She shrugged. "Why does it matter?"

"It's a loose end."

"There's always loose ends."

"They bother me."

We talked about the case for a while more, then drifted off into other topics. One of them, as I knew it would, turned out to be my personal life. I told her then about my date with Grayson and my abrupt exit from his bedroom. I hadn't discussed it with anyone, even Janet, until that moment.

"Do you think I overreacted?" I asked.

"You might have been a little excessive."

"I just didn't want to be there with him anymore."

"Then you were right to go."

"The minute he made the Lucy Devlin remark, I just lost it."

Janet looked at me with a worried look on her face now.

"Like we said, Clare, the Lucy Devlin story is over. And that's all it was, just a story. I know how badly you feel and how close you got to the family and all that, but it is still just another story. You accidentally stumbled into it a long time ago and you've never really let go. Now it's time. You're the one who always preached about how you can't let any story become personal. Right?"

I looked down at the pizza box. There was still one piece left. If I ate it, I was going to hate myself in the morning.

"This is more than just another story," I said.

"What do you mean?"

"I've never talked about it to anyone before. It happened a long time ago, and I was a different person then. I didn't even know you. You're my best friend, Janet, but I always resisted telling you this because I thought you might think less of me. But now, well . . . since Lucy's dead, maybe this is the time. I just feel like I have to share it with someone. I guess you're nominated."

Janet sat and waited.

"I didn't accidentally happen onto the Lucy Devlin story fifteen years ago," I said.

"Okay."

"I was sleeping with Patrick Devlin."

She stared at me. "You slept with the father of Lucy Devlin while the entire city was looking for her?"

"No, before."

Janet looked confused.

"I met Patrick Devlin on a story I was doing about new construction projects in the city. He took me out for a drink, one thing led to another, and we wound up in bed. After that, we started having regular trysts on our lunch hours—sometimes back at his Gramercy Park town house. His wife worked during the day, and his daughter, Lucy, was at school, he told me. We had the place to ourselves.

"Except that last day, Lucy came home early. She walked in and saw us in bed together. She got very upset. She started to cry. Patrick calmed her down, and I thought the crisis was over. But soon after that she was gone.

"I've often wondered if that was the reason she ran away or put herself into a situation where someone could harm her that day. It all came back to me when Anne Devlin said Lucy had told her something about her father and sex. Anne was afraid that meant with Lucy. But Lucy was talking about me, the woman she found in her father's bed. I'll never know if I was somehow the impetus for everything that happened to her.

"The strange thing is that Anne Devlin and I got so close afterward. We both shared this devotion and this vow to never rest until we found out what happened to Lucy. She thought I was just being kind. But part of it was my guilt. My guilt for what I'd done to her and to her family."

"And that's why you were hoping against hope that one day Lucy would be found?" Janet asked.

"Yes."

"So you wouldn't have to live with the guilt anymore?"

"I forgot about it most of the time. Time is the great healer. As the years went by, other stuff happened and Lucy Devlin and her mother faded more and more into the background. Or at least I tried to compartmentalize it down deep inside of me. But this brought it all back. All the pain. All the sadness. All the guilt."

"Lucy's dead and her mother's dying, too," Janet said softly. "There's nothing more you can do about it now."

"I know," I said. "That's what's eating me up."

And then, for the first time in a long time, I began to cry.

I cried for Lucy Devlin.

And for Anne Devlin.

And for those six children found in a lonely grave in New Hampshire.

And, maybe most of all, I cried for myself, too.

PART II

SUMMERTIME NEWS

CHAPTER 35

IT WAS ONE of the hottest summers that anyone could remember in New York City.

The temperature soared over one hundred for eight days in a row at one point. It was in the nineties for much of July and virtually all of August. The humidity was so oppressive that even a short time outside left your clothes wet. There was no blackout this summer, but a few power scares. Con Edison kept issuing appeals for people to turn their air-conditioning down to conserve electricity, which everyone ignored. Being without lights didn't seem as bad as sweating under the blazing sun. Everywhere you went, the conversation was always about how hot it was.

At Channel 10, we led the news most days with an in-depth weather update package—talking about all the records that we were breaking in this one-of-a-kind summer.

There were tips about how to beat the heat.

Advice on how to avoid heat stroke or dehydration.

Cool places to go like the beach and air-conditioned museums and city parks.

Features on the New Yorker who had the hottest job—it was a tie between a pizza parlor worker and a guy who poured asphalt on the highway—and the New Yorker who had the coolest one—a butcher who worked in a meat freezer.

One day we even tried to prove the old adage that says: "It's so hot you could fry an egg out there." We dropped an egg on the sidewalk outside our Manhattan office to see if it would really fry. It didn't.

But you want to hear the truth?

It really wasn't any hotter than it always is at this time of year. It's always hot and miserable during July and August in New York City. When I worked at the *New York Tribune* as a newspaper reporter, my editor there used to avoid doing weather stories like that. "We're going to tell them on our front page that it's hot out?" he used to say. "I think they already know that. Where's the news?" In TV news, we had no such hesitation about telling people what they already know. Hence, it was all weather all the time.

Even the stories that weren't technically about the weather seemed to be mostly weather related.

We had a shark scare at one of the beaches off the coast of New Jersey, which gave a few good weeks of scare coverage. Footage of killer sharks, clips from *Jaws*, interviews with shark experts about what to do if you see one—"get the hell out of the water" seemed to be the general consensus. The shark that had been spotted turned out to be one of the harmless sand shark variety, but by then TV news had moved on to other stuff anyway.

There was also a big series about the water quality at area beaches. "ARE YOU MAKING YOURSELF SICK THIS SUMMER?" was the title. By the time we were finished with that and the shark series, people were afraid to go anywhere near the water.

Then there was the story of the street vendor who got busted for selling ice cream cones to kids in Central Park on a hot summer afternoon. An overzealous police officer not only wrote him a ticket for operating without a valid license, but actually hauled him off to jail. You had outraged kids, outraged parents, and outraged civil liberties groups. By the time the fiasco was over, the vendor wound up on the Jimmy Fallon show and the cop who arrested him was walking a beat in the Bronx.

The good thing for me was that all of this kept me from thinking too much about everything that had happened.

I spent most of my summer consumed with covering warm fronts, humidity indexes, and temperature fluctuations.

I hardly had any time for anything else.

I almost never even thought about Lucy Devlin.

Almost.

* * *

The Senate election was the other big story.

Elliott Grayson had a comfortable lead over Teddy Weller in the race for the Democratic nomination even before Lucy Devlin.

But, after the news about the killing of Marston and Big Lou and the discovery of Lucy Devlin's body, he began to pull away even further from Weller in the polls. By June, he had opened up a double-digit lead. By July, it was even higher. By August, with the Democratic primary only a few weeks away, some political observers were calling him unstoppable unless some scandal or mistake happened.

Grayson was playing the Lucy Devlin card as hard as he could. He talked about it constantly during speeches and campaign appearances and interviews. Hey, I'm the guy who solved the case that had been unsolved for years, he told everyone. It was a powerful argument for what a great crime fighter he was, and it seemed to be working with the voters.

Sometimes, when I saw him on TV, I thought about that night in his apartment. I wondered if I'd made the right decision by walking out on him. Not that it really mattered at this point. He never tried to call me or reach me anymore after that. At press conferences, he continued to avoid any contact with me. Whatever appeal I'd once held for him seemed to be gone now.

I thought about what Cliff Whitten had said about how Grayson would do anything to win. What if he somehow set up the whole Lucy Devlin story to get an edge in the election? It was a nice conspiracy theory, but nothing more. After all, I was the one who set everything in motion. No, he just got lucky. That's what happens to people like Elliott Grayson. They get lucky. They always wound up in the right place at the right time.

* * *

Anne Devlin was still alive, but just barely.

She'd rallied for a while and been released from the hospital, but she suffered a relapse over the summer that required more treatment. It was just a matter of time, of course, and the doctors said that time was now measured in weeks instead of months.

She'd been a poignant, heartbreaking figure at the memorial service that was held for Lucy, crying softly throughout the eulogies and collapsing to the ground in grief at one point before it was over. I thought that maybe she'd been holding on just for that, a last chance to say good-bye to her daughter, and that I'd hear about her death soon after that day. But she was still around, fighting an unbeatable battle against cancer until the very end.

I visited her a few times over the summer, but the truth is we really didn't have much to say to each other anymore, now that Lucy was truly gone.

Patrick Devlin didn't even bother to show up for Lucy's funeral, which shocked a lot of people. I mean, I understand that the guy had a new life and a new family now. But I wondered how he could be so indifferent to his own daughter's death. I wondered how he could completely turn his back on his former wife at such an emotional moment. I wondered how I could have ever been attracted to—and slept with—a man like that. I had made a lot of bad choices when it came to men in my life, but Patrick Devlin was right up there at the top of my list of regrets.

* * *

There was a small crisis in the office during July when the news director of another station made a run at Cassie O'Neal—trying to get her to jump to his station.

"They're offering her $50,000 more than she gets here," Jack Faron said when he told me about it.

"Gee, that works out to $1,000 an IQ point for her," I said.

"I wish you'd take this seriously, Clare."

"It's a little hard to take a woman like Cassie seriously who thinks *The Maury Povich Show* is intellectually challenging television."

"She never said that."

"Okay, but she did ask me once if the *New York Times* came out weekly or every day."

"She looks good on camera and all our viewer surveys show that she's very popular. I don't want to lose her. That's the bottom line."

"Give her the friggin' $50,000."

"No, you give her the $50,000, and it comes out of your news budget."

"I was going to hire another reporter with that money."

"Well, you get to keep Cassie instead."

"Lucky me."

Basically, we were going to give her a $50,000 raise because she looked good on the screen. There was something inherently wrong about that. I knew what was going to happen next, too. After Cassie turned them down, someone was going to come after Janelle. Then we'd pay her more money. That seemed obscene, too. When it was all over, Cassie and Janelle would be making more money than me—who was their boss. Brett and Dani were already making more than I was.

Damn.

I understood the reality of it, but that didn't mean I had to like it. No one was going to offer me more money, because I was over forty—and none of the men who ran the stations wanted to see women past forty on TV.

* * *

In late August, I spent my two weeks of vacation at Jack Faron's summer house in Sag Harbor on the eastern end of Long Island.

I was uncomfortable at first going there by myself. But it worked out all right. Jack and his wife and his kids were there on the weekend, and I liked them. Janet came out for a few days, too, to keep me company. Mostly, though, I enjoyed the solitude. I read, tanned myself at the beach, and took long walks beside the ocean.

For the first time in my life, I was thinking a lot about the future.

I was forty-five years old. I had no husband and no children and no family. I did have a good job, but I didn't feel the same passion for TV news that I used to for newspapers. The truth was there was really nothing I was passionate about anymore. That sort of bothered me.

Maybe I was just going through a midlife crisis.

I called Sam, my last ex-husband, one night. It was late and I was lonely and I just dialed his home number. I wasn't sure exactly why. Maybe I hoped he'd broken up with this Dede woman he'd told me about the last time we talked. Or that he'd lied about her just to make me jealous. Or that the sound of my voice would fill him with so much passion that he'd dump Dede and their unborn child and run back to my arms. I should point out that I had drunk a large amount of alcohol at this point and may not have been thinking as clearly as I would have otherwise. But it didn't matter anyway. A woman answered the phone. Dede, I assumed. I didn't say anything to her. I just hung up.

I talked to another one of my ex-husbands again, too. The first one, the doctor. I went to a Fourth of July barbeque, and he was there. He had his wife and their two kids with him. A boy who was nine and a girl he said had just turned eleven. I thought about how she was the same age as Lucy Devlin was when she disappeared. My ex was friendly enough, and his wife was very nice to me, and the kids were cute—but the whole encounter depressed me. I made some excuse about having another place to go and left the barbecue as quickly as I could.

Janet fixed me up with a couple of other men that she thought might be good for me, but none of them ever called back for a second date. Which was fine with me. I was tired of dating anyway. I was tired of all the games. I was just tired.

* * *

When I got back to work after Labor Day weekend, there was a phone message waiting for me. It was from Oscar Robles. At first, I didn't even remember the name. Then it came to me. He was the police chief of Mountainboro. The guy who saved me from the bikers at the bar in New Hampshire. The message just said I should call him.

"What's up?" I said when I got him on the phone.

"When you were up here a few months ago, you asked me to contact you if I ever thought of anything else," he said. "I might have something."

Like I said earlier, every story has a life of its own.

There's always a moment when the story can either die or suddenly lurch back to life. I figure there were times even in Watergate when Carl Bernstein and Bob Woodward could have made a decision or a move that would have killed the story right there. Sometimes it's about being smart, sometimes it's about instincts, sometimes it's just about blind luck. In this case, it was probably a bit of all of that.

I'd chased after a lot of leads, hoping one of them would pan out. Most of them didn't. But Oscar Robles did.

"I couldn't stop thinking about something you said. About how there might be some common link between all six of the dead kids that got them killed. So anyway, one day I just decided to run some checks. We got this new FBI hookup here not long ago that gives us access to all kinds of computer stuff if we want it. I ran all six of the victims' names through the computer, just to see what turned up. I got a hit with one of them. It turned out one of them had a police record. Joseph Manielli."

"What'd it say?"

"That he stole a car."

"I already knew that. His parents told me. He was only twelve, so the Pennsylvania authorities just let him off with some kind of juvenile probation. I checked later."

"This was in San Jose, California."

"California? How would a twelve-year-old kid get to California?"

"It happened last month."

It took a second or two for the enormity of what he was telling me to sink in.

"Last month," I repeated.

"They took the kid's fingerprints back in Pennsylvania for that first car heist, even though he was so young. So they were always in the system. Guess what? They matched up to this guy who's arrested in San Jose. He's using a different name, of course.

But he's the same one who was arrested at the age of twelve in Pennsylvania. How does a kid who died years ago get arrested for car theft after all this time? Simple answer. He never died."

"Who's the body they dug out of the grave that's supposed to be Joseph Manielli?"

"I have no idea. Raises some interesting questions though, doesn't it?"

Yep, it sure did.

Elliott Grayson had been the one who identified the bodies of the six children in that grave.

Now Grayson was on the verge of being elected to the Senate. After that, everyone agreed he had a big political future ahead of him. The possibilities were endless for Elliott Grayson. Maybe even the White House one day.

But he had lied—or at the very least been wrong—about Joey Manielli.

If that wasn't Joey Manielli in the grave in New Hampshire, what about Becky Gale, Donald Chang, Tamara Greene, William O'Shaughnessy, and Emily Neiman?

And what about Lucy Devlin?

PART III

ELECTION DAY

CHAPTER 36

WITH JUST DAYS to go now until the September Democratic Senate primary election, the latest polls showed that Elliott Grayson continued to hold a seemingly insurmountable lead over Teddy Weller.

The experts also still predicted Grayson would have an easy time beating the Republican opponent in November.

He sure had the look of a winner. His campaign speeches were no longer attacks against Weller. He talked instead about his vision for the future of America, how he was going to represent New York in Washington, the kind of Senator he wanted to be. The message was clear: This election is already over—everyone better get on the victory train now, before it pulls out of the station.

But Grayson was more than just a successful politician. With his good looks and his charisma, he had somehow achieved a kind of rock star popularity. Young people were returning to politics in droves to campaign for him and ring doorbells and hand out literature. In an era when young people—and most voters in general—seemed to have apathy and disdain for politicians, Grayson had figured out how to connect to voters like no other candidate had in years.

He was making the gossip columns regularly, too. For the past couple of months, he'd been dating an actress who was a star in one of the daytime soaps. They showed up everywhere together—movie premieres, the best restaurants, and even some campaign appearances. She was drop-dead gorgeous. Just like him. Even I had to admit, they made a terrific-looking couple.

A lot of people suggested the actress was the final part of the puzzle for him. Since he wasn't married, voters might have started to wonder if they didn't hear anything about his personal life. But here he was dating a high-profile woman. Yep, that Elliott Grayson was a cool guy, all right.

I wondered idly if maybe that was the reason he'd asked me out back in the spring. I was a TV newswoman, which is a pretty high-profile person. Maybe he thought I would be good for his campaign at the time, too. The ultimate politician and the hotshot Pulitzer Prize–winning newswoman arm-in-arm. No question about it, he could have used me for political purposes. On the other hand, maybe he really did like my legs. Of course, there was no way I was ever going to find out the answer to that one now.

I thought again about how I'd just walked out on him that night in his bedroom when he brought up Lucy Devlin just before we were about to have sex.

Why did I do that?

Even I had to admit it was an over-the-top reaction to a seemingly innocent and joking remark he made. And Grayson apologized right after he said it. Hell, I've said a lot of politically incorrect things—cracked a lot of dark humor jokes—when I talk about people in the news like Lucy Devlin. Believe me, I'm really used to that kind of stuff from working in a newsroom for so long.

Except this was different. I couldn't explain why to anyone. I suppose I couldn't even explain it logically to myself.

But—deep down somewhere in my subconscious—I knew why I had walked away from Elliott Grayson like that.

Even if I didn't want to admit it to myself.

I found an article in the clips that had an interview with Gwen Thompson. She was Grayson's special assistant, the one I'd had the run-in with on the phone before my first meeting. She gushed about how wonderful he was and how dedicated she was to his career and campaign. She said she'd wanted to do something to make the world a better place. "I remember reading about John F. Kennedy in the White House in history class," she said. "How people loved Camelot and the New Frontier. How he made people care about politics again. Well, that's how I feel about Elliott Grayson. He's the John F. Kennedy of our times."

No question about it, everyone loved him.

Well, almost everyone.

His primary opponent, Teddy Weller, kept hammering away at alleged questions about his character and his record as a prosecutor and his fitness for the Senate.

"Is this the kind of man you want to represent you in Washington?" Weller implored voters at nearly every campaign appearance now. "Is this the kind of man you want making decisions about the future of your children and your families? Is this the kind of man worthy of the public trust of a great state? I've shown you by my record over many years in office what kind of a man and what kind of a public official I am. What has Elliott Grayson shown you? A lot of slick tricks, public relations hocus-pocus, and self-aggrandizing law enforcement stunts. You cannot put a man like this in the seat of power in the Senate. He simply is not worthy of this office, and the true story and the true character of Elliott Grayson will eventually come out. Believe me, it won't be pretty. There is a clear-cut choice in this election. I offer you substance over slick PR image, leadership over rhetoric, and honesty over deception. I will never betray the public trust. Remember that when you go to the polls to decide between me and Elliott Grayson on Election Day."

But there were never any specifics. All Weller had were just a lot of vague generalizations and innuendo. He seemed desperate, an almost pathetic figure flailing at the wind.

I remembered Cliff Whitten telling me how Weller—despite proclaiming himself as the honorable candidate in this race—had always had a reputation as a dirty, no-holds-barred politician who would do anything to win an election.

I also remembered Janelle telling me how the people in the Weller campaign kept talking about some big scandal that was about to bring Grayson down.

What were they all talking about?

It was possible, I suppose, that Weller had set this all in motion by sending the original e-mail to Anne Devlin about the mysterious biker named Elliott or by getting Marston and Big Lou on his payroll or something. Part of a smear campaign to ruin Grayson's reputation.

If so, it had backfired badly on him.

That made me wonder again if Grayson himself could have been the one who sent that e-mail to Anne Devlin, somehow knowing it could only help him in the end. But that still didn't make a lot of sense either. How could Grayson have even imagined the sequence of bizarre events which followed that propelled him into such a big lead in this Senate race?

Whatever the reason, the results spoke for themselves.

"The election is pretty much over," one political columnist wrote the week before the primary. "The only thing that can stop Grayson now is some big scandal or monumental gaffe or terrible revelation about him. Teddy Weller keeps promising us some kind of smoking gun in his accusations against Grayson. Is there a smoking gun like that out there? I don't think so. If there is, someone better produce it pretty fast."

A smoking gun?

Not yet.

Not until now.

Now I just might have something.

All I had to do was figure out what it meant.

CHAPTER 37

I TOLD JACK Faron the next morning I needed to see him right away in his office about a story.

"What's the story?" he asked when I got there.

"Elliott Grayson."

"His political campaign?"

"No—his possible involvement in the story about Lucy Devlin and the six dead children."

Faron sighed.

"My God, you're not going to start obsessing about that Elliott Grayson conspiracy theory stuff of yours again, are you, Clare? I thought we decided a while ago it was time for you to drop all of this stuff."

"That was then."

"What's changed?"

"I have new information."

I told him the story about Joey Manielli's arrest in California, years after his body had been identified by Grayson's task force as one of those buried in the mass New Hampshire grave.

"Everything about this case—all of the information—comes from Elliott Grayson," I said. "The deaths in the shootout with Marston. The discovery of Lucy Devlin's body based on evidence Marston supposedly supplied because he had abducted and killed her. The identification of the six bodies in New Hampshire. Now we find out that a key piece of information—something we took for granted, the identity of one of the kids' bodies in the grave—was wrong. That means—"

"Everything else could be wrong, too."

"Nothing is what it seems here, Jack."

I'd thought I was wrong about Grayson before. I thought that I had simply jumped to some hasty conclusions and assumed he could have a violent past that he was now trying to cover up. I decided then I was mistaken. Now I wasn't so sure anymore. Maybe my first instinct about him had been right, after all.

"This doesn't have anything to do with the abortive relationship you had with Grayson, does it?"

"C'mon, Jack, I'm more professional than that. I've had abortive relationships with a lot of men. I don't generally take my frustration out on them this way."

"We're all human, Clare. People react in different ways to certain situations. Maybe that's what's happening here with you. A woman spurned and all. So you try to get back at Grayson by—"

"I wasn't spurned by Grayson," I pointed out. "I walked out on him. I'm the spurner. He's the spurnee. So that theory doesn't hold up."

I was kinda pissed at Faron that he would even suspect it.

Okay, maybe I was overreacting. Maybe I was being paranoid. Maybe I was just being a little bit vindictive and petty because things hadn't worked out between Grayson and me. Or maybe, just maybe, there was some significance to the fact that he kept turning up everywhere I looked.

"What does Grayson say about all this?" Faron asked.

"I haven't asked him yet. But I have to do it quickly. Before Election Day. This could be a game changer for the Senate race."

Faron shook his head.

"Clare, we have to be very careful here. Elliott Grayson is about to become a powerful man in Washington."

"Or he could be about to go to jail."

"What are you saying?"

"Someone killed those six kids. Lucy Devlin, too."

"Now, wait just a minute . . . there's a big difference between finding out Grayson misidentified a body and suggesting he's a killer. And this could have all been an innocent mistake anyway. Why would Grayson give the wrong identity on purpose? What's he got to gain from it anyway?"

"What if Sandy Marston wasn't the one who really killed Lucy Devlin?" I blurted out.

"He confessed."

"Allegedly."

"He even told the authorities where to find the body."

"What if they already knew?"

"Why would they already know that?"

"Elliott Grayson was the chief law enforcement official in the shootout where Marston died. He also was the lead investigator in the excavation of the six bodies of those children in New Hampshire. And Louise Carbone claimed he was there with a little girl who looked like Lucy Devlin."

"So what does that all mean?"

"I'm not sure, Jack. Not yet. But there's something wrong with this guy. I've felt it all along. We've got to stop him before it's too late."

Faron let out a huge sigh. "Every expert, every politician, every poll is convinced that Grayson will be the next Senator. The voters love him. Our viewers love him. Hell, my own wife and kids love him. Not only that, the owner of this station had a dinner party the other night where Grayson was the guest of honor. He's one of the most powerful men in this city. And now we're looking to accuse him of all sorts of potential wrongdoing and crimes, even though we're not sure yet exactly what they are?"

There's a scene I always remember in a movie version of *Farewell, My Lovely*, the Raymond Chandler book. It's set in 1941, and at the end, Robert Mitchum as Philip Marlowe muses about how Yankee superstar Joe DiMaggio's fifty-six-game hitting streak finally ended.

"Bagley and Smith, a couple of run-of-the-mill pitchers, stopped DiMaggio," Marlowe says. "I guess maybe they had something extra that night."

I like to think that's true of a lot of us. Most of us aren't superstars. We're not heroes every day. We don't do great deeds all of the time. But there are moments—every once in a while there are special moments—where we can reach deep down inside and summon up just a little bit of greatness.

As I said before, Jack Faron was one of the pretty good guys in the TV news business.

And maybe this day, just like Bagley and Smith against the great DiMaggio, he had something extra.

"Okay," Faron said to me. "What do you want to do next?"

"Check out everything Grayson has ever said and done. In the Senate campaign, as US Attorney, as a prosecutor before that—whatever it takes. We need to find out whatever there is to know about him. Not the Elliott Grayson we see in the press and in the public eye, the real Elliott Grayson. If nothing is what it seems, then we must assume that everything Grayson has said is a lie. We have to find out exactly what is true and what isn't."

"Starting where?"

"There's one obvious place."

"Joey Manielli."

"That's right," I said. "I'm going to go to California and talk to Joey Manielli. I want to find out what he has to say about his miraculous return from the dead."

CHAPTER 38

JOEY MANIELLI MET me in the prison visiting area.

"Who are you again?" he asked.

"Clare Carlson. I'm a TV reporter from New York City."

"What the hell does a TV reporter from New York want to talk to me about?"

"They didn't tell you?"

"Someone just said I had a visitor."

"And you didn't bother to ask what it was about?"

"I've got plenty of time to kill." He smiled.

I'd flown to northern California that morning after calling ahead to the prison to make arrangements to see Manielli.

His name now was Joseph Wilkinson, and he'd been arrested for stealing a BMW a few weeks earlier. It got worse after that. The cops discovered the stolen car had been used in a series of gas stations holdups by Manielli and another guy. The last one had gone bad. The gas station owner pulled a gun, and the guy with Manielli shot him. For a while, it looked as if he might die. He recovered, which is the only thing that saved Manielli and his pal from a murder charge. But he was looking at a lot of years in prison.

As I sat across from him now, I thought about how much he reminded me of his father. There was a big tattoo on his arm, just like Ralph Manielli had had when I saw him at the trailer park in

Allentown. Same look, too, right down to the sneer on his face. He was wearing a pink prison jumpsuit. But put him in a t-shirt and cutoff shorts like Ralph Manielli was wearing that day, and you'd have a younger version of his father. It's amazing how we turn into our parents as we get older, whether we want to or not.

"Your name is Joseph Wilkinson?"

"That's right."

"What happened to Joey Manielli?"

"He died."

"Except he didn't."

"Yeah, well . . ."

"You're really Joey Manielli."

"Who would have figured they still had those fingerprints on file, huh?"

"Tell me what happened."

The thing about talking to prisoners, I've found out over the years, is that it can go one of two ways. Either they clam up and say nothing at all, or you can't shut them up. Fortunately, Joey was the second kind. I think he liked the fact that he was suddenly important and a TV newswoman wanted to talk to him. I think he also liked the fact that I was a woman, since he kept checking me out with an interested eye throughout the whole interview. Or maybe he just was glad to "kill some time," as he put it. Whatever the reason, he told me his story.

"My mother back in Allentown was a drunk. Not just any drunk, but the queen of the drunks. The first sound I used to hear when I woke up in the morning was the popping open of a beer can. She kept a six-pack by her bed so that she didn't have to walk into the kitchen. By the time I left for school, she already had a nice buzz going. When I got home at the end of the day, she was either asleep or passed out.

"My father, he was the real asshole. He drank, too, but he didn't pass out. He just got mean. The more he drank, the meaner he got. Sometimes my mother or someone else was his target, but mostly it was me. I guess I was more of a challenge because I fought back. Of course, that just made him beat me harder. Sometimes he used his fists, sometimes he used a belt, and sometimes it was a wrench from his toolbox. Sometimes he did all of these things, plus other stuff I can't even remember.

"I tried to run away a lot of times, but where was I going to go? I was a little kid. I had no money, no way of getting away. That's why I stole that car back then, even though I didn't get very far. Most of the time, though, I'd just go down to the highway near where I lived. I'd sit there for hours, thinking about how great it would be to ride away on one of the trucks that passed by. Then, when it got dark, I'd go home. Most of the time they didn't even know I was gone.

"Those are the things I remember about being a kid. No father-son talks, no discussions around the dinner table. Hell, we hardly ever had dinner. My mother was usually too drunk to cook, and my father was hardly ever around. Once in a while, one of them would stop at a McDonald's or a Kentucky Fried Chicken and I'd get some of that. But most of the time I just had to fend for myself when it came to eating. Just like everything else."

"Did you ever go to anyone for help?" I asked him.

"Like who?"

"A teacher or a guidance counselor at your school?"

"What could they do? Just contact my parents and tell them I was complaining about them. Then I would have gotten beaten up again when I got home. I knew how things worked. No one at that school or anyone else in that town was ever going to help me."

"What happened?" I asked.

"One day I was sitting by the highway, watching the trucks like I always did, and this guy came up to me. He sat down next to me and started talking. He came back the next day, and the day after that. He told me he wanted to be my friend. My special friend was the way he put it. Well, one thing led to another, and he asked me if I wanted to go away with him. I couldn't imagine anything worse than where I was living. So I said yes."

"Did this man . . ." I wasn't sure exactly how to ask the question . . . "have sexual relations with you?"

"Nah, nothing like that."

"Are you sure?"

"Believe me, I'm sure. I knew all about that even when I was that young. To be honest, I figured that was what he was after. I was even prepared to let him do some stuff to me if it got me out of there. That's how desperate I was. But it never happened like that. We just traveled around the country together."

"Where?"

"Lots of places. I didn't care, I just was glad it wasn't Allentown. We stopped at little motels, camped out in the woods some-times—it was fun. Then one day we wound up at this big house. There was a man and a woman there. The guy said these two were going to be my parents now. That was all. Then he left. I never saw him again."

The bastard had sold the kid, I thought to myself.

"I lived with them," he continued. "They were real pushovers, real goody-two-shoes. At first, they were real easy with me, let me do whatever I wanted. Then they tried to impose all these rules— curfews, making me do homework, telling me who I could hang out with. But I ignored them. I mean, they were nice and all, but they were really kind of pathetic. Even when they tried to punish me, that didn't mean anything. Not after what I'd been through.

As I grew older, I got bigger and tougher and I think that scared them. One time I pushed the old lady down a flight of stairs when she started giving me lip. Another time I grabbed the guy by the throat and threatened to beat the crap out of him if he didn't leave me alone. That night I heard them talking, complaining about how they'd made a big mistake in taking me in. Hell, I was ready to move on, too. And by then I was old enough to be on my own. So, one day I just left."

"Did you know about the body back in New Hampshire with your name?" I asked.

"Not until they told me here."

"Did you ever use the name again after you left Allentown?"

"Nope."

"Why would someone want to make it seem as if you were dead?"

"I have absolutely no idea."

I'd thought this was about sex and perversion, but it wasn't. Whatever happened to Joey Manielli was about something else. These people didn't take him out of some kind of sick lust for children, they were running an adoption scam. Taking kids like him who wouldn't be terribly missed and selling them to desperate would-be parents. So, a kid from a dead-end, go-nowhere existence like Joey Manielli somehow wound up in a house with rich people who could afford to pay for a black-market child.

"Tell me about the man you ran away with," I said.

"What do you want to know?"

"His name."

"He never told me."

"How did you get around the country? Car? Truck? Bus or train?"

"None of those things."

"But you said you traveled everywhere."

"Sure, by motorcycle."

Motorcycle.

"The funny thing is, I never did know who he was all these years. Then one day, not long ago, I'm watching TV, and the news comes on. There's his picture right there on the screen. He was older, but that was him."

I took out a picture of Elliott Grayson and showed it to him.

"Is this the man who took you away?"

Joey glanced at the picture briefly, then shook his head no. "Nah, he didn't look anything like that."

"Are you sure?"

"Sure, I'm sure. This guy had long hair and these kind of real piercing, intense eyes. I recognized him right away when I saw him on TV. I couldn't figure out at first why he was on the news. It turns out he was killed during some big shootout with the law out in Idaho a few months back. Do you know who I'm talking about?"

Yeah, I did.

I knew exactly who he was talking about.

Sandy Marston.

CHAPTER 39

I HIRED A freelance film crew from the area to shoot some video of Joey Manielli at the prison for us.

I thought I might have a hard time getting official approval, but the warden was fine with it. All he asked was that he appeared on camera. He was an ambitious guy, and he figured being part of a TV news story kept him in the public eye.

Manielli was fine with it, too. He preened and mugged for the camera, clearly enjoying his moment in the spotlight.

Watching him, I thought about how funny life can be sometimes. I mean, Joey Manielli got dealt a bad hand in life as a kid—having a couple of loser parents like Ralph and Janis Manielli. Then he lived with a different family, a better family, a family who apparently tried to raise him the right way. But he still wound up here in jail. Had he always been doomed—from the moment of his birth—to this kind of life? Or were there moments along the way that could have changed the course of events for Joey Manielli, but never worked out right?

I suppose it all went back to the age-old question of heredity versus environment. Which one was the most important in determining the direction of a person's life? Heredity or environment? And can one's destiny or future truly be altered in the big scheme of things?

My piece that ran on Channel 10 showed Manielli telling pretty much the same story he'd told me. About growing up in that trailer park in Pennsylvania. About going away with Sandy Marston. About being handed over to the new family in California. About finding out recently that he was supposed to be dead.

Afterward, I came back on camera and wrapped it up by saying:

> And so long after he was declared dead, and even longer since he disappeared, the questions about Joey Manielli's abduction are finally answered.
>
> But this raises many other questions.
>
> Who was the dead child found in that grave?
>
> How did Elliott Grayson and law enforcement officials make such a mistake by identifying the person?
>
> And, of course, does this mean there are any questions about the identities of those other five children found dead in Mountainboro, New Hampshire?
>
> Those are questions that Channel 10 will continue to look into . . .

* * *

But that turned out to be easier said than done.

They couldn't exhume the body that was supposed to have been Joey Manielli because it had been cremated. The Manielli family had found some bargain-basement funeral director who offered them the cheapest way to get rid of the body. No funeral, no casket—just a quick cremation and scattering of the ashes. "Why should I spend a lot of money on some damn pine box?" Ralph Manielli said in explaining his reasoning for the cremation and lack of a funeral service. "I mean if the kid was already dead, what difference did it make?"

I assumed Ralph and Janis Manielli would be underwhelmed, too, at the news that their son was still alive. But I was wrong about that. They were ecstatic. That's because they'd hooked up with a lawyer who told them they could probably get a lot of money from the government for the screwup. They were planning on suing for the "pain and suffering and emotional distress" they suffered from wrongly believing their son was dead. Beautiful.

Elliott Grayson held a press conference where he apologized profusely for the mistake and expressed his regrets for the pain it caused to the Manielli family. He gave a detailed account of a mix-up in records by a technician that they had determined must have led to the misidentification. The technician, he said, no longer worked for the government and could not be found to provide any further explanation.

He also said that the records of all the other five cases had been rechecked, and there was absolutely no doubt they were the same children that had been identified. He looked into the camera and said solemnly that he had personally conveyed this information to all five of the families. He talked about how sorry he was that they had to suffer through this additional anguish.

It was another impressive performance, and most people seemed to accept his explanation. The parents of the five other children. The rest of the press. And, most importantly of all, the voting public.

"Am I going to vote for Elliott Grayson for Senator?" said one woman we put on the air. "Of course I am. Okay, he made a mistake. We all make mistakes. I liked the way he stood up like a man and admitted it. He's done so many great things, I think it's a shame anyone makes a big deal out of something like this. He's still the man I want to send to Washington."

Teddy Weller, of course, tried to turn it into the biggest political scandal he could. He talked at his campaign appearances about how this showed Elliott Grayson was incompetent; that he was irresponsible; that you couldn't believe anything he said; and this showed a longtime trusted civic leader like Weller was the right man to represent New York in the Senate.

He dramatically demanded at one press conference that the five other bodies be exhumed now to determine for certain that they were the five missing dead children that Grayson had said they were several years earlier.

But that didn't go anywhere, because none of the families of the other five wanted their children dug up. They accepted Grayson's explanation of what happened and didn't want to go through the trauma and public spectacle of having their children's bodies exhumed again. "My little boy Donald suffered enough in life at the hands of the inhuman monster who killed him for no reason," the father of Donald Chang said. "Please just let him rest in peace now." Emily Neiman's parents called the idea of digging up their daughter's remains after all this time "ghoulish."

In the end, political experts agreed that the Manielli misidentification was just a minor glitch—not a fatal one—for Elliott Grayson's Senate prospects.

And they said he'd handled his damage control press conference so well that there wasn't likely to be any lingering questions about this.

People believed his explanation.

They believed everything he said.

He was a believable guy.

Of course, someone from the families might change their mind at some point and demand that those other five bodies be dug up—wherever they were now—to make sure they were who he said they were. But, even if that did happen, it probably wouldn't have any impact on the election. After all these years, positive

IDs would take a long time and most likely have to be done by DNA testing, medical experts said. This could take months to complete. Whatever the outcome, Grayson would probably be already elected by that time.

There'd still be a big controversy then, but most observers didn't expect anything that dramatic to happen.

Like I said, people bought Grayson's story.

Why would he lie, they asked.

I'd hoped this was going to be the break I needed to go after Elliott Grayson and reveal the true story about him—whatever that might be.

But it wasn't enough.

I was going to have to find something else.

CHAPTER 40

THE BIGGEST PROBLEM with a story like this one—about crimes that happened a long time ago—is that the trail is so cold.

People die over the years, they move away, or they just disappear.

Like Phil and Nancy Wilkinson. They were the family who raised Joey Manielli after getting him from Marston. I'd hoped to be able to get them to open up about the whole deal—how they met Marston, how much they paid him, and who else might have been involved. But I found out the Wilkinsons had both been killed in a car crash a few years earlier.

At first, the tabloid reporter instinct in me had speculated wildly about how maybe it wasn't an accident after all—that they'd been killed by Marston or Grayson or someone else to cover up the Manielli adoption truth.

But, after I looked up the details of their deaths in some old newspaper articles, I realized that wasn't the case.

It was front-page news in several of the northern California papers. A tanker truck filled with gasoline had overturned on a busy freeway, exploding into flames that engulfed several cars near them at the time. Investigators later determined that the driver had gone thirty-two hours without sleep on a cross-country trip—and then dozed off at the wheel, losing control of his fuel-filled vehicle. Five people died in the tragedy, including Phil and Nancy Wilkinson.

Nope, they were just in the wrong place at the wrong time.

Too bad for them—and too bad for me because they took whatever secrets they had about how they got Joey Manielli to the grave with them.

Who else was there to talk to?

I'd already talked to the other five families of the bodies identified in the New Hampshire grave besides Joey Manielli. But I went back now and talked to each family again. All of them had different stories. Some had been forever devastated by the loss of their child, while others were able to pull themselves together and continue on with their lives.

Tamara Greene's parents had gotten divorced, just like Patrick and Anne Devlin. David Chang's family had had another little boy who they said proudly looked just like David had when he was younger. William O'Shaughnessy's parents had moved from Florida to another state because they said the memories were too difficult to deal with once he was gone—and then the father later killed himself. Emily Neiman's mother had thrown herself into a volunteer organization that ran a day camp and other outdoor activities for city kids in the Houston area. And Victoria Gale told me again about all the good work she was doing for the Lord at her church in Princeton in memory of her beloved daughter Becky.

All of them said they believed Elliott Grayson—that they were convinced it was their children buried in that mass grave in New Hampshire.

And what about the sixth body in the grave? The one that had been misidentified as Joey Manielli? All we knew for sure was that he was a young boy about the same age as Manielli had been when he disappeared. But any other possible clues to his identity were destroyed when the Manielli family had him cremated so that they didn't have to pay for an expensive funeral. And there was no DNA crime scene evidence on file to check—DNA wasn't being used as commonly as a law enforcement tool fifteen years ago as it is today. Damn.

This was all interesting enough, but it didn't give me any answers. I was at a dead end again.

I went back over my notes and looked through all the interviews I had done with the families of the six children who had disappeared back then. Trying to find any kind of loose end I could go after. Manielli. Chang. O'Shaughnessy. Greene. Neiman. Gale. Who else was there?

That's when I remembered the sister. Becky Gale's sister. Becky's mother had said that she'd lost her other daughter, too—that Becky's younger sister, Samantha, lived in New York City now and she hadn't seen or talked to her in years. Maybe I could find out something from the sister.

I sat down at my computer, punched in the name of Samantha Gale to an online phone listing site for Manhattan—then waited to see what came up. I didn't know for sure she lived in Manhattan, of course. But her mother had said she lived in New York City—so that seemed like the best place to start.

There were no Samantha Gales in the Manhattan phone listings that I found. But there were some S. Gayles. I went through all of them—calling the numbers there one by one until I finally found an answering device where the woman identified on the phone message identified herself as Samantha.

Except the address listed with that number turned out to be for a fortune-telling place in Chelsea.

I called Victoria Gale to ask if that could be right.

"Yes, that's my daughter," she said.

"An astrology parlor?"

"She tells fortunes for a living."

"Why?"

"I have no idea," Victoria Gale said sadly. "If you find out from her, please tell me. I'm sorry, but I have to go now. I'm on my way to pray at our church."

CHAPTER 41

THE SIGN ON the window of the storefront building near Eighth Avenue in the West 20s said: "Astrology, Tarot Cards, Crystals, Palm Reading. Come Inside." A bell tinkled when I pushed the front door open. There was a small, darkly lit waiting room. On the wall was a framed document that proclaimed Samantha Gale was a licensed practitioner in astrology, who had been approved by some international astrology organization based in Barstow, California. Guess that made the suckers feel better.

I have a very low threshold of patience for people who think that stuff like stars tell their future. Sure, I look at the newspaper column once in a while to see if I'm going to find true love that day or not. But mostly I think it's ridiculous. I remember a newspaper where they fired the astrology columnist. When she got the bad news, she was very upset. "Hey, if you were any good, you would have seen it coming," the editor told her. That's pretty much the way I feel about astrology and the people who practice it.

A woman came out of a door in the back. She was young, in her twenties, with long dark hair, big brown eyes, and a pretty, almost angelic face.

"Samantha Gale?" I asked.

"Yes."

"I've been looking for you."

"Well, you're not here for a reading."

"How do you know that?"

"I'm a psychic, remember?" She smiled.

"Okay, then . . . why don't you tell me why I'm here?"

"Your name is Clare Carlson," she said. "You work for a TV station, Channel 10. And you're doing a story about my sister, Becky, so you want to ask me some questions about her. How am I doing so far?"

I stared at her in amazement.

"How'd you know that?"

"It's all in the stars and the spirits," she said, waving her hands and making a spooky sound with her voice.

"Really?"

"No," she said. "I watch TV. I recognized you right away. I saw your newscast, the one which mentioned my sister. I knew from that you'd been to see my mother in New Jersey. Then you walk into my store and say that we need to talk. Ergo, I figure it must be about Becky."

I smiled. This was a smart woman. I remembered her mother saying she could have gone to Princeton. What the hell was she doing reading fortunes in Chelsea?

"Let's talk about Becky," I said.

"There's nothing to say. She's dead."

"Okay, then let's talk about your mother. She's alive."

Samantha made a face. "Is the old lady still keeping Becky's room the way it was? Like Becky's going to come back one day and find it the same as she left it. Is she still going to church every day to pray for Becky's soul? All that grief, all that sorrow, all the energy she puts into being the heartbroken mother. Maybe it would have been better if she'd cared a little more about Becky when she was alive. Maybe she could have done something useful for Becky then."

"What do you mean?"

"I mean the guilt is her payback for what happened."

"I don't understand . . ."

"Of course you don't."

"What did your mother do?"

"She didn't do anything. Not a damn thing."

"Okay."

"That was the problem."

She led me into another room. There were black curtains on the windows, and it was dimly lit. A smell of incense filled the place and a single candle flickered on a table in the center of the room.

"I was just a little girl, of course," she said. "I didn't understand a lot of it. But I knew something was wrong in that house, even then. One day, Becky came to me and said she had a secret. She said our father . . ." Her voice wavered at this point . . . "Our father had done things to her. They were sexual things. He'd come into her bedroom late at night and force her to do this stuff. She said it made her cry. She was confused and afraid."

I stared at Samantha Gale.

"What did you say?" I asked.

"I told her she needed to tell our mother."

"Did she?"

"Yes, for all the good it did."

"Your mother didn't believe Becky."

"She claimed she was lying. She told her God would punish her for saying terrible things like that. She didn't even want to think about the possibility that it might be true. She couldn't believe this man she'd been married to for all those years could be capable of something like that."

I nodded. Denial was common in cases like this. I'd come across it in stories I'd covered on the subject before.

"The weird thing is I didn't really understand it," Samantha said. "I mean, I loved my father. I was almost jealous that he wanted Becky more than me. Then, after she was gone, he started coming into my room. That's when I really knew what my sister had suffered through all those years."

"Did you go to your mother?"

"No, not then."

"Because you decided she wouldn't believe you, just like she didn't believe Becky?"

"I'm not sure."

"But she knows now?"

Samantha nodded.

"My shrink tells me I repressed the whole thing for a long time. All I knew was how miserable I was growing up after Becky was gone. Then, when my father died, I guess it all came pouring out. The shrink said I was finally confronting my demons or something like that. Anyway, that's when I went to my mother and told her. She realized then that Becky had tried to tell her the same thing, but she never listened. That's why she talks to God all the time now. To get rid of the guilt."

"And your mother never suspected anything?"

"So she says."

"You don't believe her?"

"How could she not know? He was getting in and out of bed in the middle of the night to come into our rooms. What'd she think he was doing? No, I guess she was just in denial. That's what her whole life has been about. Denial that her husband was a sick pervert. Denial that I was long gone from that house and from her. Denial that Becky was dead.

"I realize now that she must have known something was wrong. But she hid her head in the sand and pretended she didn't see it. My father . . . well, he was just sick. But my mother had the opportunity to save Becky and me from the unspeakable things he was doing, and she did nothing.

"It's funny, but my parents provided us with so many things on one level. A good house to live in, food on the table, a good education, anything like that we wanted. Anything except for the most important thing. They couldn't protect us from evil, the evil that was right in that house. I couldn't even look my mother in the face after that.

"I was supposed to go to Princeton. I wanted to major in English literature. I wanted to teach it, maybe be a professor there. Be close to my family and all that crap. But now I wanted to be as far away from that house as possible. I moved to New York, lived here until I decided what I wanted to do, and then a friend of mine turned me on to astrology. I know you probably think it's no way to make a living, but I like it. It's honest. I help people. Or at least I make them feel better. I'm not a phony like my mother and father.

"I've never been back to Princeton. My mother called and tried to see me at first, but I wouldn't talk to her. After a while, she just gave up. I guess I'm dead for her now, too. Just like Becky."

* * *

I called Victoria Gale again when I got back to the office and she confirmed it all.

Then she started to cry over the phone.

"I've often wondered if this somehow played a part in what happened," she sobbed. "What if Becky was so upset by what her father had done that she was running away? She'd tried to talk about it with the only person she could. Me. And I hadn't believed her. Maybe, in the end, that's what got her killed.

"When Paul was dying of cancer, he was in terrible pain. They gave him drugs at first, but after a while even that didn't help. He would lie in his bed and cry out in agony for the Lord to have mercy on him. Now I wonder if that was the Lord's punishment for him. That he had to suffer like that for the terrible things he did to his own daughter. Do you think that's possible, Ms. Carlson?"

I didn't know the answer to that.

What I did know was that Joey Manielli and Becky Gale—even though they came from completely different backgrounds—had been abused in some way by a member of their family.

Joey from the beatings he got from his father.

Becky Gale by her father's sexual coercion.

And I remembered all over again what Anne Devlin had told me that Lucy said the day before she disappeared. About her father and sex. Like I said earlier, I at first assumed that was a reference to having caught me in bed with her father. But what if Patrick Devlin—despite his denials—really had been doing things to his daughter, too? That would mean all three of them were suffering from horrible abuse in their homes before they disappeared.

Did someone take advantage of this? Someone who zeroed in on kids who had been abused and were unhappy and despondent about their own family? Someone who used that to convince them to run away—and then murdered them himself?

I'd been looking for a connection between the six children whose bodies turned up in that New Hampshire grave.

Now maybe I had one.

Maybe even a connection to Lucy Devlin, too.

Maybe.

CHAPTER 42

THERE'S A PATTERN to every story.

Most of the time we never see this pattern because the story only lasts for a day or two. It goes on the air or in the newspaper and then we move on to the next story. Nothing is so easily discarded as yesterday's news, and all of us in the business have a very short attention span.

But when a journalist really digs into a story in depth—like I was doing now—things sometimes begin falling into place in a way you never thought would happen.

When I was a reporter for the *Tribune*, I covered a popular TV newscaster that everyone loved. A great guy, they all said. Then one day it turned out he was beating his wife. He got arrested and suspended from the station. After that, more people started telling stories about him. How he'd been picked up for drunk driving a few times. How he had a bad drug habit. How he hadn't paid his income taxes for several years. In the end, he went to jail and wound up committing suicide a few years later. Everyone said they saw it coming, and how troubled he was. Except that wasn't true. No one predicted anything like that, no one saw anything wrong with the guy until they started digging into his life.

That's what was happening with the families of the children found in the New Hampshire grave.

Everyone had assumed they had been taken by chance—at complete random—by a crazed mass murder. All that mattered was the person who abducted them. No one paid much attention to what happened before they were abducted. They didn't think it mattered, and maybe it didn't. On the other hand, it might prove to be a clue that would point to whoever committed the crime.

Joey Manielli had had a wretched existence as a child. A bully of a father, a drunk of a mother—no supervision, no love, no hope for anything for him in that run-down trailer park in Allentown, Pennsylvania. Everyone—including me—had just assumed that was simply a description of his life before he disappeared, not that it might have something to do with his disappearance.

Because Joey Manielli's life didn't seem to match up with the lifestyle elements of any of the other five children found in the mass grave.

But now I'd determined that Becky Gale—who seemed outwardly to live a perfectly happy life with a loving family in a beautiful town like Princeton—had been living her own nightmare as she grew up.

What did that say about the other four?

* * *

Emily Neiman, William O'Shaughnessy, Tamara Greene, and Donald Chang were all from different parts of the country. Different kinds of families, economic backgrounds, ethnic heritages. They didn't seem to have much of anything in common. But they'd turned out to be a connection between Joey Manielli and Becky Gale. Both had been victims of abuse at home. Joey, an obvious one. Becky, not so obvious. Maybe that was true of them, too.

I'd talked to the parents of those children, letting them tell me what they wanted me to hear. Just like I did with Victoria Gale. Until I found out the truth from the sister, Samantha. Now I needed to find out the truth about all of them. I needed to know if there were any secret dark sides to the other four families, too.

I spent hours checking deeper into their backgrounds. But it was worth it. I uncovered a lot of stuff I hadn't known about them before.

William O'Shaughnessy had gone to the school nurse several times after teachers spotted bruises on his body. He claimed he'd fallen down the steps, but they didn't believe him. The police were notified and they talked to the family. But everyone stuck to their story, and there was nothing anyone could prove.

Emily Neiman had tried to kill herself when she was ten. She slit her wrists with a kitchen knife. Her mother found her and rushed her to the hospital in time to save her life. Emily kept telling the doctors there that she just wanted to die. She was under psychiatric care at the time of her disappearance.

Neither Donald Chang nor Tamara Greene had tried to kill themselves, nor did they show any obvious signs of abuse. But each of them seemed to be a troubled kid. Low grades, trips to their school counselors, even a few run-ins with the law. Yep, there was definitely a pattern here. These were unhappy kids. These were kids with problems. These were kids who had a reason to be depressed about their lives.

That was the common denominator between all six.

But what did it mean?

I kept coming back to the theory that this made them perfect targets for a predator that could use that unhappiness to his advantage.

Who? Well, one obvious possibility was someone who came in contact with troubled kids. A school guidance counselor or teacher or principal, for instance. But that didn't explain how all of these kids came from different parts of the country. A counselor in a school would have access to such information in only one area.

It had to be someone else. Someone who moved around the country a lot and might have come across—and taken advantage of—troubled kids on a wider scale. Someone like a truck driver. Or a traveling salesman. Or maybe even the member of a motorcycle gang. A modern-day Easy Rider who pedaled murder, not drugs.

Sandy Marston had been in a motorcycle gang.

So had Patrick Devlin.

And Elliott Grayson.

I remembered something else about Grayson. I'd asked him if he was an only child. He said he'd had a sister, but she died. I was curious to find out more.

He'd grown up in Pennsylvania in a place called Clarion and talked in interviews about his small-town roots. He also talked about his mother and his father, who was a firefighter in Clarion. He talked about the American values this kind of upbringing had instilled in him. But he never talked much about a sister.

It took some digging, but I finally found a story about his sister's death in the Pittsburgh paper. It had gotten pretty decent coverage at the time. Her name was Sarah Grayson. One morning, she'd left for school with her brother, Elliot. He was twelve and she was ten. Elliott came home at the end of the day, but she didn't. Her teacher said she never showed up for the first homeroom class. Elliott said he'd left her outside the school, where he'd seen her talking to some man in the school playground.

Her body was later found in a wooded area near the town. She'd been beaten and sexually molested, police said. They assumed she'd been abducted by the man Elliott had seen her talking to—and then assaulted and murdered. No one was ever caught. It was the first murder in fifty years in the town, and it remains on the books today as an unsolved case. A few months later, the Graysons moved away from Clarion, saying the memories were too much for them to bear.

Big Lou had claimed she saw Elliott Grayson with Lucy Devlin soon after she went missing at a motorcycle convention in Mountainboro, New Hampshire.

Then it turned out he was the federal investigator who directed the unearthing of six children's bodies years later in the same small town.

I'd decided this was all a coincidence.

Now I found out that his own sister was abducted and killed—just like all the others—when he was young.

Elliott Grayson was the last person to see his sister alive. He said he saw her talking to a man in the school playground, but he never told anyone that until after she was gone. Why not? What if there was no man in the playground that day? What if Elliott had made that all up? What if Elliott had killed her himself? What if he was a pathological killer who'd started at a young age and then gone on to kill a lot of other people over the years? What if he was now trying to desperately cover up his murderous past as he ran for the Senate?

All of this was just speculation, of course.

I needed to concentrate on what I knew, not what I thought I knew, if I was ever going to put this on the air.

If I didn't have any hard evidence against Grayson, that meant I had to attack the problem from a different direction.

Go with the facts I did have.

Well, one indisputable fact was that Sandy Marston had been involved with both the Lucy Devlin and Joey Manielli disappearances—Marston was the first real link I had between Lucy and those bodies in New Hampshire.

I decided to follow that trail for a while and see where it led.

CHAPTER 43

I'D DONE ALL right the first time I went into a biker lair at the Warlock Warriors headquarters in Hell's Kitchen.

I hadn't done so good the second time at the biker bar in New Hampshire.

Now it was time to try again, and I wondered if my luck might be running out.

The guy who answered the door at the Warlock Warriors headquarters this time looked a bit like Sandy Marston, only bigger. He was maybe six foot eight and most of it was muscle. He was wearing black jeans, a black t-shirt, and black combat boots.

"I can't believe you have the nerve to show your face around here," he said when he saw me. "Sandy's dead. Louise, too. We've had people hassling us ever since then. Our landlord, he's tired of all the trouble—we're getting thrown out of our place. Now you show up at the front door. That's just perfect."

"You blame me for all this?"

"Why not?"

"Hey, I liked Big Lou," I said. "I actually kind of liked Marston, too, if that makes any sense. I'm not sure we know the entire truth yet about what happened and what they did. I'm trying to find out. I just want to talk to you and some of the others here and ask some questions. What do you say?"

"What is it that you think you're going to find out, lady? There's nothing more to say."

"I don't think Sandy Marston did it," I blurted out.

He'd already started to close the door in my face again, but stopped now.

"I know Marston was no Boy Scout," I said. "But I don't see him killing the Devlin girl. I think there's someone else involved in this. Someone who wants to make it look like Marston did it. He's a bad biker guy, and now he's dead—end of story. But I think there's a lot more story here. I want to find out the real answers to what Marston did or didn't do. How about you?"

He stared at me for a long time, apparently trying to decide whether or not he wanted to talk to me.

"C'mon in," he said finally.

I followed him through the house to a room where a half dozen people—five guys and a girl—were sitting around. The big guy said his name was Dale. He introduced me to Buddy and Nick and Carol and a few others whose names I couldn't remember. They were reluctant to talk at first, but started to come around after a while.

"Did you ever notice Sandy having any abnormal interest in children?" I asked.

"Nah, he wasn't like that," one of the guys said. He had a tattoo on his arm of a Harley 1200 that was so prominent I had to stop myself from staring at it. "Sandy was a regular guy. He liked women. Grown-up women. Hell, look at Big Lou. She was his lady, and she was no kid."

"Maybe he had unfulfilled sexual fantasies that he needed to act out," I suggested.

"Huh?"

"He wanted to have sex with young kids."

"We never saw that," one of them said.

"He liked kids but not like that," the woman named Carol said. She had dirty-blond hair and acne and tired-looking eyes. She looked to be about twenty-two, going on forty-five. I wondered if she'd wind up like Big Lou. That is, if she lived that long. "When I got knocked up a few years ago, he looked out for me and my kid. Made sure the baby was well taken care of. He was a tough guy, but could be gentle, too. I never understood how he could have killed that little girl the way they said."

"Then why did he confess to it?" I asked them.

"Maybe he didn't," tattoo guy said.

"You think the confession letter was a fake?"

"Sandy's dead. He can't speak for himself. All we've got is the law's word. I don't believe it, do you?"

Everyone shook their head no.

"It doesn't make sense," Dale told me.

They described how the cops and feds and all sorts of other law enforcement types had descended on the place after Marston and Big Lou had gone missing, then again after the big shootout in Idaho.

"They took everything that was here," one of them said. "All of Sandy and Lou's clothes and belongings. They were real bastards about it all, too. Walked around here like they owned the place. That never happened before. Not to us."

"Before this, we used to get a free pass most of the time from the cops," Dale explained. "They didn't mess with us, we didn't mess with them. It was like we had this kind of understanding or whatever. I was never sure why. But Sandy always said he could handle the cops. I figured he must be paying them off. But now I think it was more than that. It was almost as if they were scared of him or something."

"Or something," I said.

I wanted to see the room where Sandy and Big Lou had lived. They said there was no point, since all their stuff was gone. The cops had taken it all away. I said I wanted to see the room anyway.

Dale took me up to the second floor. When we got inside the room, I realized it was the same place I'd seen Big Lou staring down at me from that first day. Which seemed like such a long time ago now. Of course, Dale was right about it being a wasted trip. There was nothing there.

"Were you here the day Sandy and Big Lou left?" I asked.

"Sure, I said good-bye to them."

"Did they tell you where they were going? Or why?"

"He just said they had to get out of town in a hurry. He said there was trouble. I said we'd all help him take care of it. He said even we couldn't take care of this kind of trouble. Then he and Lou got on their bikes and left. That was the last time I ever saw either of them until I found out they were dead."

"So, Sandy and Big Lou are just sitting around the house here when they announce they're leaving?"

"No, they came back."

"Came back from where?"

"They were out somewhere on their bikes. They came back here, got some stuff from upstairs, and then left again for good."

"You think they came back to pack?"

Dale shrugged. "I don't know . . . Sandy wasn't much for changing clothes. He sometimes wore the same outfit for days. Same with Lou. If he was really on the run, he wouldn't ever have come back just to pack clothes."

"So that means he came back here for something else?"

"I guess."

Sandy Marston was scared. He wanted to get out of town with Big Lou, and he wanted to do it in a hurry. But he came back here first for something. What was it that was so important to him? And where was it now?

If he took it with him to the farmhouse in Idaho, the feds had it. But if not . . .

"Did Sandy have any kind of a safe deposit box or place where he might store something valuable for safekeeping?"

"Nah, Sandy didn't believe in banks."

"How about a close friend?"

"He didn't have any friends except us."

"Maybe a family member, then . . ."

"Sandy didn't have any family."

No, he didn't have a family.

But Big Lou did.

And I knew where to find them.

CHAPTER 44

BEFORE THEY LEFT town, Sandy Marston and Louise Carbone had visited two places where her family lived.

The first place was the house of Louise's ex-husband and her daughter. I drove out to Lodi, New Jersey, again to talk to Dave Weber. I told him what I was looking for.

"No, Louise didn't leave anything here that day," Weber said. "Like I told you before, they didn't stay very long. She really just wanted to see Maureen, our daughter. When Maureen wouldn't talk to her, she and Marston left. That's all that happened. I wish I could help you."

"Where is Maureen?"

"She's at school. She's had a hard time with all this. Maureen had mixed feelings about her mother, I guess. On the one hand, she hated her for leaving us the way she did. On the other hand, well . . . she was her mother. Now that she's dead, she's having trouble coming to grips with how she feels about her. Me, too, I guess."

"So, that day here was the last contact you and your daughter had with her."

"In person, yes."

"What other kind of contact did you have?"

"Just the letter."

"What letter?"

"A day or so after she died in that shootout, we got a letter from Louise. She must have mailed it from somewhere on the road just before she and Marston died. It was addressed to Maureen, but it was really about the both of us. We cried together when we read it. I don't know if Louise knew she was going to die when she wrote it, but it sounds like it."

"Do you still have the letter?"

"Of course. I'll show it to you, if you want."

The letter was written on motel stationary from a place in Minnesota where she and Marston must have stayed during their run from the law. The handwriting in the beginning was neat and precise, but turned into more of a scrawl as it went on—as if she was in a hurry to finish it. Like her husband said, maybe she knew she didn't have much time left.

The letter from Big Lou to her daughter said:

Dear Maureen,

We make a lot of decisions in our life, and sometimes wish later that we could take some of them back. To go back in time and change everything and make it right again. That's what I wish I could do with you and me. But I'm afraid it's too late for that now.

I know you're mad at me, and you don't understand why I'm not there for you. Why I haven't been there for you in a long, long time. Maybe in time you'll understand my reasons for what I've done with my life. (actually I'm not sure I do!)

The simple answer is I just lost my way. I went looking for something that was never really there. And all the time what I really cared about—you, Maureen—was there for me, if I had just realized it. I'm telling you this because I don't want you to wind up like me. I want you to have a better life than I did.

Your father, he's a good man. He probably wasn't the right man for me, but that was my fault not his. Listen to him. Let him into your life. Love him. I never did any of those things, and I would be so much better off today if I had.

You've probably heard a lot of the things they've been saying about me on the news. Some of it is true, and some isn't. But I'm afraid this will end badly, and I know it must be hard for you to understand how your mother ever reached such a point of no return.

That's why there's one thing I want you to know.

I love you, Maureen. I love you with all my heart.

That first day in the hospital I held you in my arms for the first time as a baby was the greatest moment of my life. I've screwed things up a lot since then. But that's one thing that no one can ever take away from me. My love for you. No matter what you think of me, no matter what I do—I'll always love you, Maureen. Remember that, no matter what happens.

A mother's love for her daughter can never die.

They can never take that away from me.

All my love,
Mom

I looked up at Dave Weber. There were tears in his eyes.

I thought about how different Louise Carbone's life might have been if she'd stayed in this house with him and her daughter instead of running off with Marston and the Warlock Warriors. How different her husband and daughter's lives would have been. Could she have survived as a suburban housewife in Lodi, New Jersey? Probably not. Any more than I could. We all make decisions in our life, she said, and then we have to live with them.

"They're saying all these terrible things about Louise now," Dave Weber said. "How she might have been involved in abducting and killing children. It's like they're talking about someone else, not Louise. Sure, she wasn't perfect. But I can't believe those things about her. Louise was no killer. She was a good person at heart."

He shook his head sadly as he looked down at the letter.

"Is this what you came here for?"

"Not exactly, but it helps."

"What are you looking for?"

"Something she and Marston may have stopped somewhere to leave off before they hit the road."

"I'm sorry, but she didn't leave anything here."

"There's one other place she stopped," I said.

* * *

Irene Carbone said her daughter and Marston had stayed there for no more than half an hour.

"Did she leave anything behind?"

"Like what?"

"A suitcase. A duffle bag. A briefcase. Anything like that?"

"There was a package. She said they had too much stuff to carry on the bikes, and she'd come back for it later."

"Where is it?"

"She put it down in the basement, I think."

"Did you look inside?"

"I haven't been through any of her stuff yet. It's too painful."

The package was hidden behind the furnace. Maybe Louise did put it there because she figured they'd come back for it later. Or maybe she hoped someone would find it after they'd gone. Whatever, it was important enough that they'd apparently gone back to the gang's headquarters in Hell's Kitchen to get it before they left. And important enough to store at her mother's house, so it wouldn't be with them if they got caught.

I opened the package. There were file folders inside with documents and papers and clippings. The documents were missing person reports and posters from the FBI. There were six of them.

Joey Manielli. Becky Gale. Tamara Greene. Donald Chang. Emily Neiman. William O'Shaughnessy. The six children whose bodies Grayson had identified as being in that mass grave in Mountainboro, New Hampshire.

There was a piece of paper with a list on it. It had all of the names of the same kids on it. But it had something else, too. Details on how and when and where they had been abducted. Specific details that no one had ever heard. They said Joey Manielli had been taken at a highway rest stop outside Allentown, Becky Gale from a shopping mall near Princeton. There were details for how the others disappeared, too. There was no proof of any of this, of course. But I knew in my heart it was all true. Why would anyone keep a record of this kind of thing otherwise?

There was also a picture. A little boy with a man. I didn't recognize the boy. It could have been one of the missing children in the posters, but I wasn't sure. I recognized the man though. Elliott Grayson. It wasn't easy at first because Grayson wasn't looking directly at the camera. It appeared as if the photographer had taken it without Grayson's knowledge. But it was definitely him.

There was a series of newspaper articles and computer printouts from online websites about Elliott Grayson. His appointment as US Attorney. The press conferences after some of his big arrests. His campaign announcement that he was running for the Senate. In it, Grayson had pledged at one point to bring "a return to integrity and trust" to the criminal justice system. Someone—presumably Marston or Louise Carbone—had written the word "LIAR!" in big letters with a magic marker over that article.

There was a pair of older, wrinkled newspaper clippings, too. The first one was from a small paper in Pennsylvania called the *Clarion Dispatch*. It had the same story I'd read in the Pittsburgh paper about the disappearance of Grayson's sister, only with more facts and details.

The headline said:

MASSIVE SEARCH FOR MISSING GIRL

By Richie Briggs

Hundreds of Clarion police, state troopers and local volunteers combed the area yesterday looking for 10-year-old Sarah Grayson.

The fifth grader was last seen three days ago outside the Valley Grade School, where she arrived for school shortly after 8 a.m.

The last person to see her was her brother, Elliott, 12.

"She was talking to a man in the playground," Elliott Grayson told police.

The boy gave a description of the man, saying he appeared to be in his 40s, with gray hair, wearing a green windbreaker and a black cowboy hat. He said he had never seen the man, who is now being sought for questioning...

The second clip was also from the *Clarion Dispatch*.

10-YEAR-OLD GIRL'S BODY FOUND

By Richie Briggs

Police last night discovered the remains of Sarah Grayson, the 10-year-old who disappeared from her school playground this week.

A dog walker found her body shortly after 8 p.m., hidden under a pile of leaves about a mile into the Atchison Woods on the south side of town.

A preliminary examination showed she had been beaten badly and also appeared to have been sexually assaulted.

There were no suspects in custody, although police continued to search for an unidentified man seen talking to her in the school playground, just before she disappeared . . .

* * *

Six bodies in a grave. Now it turned out that at least one of them—and I was betting all six—were not who they were supposed to be.

That meant those were the bodies of six other missing children buried a long time ago in that New Hampshire grave.

Then there was ten-year-old Sarah Grayson who also went missing and was found dead.

Plus, all the tantalizing connections to Lucy Devlin.

That added up to fourteen cases.

No matter how you did the math, the answer to this puzzle always came out the same way.

One man.

Elliott Grayson.

CHAPTER 45

RICHIE BRIGGS HAD retired from the Clarion paper a few years ago, but he was still alive. I tracked him down by phone with a bit of help from a woman in the *Clarion Dispatch* personnel office who somehow was under the impression that I worked for an insurance company that had a cash payment for him. That was probably because I said I was from State Farm insurance company, and we had a cash payment for him.

She said she'd call Briggs for me, tell him the good news, and ask him to call me back. It was a scam I'd worked as a journalist many times in the past when I wanted to talk to someone. People were always a lot more likely to return your calls if they thought you were giving them money.

As it turned out, I could have saved myself the bother. Richard Briggs was listed right there in the Clarion telephone book. He'd never left the area.

"I checked out a lot of the areas where people retire to," Briggs told me when he called. "Florida. Arizona. North Carolina. You know what I found out? I was better off staying right here in Clarion. I live in my own house, my own town, with people I've known all my life—why do I have to be rushing off to some new spot just because someone says that's what you're supposed to do when you're sixty-five?"

I listened politely to him. Retired people always like to talk about how happy they are not working anymore. Most of the time I figure it's just a kind of defense mechanism—a denial to themselves that they're no longer a productive part of society. But Richie Briggs really seemed to mean it.

"Tell me about this money I've got coming to me," he said finally.

"There is no money."

"I knew that," he chuckled.

"How did you know?"

"I'm seventy-five years old. In all that time, no insurance company has ever called me up to tell me they have money for me."

"It could have been real . . ."

"Also, I don't have a policy with State Farm."

"Right."

"So why would they be sending me any money at all?"

"Then why did you even bother to make the call?"

"I recognized your name. I still follow the news. I saw you being interviewed on CNN after that shootout in Idaho. I file away names and places and details like that. An old habit, I guess. When I heard your name, I remembered it right away. I wondered why a TV reporter from New York City would be calling me. There was only one answer, of course. Elliott Grayson."

"You must have been a pretty good reporter," I said.

"Oh, I had my moments."

The Sarah Grayson abduction and murder was the biggest story he'd ever done, he recalled. There weren't many abductions in Clarion and even fewer killings. Everyone knew the Graysons. Tom Grayson, Elliott's father, was a local fireman and a deacon at the Methodist church. His mother was on the board of the

PTA. The two children, Elliott and Sarah, were both straight-A students and budding athletes. She was on the swim team, and he played Little League baseball in the summer and ice hockey in the winter. The entire town liked the Graysons.

So there was immediate concern when Sarah didn't come home from school that day. She wasn't the kind to just wander off on her own. The townspeople's worst fear was realized when the searchers discovered her battered body in the woods a few days later.

"Everyone was terrified," Briggs recalled. "This wasn't New York, where this kind of thing happens a lot. There was a killer loose here, walking around among us in our quiet town. Until he could be caught, no one would be safe. We ran stories for days about people buying guns and putting extra padlocks on their doors and keeping their children home from school. Sort of a mini version of what the big cities like New York or San Francisco went through with Son of Sam or the Zodiac killer, I guess. Then, of course, there was the funeral for Sarah Grayson. The whole town was in mourning. Never saw anything like it before, never saw anything like it since. No one could believe that this beautiful little girl's life had been snuffed out so horribly. All everyone talked about was poor Sarah. And about what they wanted to do when they found the bastard that did this to her."

"Did they ever catch him?"

"Never did."

"No leads, no clues?"

"The police figured it was a drifter. Someone who was passing through, saw little Sarah outside the school, somehow managed to get her away from there and attacked and then killed her."

"The man her brother saw her talking to outside the school?"

"That was the theory."

"And no one else ever saw that man?"

"No, just Elliott. Poor kid. Can you imagine something like that happening to you when you're only twelve years old? You love your sister, and you see the man that killed her. But you don't realize the danger she's in until it's too late. That must be a terrible thing to live with. It's amazing that Elliott was able to survive that and live the successful life that he has."

I worded my next question very carefully. The guy was still smart at seventy-five, and I didn't want to give away too much of what I knew. But I needed to find out his answer to something.

"Did the police ever question Elliott?" I asked.

"You mean about the drifter? Of course."

"No, I meant about his sister's murder?"

"What about it?"

"Was there ever any suggestion that . . . well, he might have done it?"

"Elliott?"

"Yes."

"Why are you asking that?"

"He was the last person to see her," I said. "Sometimes the police zero in on that. I just wondered if that ever happened in this case."

"Elliott was a twelve-year-old kid. His sister was tortured and raped. No kid did that. No one from this town was capable of something like that. It had to be some sick pervert who came through here, then moved on. God knows if he did it to other children, too. It never happened again in Clarion, that's the one solace. But that didn't help Sarah Grayson or her family."

"What happened after that?"

"The Graysons moved away a short time later. There were too many memories for them to stay, I suppose. Eventually, people forgot and moved on with their lives. I didn't even think about the Graysons for a long time until I started reading about Elliott in New York. Catching criminals and appearing on TV and now running for the Senate. We're all very proud of him here. I even came out of retirement briefly to do an article about him for the paper. Local boy makes good and all that. I called him up, did an interview—he couldn't have been nicer."

"Did you talk about his sister?" I asked.

"No, Elliott didn't want to talk about her. He said it was still too painful even after all this time. He said it was the most trau-matic thing that had ever happened to him. He said that day in the school yard, it had . . . well, he said it had changed him forever."

I thought about little Sarah Grayson's battered body lying in the woods.

About how the police had never caught the person who did it.

About how Elliott Grayson had been the only person to see the drifter and the last person to see his sister alive.

Maybe that day had changed him.

"Everyone in town has been talking about Elliott these days, and how great it is that he's going to Washington now as a US Senator," Briggs told me. "For a lot of people, their lives could have been destroyed by a tragedy like he went through. But he survived. And he's gone on to do such great things. We're all very proud of him here in Clarion. He's a real inspiration to the people of this town."

"He's a real inspiration to us all," I said.

CHAPTER 46

I HAD A problem.

Well, two problems, actually.

Okay, three.

My first problem was that I had too much information. This sometimes happens in the news business. You knock yourself out trying to chase down a few basic facts, and then suddenly you're inundated by them. You've got facts and information and hot leads coming out your ass. Having too much information is still better than having none at all. But enough is enough.

The next problem I had—which was a direct offshoot of the first problem—was that I didn't know what to make of the information I had. There was no straight line, no pattern—the trail took off in different directions every time I tried to follow it. Was Grayson responsible for everything that happened or just some of it? What about Sandy Marston? And how did Patrick Devlin fit in? I had lots of suspects, lots of clues, and lots of unanswered questions.

My third problem—and this was undeniably the biggest one of all—was what to do with all this information I did have. The simple answer was to put it on the air. Only it wasn't that simple. I couldn't just throw it out there to the TV audience and tell them: "You decide!" I didn't have real proof for a lot of it. Marston couldn't sue me for slander or libel, because he was dead. But Grayson could and Patrick Devlin could and so could anyone else I tried to implicate.

Anyway, it was more than just the potential legal consequences that I was worried about here. I wanted to do the right thing journalistically, too. You need to follow the rules as a journalist when you go after bad guys like Elliott Grayson. Otherwise, you're no better than they are.

* * *

I was still mulling over my options on what to do now about the Elliott Grayson story when I got to the office the next morning. I decided I needed a second opinion. I called Maggie into my office and laid it all out for her—everything I'd found out about Grayson and the rest over the past few days.

"You don't really have much there we can work with, Clare," Maggie said when I was finished.

"I've got plenty."

"Okay, but not much we can put on the air."

"Well, that is a slight problem."

"Grayson would sue our ass off if we suggest he had any connection at all to these murders and kidnappings."

"True."

"There's all sorts of other issues, too. For instance, did the Carbone woman's mother know about the stuff you took from her house?"

"I neglected to mention that to her."

"So, you just took it."

"I borrowed it."

"You stole it."

"There's solid evidence there, no matter how I obtained it."

I was starting to regret talking about this with Maggie. The damn kid asked too many questions. Sure, they were good questions, tough questions—the kind any smart journalist would ask.

But she was still pissing me off by asking me all this stuff. Mostly because I didn't have any answers for her.

"What about the list of the six dead kids that Grayson identified as being inside that grave—and the details of how they were abducted?" I said.

"It proves nothing at all. The names were always out there. Marston or anybody could have made the rest of it up."

"Okay, then how about the picture of Grayson with a kid?"

"We don't know who the kid is. Maybe it's just a relative, maybe he's in a big brother program, maybe the kid wanted to grow up to be an FBI agent and his parents asked Grayson to pose for the picture..."

"Whose side are you on anyway?"

"I'm on your side, Clare. I'm just trying to save you from doing anything that might ruin your career. Elliott Grayson is a very important, a very powerful person. You can't take on someone like that unless you have the evidence to back you up. It's one thing to think you know something, but you need facts to put it on the air. You don't have a story without those facts. C'mon, Clare, you taught me that a long time ago. You've preached that to every reporter in this place at one time or another."

That shut me up. She was right. Tough to disagree when someone throws your own words back at you.

*　*　*

We spent the rest of the meeting in my office talking about more immediate issues—like that night's newscast. There had been a subway fire that forced the evacuation of a jam-packed Number 6 train during the morning rush hour. Meanwhile, the city council was slated to hold a crucial vote on school funding.

"Subway fire trumps city council school vote," I said.

"Are you sure?" Maggie asked. "No one was hurt in the fire, and the school funding decision is pretty important."

"Do we have video of the subway evacuation?"

"Yes, some great stuff of people being led up out of the tunnels into the street around 59th."

"And the council vote?"

"I guess that'll be the press conference stuff from some of the council leaders afterward, talking about the importance of . . . education."

"I rest my case."

Maggie nodded.

"Anything else?" I asked.

"Well, there is a small crisis involving Brett and Dani."

The crisis turned out to be which of my news anchors should speak first at the beginning of the show. It always started the same way now, with Brett saying: "This is Brett Wolff. Welcome to the six-o'clock news on 10." Then Dani saying: "This is Dani Blaine. We've got you covered on everything that's happening in New York City and around the world." Dani wanted to know why she couldn't speak first, then Brett second.

Now, as an old newspaper journalist, there were a few things that really ticked me off about TV news—and this was one of them. Why did we need two friggin' people to do one simple intro? Hell, we could save a lot of money by just having one anchor altogether, instead of a twosome alternating sentences with each other. Except I knew that television news didn't work like that.

"You're kidding me, right?" I said when Maggie had finished giving me the details of the problem.

"Nope, Brett and Dani are both really serious about this. They want you to make a decision."

I thought about it for a minute.

"How about this?" I said finally. "We let them alternate intros. Brett goes first night, then Dani the second. Same with the signoff at the end of the show. They each get to go first that way—half of the time."

Maggie chuckled.

"That is brilliant, Clare."

"Hey, that's why they pay me the big bucks."

Maggie said she'd run the plan by Brett and Dani, but she was pretty sure they would both go for it. We went through some other stuff and then she got up to leave. Before she did, she stopped and looked around at me.

"So, what are you going to do about Elliott Grayson?" Maggie asked.

"I have no idea."

"It could be a really big story."

"And a game changer for the Senate election," I said.

"Exactly."

"Now all I have to do is figure out how to run it."

CHAPTER 47

"What does Grayson say about all this?" Janet asked me.

"I don't know. He won't talk to me."

"Why not?"

"I think it's because I wouldn't kiss him."

Janet sighed. We were walking down Madison Avenue. I was on my way back to the office. She was on her way to court. I'd asked her to meet me to help me figure out what to do next.

"You still don't know for sure that he's done anything wrong or that he's really involved in all of this," she said.

"I know he's involved somehow."

"How can you be so sure?"

"My journalistic instincts, Janet. I just have a feeling about this one."

"Are you sure your personal history with the guy doesn't play any part in this?" she asked me.

"What does that mean?"

"Well, maybe the abortive romance with him is clouding your judgment."

"You can't believe that. After what I told you about him?"

"I'm just saying that you don't always handle failed romances well. If you were happily married or in a good relationship, it would be a different story. But you tend to overreact when things don't work out with a man. Like the whole thing you told me about Sam and Dede and the call you made to his house. I just think it would be nice if you met a good guy and stopped playing musical chairs with all these men. I think it might help the rest of your life, too, including your professional life."

"My God, why do I come to you for advice? It's like I'm talking to my aunt Agnes."

"What is it you want me to say?"

"Something that will help me figure this all out."

"Like what?"

"You're a lawyer."

"Okay, but . . ."

"So, what should I do about Elliott Grayson? How do I get him to talk to me—and maybe trap himself in a lie? What would you do if you had a case like this?"

We stopped at a light on 51st. She thought about it for a second until the light changed. Then she started talking as we kept walking.

"Sometimes I get people to say stuff on the witness stand. They don't want to talk about it, but I get them to answer my questions by letting them think that I know more than I really do. It doesn't matter so much if I know the answer. All that matters is that they think I do. They feel they have to say something to protect themselves."

"So you're saying that if Grayson thinks I have a lot of bad stuff on him—more than I really do—and that I'm going to put it on the air . . . Well, he might decide he's better off talking to me. He doesn't know what evidence I have or don't have. It's kind of like poker. I can bluff him."

"It's just a thought."

"That's not bad, Janet."

"You never know . . . it might smoke him out."

"Yes, but first I have to make contact with him somehow."

"Well, I have no idea how you can do that if he won't meet with you or answer your calls."

"I think I do."

"What?"

"An ambush interview."

"What's an ambush interview?"

The idea of the "ambush interview" is to get the person on camera to ask him a question even if he won't say anything. You surprise him at his home or his job or anyplace you know that he'll be. Several things can happen. Maybe he'll talk to you. Maybe he'll run away. Maybe he'll cover up his head and face. Maybe he'll take a swing at you or try to smash the camera. All of these things are good, as long as you can get them on video. Even if the guy doesn't say anything about the story, it adds real action and color and drama to the report you're doing.

I explained this all to Janet now.

"That sounds pretty confrontational," she said when I was done. "Grayson will go nuts if you do that to him."

"Yeah," I smiled. "How about that?"

CHAPTER 48

THE FIRST THING you have to do in an "ambush interview" is get to a spot where you can pull it off.

In this case, it was going to be Grayson's campaign headquarters. I found out that he was supposed to be there for an endorsement from some local union organization at two p.m. I got there a little before that. The offices were located in Midtown, on East 53rd Street near Park Avenue. The Grayson headquarters took up most of the fourth floor of a fifteen-story office building. There was security in the lobby, of course. A guard checking IDs.

I decided to try the simple approach and bluff my way through. It's a lot easier to do that when you have a camera crew with you. Someone with a camera crew just looks like they belong there. I told the crew with me to follow me in the door and just do whatever I do. We walked purposefully through the lobby as if we knew exactly where we were going.

"Hey, I need your ID," the guard yelled after us.

"I already showed it to you."

"I didn't see it."

"Look, we're late for an interview with Elliott Grayson. It goes with the announcement at two p.m. of his big union endorsement. This video has got to be shot today for a campaign promo. If we're late, it's going to be someone's ass. You want to hassle us, fine. We'll tell Grayson exactly why we weren't able to get up there on time."

He shrugged. He didn't want any problems.

"Okay, go ahead."

"Thanks."

"I'll have to call up and tell them you're coming. What's the name?"

"Just say the camera crew is here," I said, as we got on the elevator and pressed the button for the fourth floor.

I figured that was pretty safe. There had to be lots of camera crews coming and going through Grayson headquarters these days. That shouldn't arouse anyone's suspicions. In the end, it didn't matter anyway. As the elevator door closed, I saw more people pouring into the lobby. The guard saw them, then put the phone down to go deal with them. He'd probably never even made the call.

Upstairs, the campaign headquarters was a madhouse. Just the way you'd expect it to be a few days before the election. It was easy to blend in amid all the confusion.

Grayson's office was in the back. Gwen Thompson, the woman that I'd had the run-in with at the prosecutor's office the first time I saw him, was sitting at a desk outside his door. I figured Gwen might be tough to get past. I was right.

"What are you doing here?" she screamed as soon as she recognized me.

"I'm here to see Elliott Grayson."

"He doesn't want to talk to you."

"Are you sure about that?"

"You called here a dozen times. Don't you get the message?"

"Oh, he's probably just playing hard to get."

"Get out of here!"

"Not until I see Grayson."

Elliott Grayson suddenly emerged from an office to see what all the shouting was about. I could tell from his expression he was surprised as hell to see it was me there. He'd been so cool and in control the other times I'd seen him. For the first time now, he looked rattled. That was good for me, I figured.

"Elliott Grayson, have you told us everything you know about Lucy Devlin?" I shouted above the noise.

"I'm not answering any questions like that from you," Grayson yelled back.

"Have you told us everything you know about those six missing children whose bodies you dug up in New Hampshire?" I asked.

"Get out of here!" he said now. "You don't belong here. You have no authorization to—"

"Tell us about the death of your sister, Sarah, when she was a child . . ."

"What?"

He looked especially agitated now that I'd brought up the name of his dead sister.

"Elliott Grayson, I have a lot of questions to ask you before the election about Lucy Devlin, the missing six children you found in that grave, the death of Sandy Marston and Louise Carbone, plus the death of your ten-year-old sister, Sarah Grayson, when you were growing up in Clarion, Pennsylvania."

"Don't you ever talk about my sister!" he said angrily, almost as if he hadn't heard any of the rest of what I said.

"If you'll just sit down with me now and answer these questions —"

"I want you out of here!" he screamed.

"Not before you answer my questions about Lucy Devlin, the missing children, Sandy Marston, Louise Carbone—"

"Out!" he yelled at me again.

"And, yes," I said, "questions about the death of your ten-year-old sister Sarah, too."

Grayson moved toward me now with his fists clenched. For a second, I thought he was going to try to hit me. While we were filming the whole thing for TV. Senate candidate fights it out with newswoman and her TV crew. Now that would be great TV. Boy, talk about a video going viral! But instead, he thought better of it, stopped a few feet away—and then yelled to his campaign staff: "Someone just get this woman the hell out of here."

"Security!" Gwen screamed and set off a loud buzzer on her desk.

The place turned into bedlam after that. Cops, security people, campaign workers all came pouring out from everywhere. Gwen herself was out in front, waving her hands in my face and yelling at me and the film crew to get out.

I told the film crew to keep shooting video of the whole thing for as long as they could.

Eventually, security people dragged us back to the elevator, down to the lobby, and out the front door.

The "ambush interview."

Sometimes it works, sometimes it doesn't.

This time it did.

He hadn't answered any of my questions, but I'd accomplished what I set out to do when I went there to confront him.

* * *

I went on the air with it that night. The newscast led off like this:

ANNOUNCER: This is the Channel 10 News. With Brett Wolff and Dani Blaine at the anchor desk. Steve Stratton with sports, and Wendy Jeffers at the Accu 10 weather central.

If you want to stay up to date in this fast-paced city, you need to keep on the go with Channel 10 News.

And now here's Brett and Dani...

BRETT: There's a five-alarm fire raging in Brooklyn.

There's been a stunning courtroom verdict that could allow a top mobster to go free.

And there's a $100 million lottery winner out there somewhere.

DANI: We're also going to take a look at some of the fun things to do in the fall around New York City. September getaways to make that transition from summer just a little easier. Some of them may surprise you.

BRETT: But first, we have a special Action 10 report on a breaking political story from our own Clare Carlson, who's uncovered some blockbuster revelations about Senate frontrunner Elliott Grayson.

ME: New Yorkers go to the polls soon to vote for a US Senator. Right now, the leading candidate is Elliott Grayson, who's expected to sweep to victory in the Democratic primary over council president Teddy Weller.

Grayson is also considered an overwhelming favorite to win the general election in November. But who exactly is Elliott Grayson? What do we really know about him? More importantly, what don't we know about him?

We know that he's been the poster boy for law enforcement. Crime buster, crusading prosecutor, terrific conviction record. This list of achievements culminated recently when he solved the long-ago Lucy Devlin disappearance case. Tracking down the alleged kidnappers to a farmhouse in Idaho, killing them in a shootout, and then finding the body of Lucy Devlin after years of mystery over what happened to her. That was big news everywhere, including this station.

But a closer examination of Grayson and his record by this station has raised some disturbing questions. Questions about his actions in the Lucy Devlin case. Questions about his investigation of other missing children cases. And questions about a lot of other things, too, including even the mysterious death of his own sister.

We've tried to get answers from Grayson to our questions, but so far, he's refused to talk to us. He doesn't return our phone calls or respond to our e-mails—and this is what happened when we went to his campaign office.

The picture cut to the video we'd taken showing the chaotic scene there. There were shots of the cops and security pushing us out of the office. Me shouting out questions to him, and him refusing to answer. Then Gwen Thompson screaming and everyone yelling at us as we were forcibly escorted out onto the street.

ME: My message to Elliott Grayson tonight is this.

Talk to us, tell us the truth, answer our questions. The people of New York City expect that from their next Senator. Otherwise, before the election, Channel 10 News will run a special report detailing all these allegations and raising new questions about Grayson. The only reason we're not doing it now is because, out of fairness, we want to give him once last chance to respond.

Many of these facts we're prepared to reveal are shocking. Many are disturbing. Many are hard to believe.

The only person who can say they're not true—and hopefully prove to us why not—is Elliott Grayson. And he's not talking.

The ball is in your court, Mr. Grayson. Otherwise, viewers . . .

Stay tuned for this special report before Election Day. It just might change your vote.

Both Brett and Dani looked stunned when the camera went back to them.

BRETT: Well, thanks, Clare . . . we'll be watching for that.

DANI: Uh, William Bero thought he was just making a routine trip to the store for milk and bread. Except he stopped to buy a lottery ticket there, too.

BRETT: Now that lottery ticket has changed his life, because it's worth $100 million! More on that after these messages . . .

When we were off-camera, I turned to Brett and Dani. "What do you think?" I asked them.

"Wow," Dani said. "Grayson's not gonna like this."

"That's the basic idea."

CHAPTER 49

JACK FARON CONFRONTED me in the hallway on the way back to my office right after the telecast.

"What the hell was that all about?" he asked.

I hadn't told Faron what I was going to do. Not about the ambush interview at Grayson's office. Not about going on the air with the ultimatum to Grayson to talk to us about Lucy Devlin and all the rest. I figured he wouldn't let me do it if he knew beforehand. I was right. He was plenty mad.

"Don't worry, Jack. I have a plan."

"What plan?"

"C'mon," I said, "we have all this stuff about Grayson, but we can't use most of it on the air. Only Grayson doesn't know that. He knows what he knows, and he knows what he did, and he knows what would happen if all this came out on the air. Which we know we can't do. But he doesn't know that. Are you following this?"

Faron looked like he was going to have a stroke.

"Anyway," I said, "the idea is we scare him into talking to us, bluff him into reacting, prod him into doing something stupid— anything to put this all in motion."

"That's your plan."

"You have to trust me on this."

"And what if Grayson doesn't do anything?"

"Then we're in trouble."

"You're damned right we're in trouble."

He paced up and down the hallway, waving his arms at me in exasperation.

"You just promised our viewing audience a big exclusive on a scandal. Only you don't have a big exclusive. What you have is a lot of suspicions, half-baked theories, and suppositions. Let's say Grayson doesn't do a thing. He doesn't take the bait. What do you tell the audience tomorrow night that's waiting with bated breath for all these revelations you promised to reveal about him?"

"What I did tonight will smoke Grayson out, Jack."

"I sure hope you're right."

So did I.

* * *

As it turned out, I didn't have to wait very long. I didn't even have to try to call Grayson again. He called me.

"What do you think you're doing?" he yelled over the phone.

"My job."

"You're going to cost me this election doing your damn job."

"Kinda neat the way that works out, huh?"

"You've got everything all wrong, Carlson."

"I simply reported the facts that I have."

"You don't know what I know."

"That's because you won't talk to me."

"I don't have time to talk to you now. I'm in the last days of an election campaign."

"Fine. Then you can find out exactly what I do know by tuning in to the Channel 10 News. I'm spelling it all out there. That ought to give the voters something to think about on the way to the polls on Election Day."

I ran quickly through everything I knew. The connection between Marston and Joey Manielli. The letter about the six young Mountainboro victims—including how they were abducted and how they died—that I found in Big Lou's stuff. And the way the trail of evidence all seemed to lead back to him. Even the long-ago murder of his ten-year-old sister. I made the whole thing sound even more damning to him than it really was, suggesting I'd connected all the dots to Lucy Devlin—even though I really hadn't. But I wanted to make him squirm. I wanted to scare him badly enough to do something.

There was a long silence at the other end of the line when I finished talking. I held my breath.

"Okay, let's meet and talk about this," Grayson said. "Maybe we can work something out."

Jesus, I thought to myself.

This idea might really work.

"Now you're being smart about this," I said to Grayson.

"But no camera crew this time. Nothing on the air."

"Okay."

"Just you and me talking."

"Where do you want to meet?" I asked.

"How about my office?"

I'm not normally paranoid about stuff like this. And the truth was I didn't really think Elliott Grayson was going to have me rubbed out if I showed up there. But I did have this image of Gwen or some other crazed Grayson fanatic coming at me with a letter opener or a staple gun. Besides, a lot of people who came in contact with Grayson over the years had mysteriously turned up dead.

"No, I want to do it in a public place."

"Why?"

"I'm the nervous type."

"You think I'm going to do something to you?"

"Let's just say I don't want to end up like Sandy Marston."

"You're crazy."

"How about a restaurant?"

"I'd be recognized. You, too, probably. You don't want that, do you?"

"Outside then," I said. "A park."

"Central Park?"

"Union Square Park," I said, because I used to live near there and I knew it well. I'd feel comfortable in Union Square Park. If anything was wrong, I'd sense it better and faster there than in a huge place like Central Park.

"Okay, Union Square Park," Grayson said. "Let's meet there tomorrow morning at ten a.m."

"At one of the benches at the north end of the park. Near the Farmer's Market. Come alone."

"You, too."

"Oh, and Elliott . . . one more thing."

"What?"

"You're not going to try to kiss me this time, are you?"

He slammed the phone down in my ear.

I took that as a no.

CHAPTER 50

IT WAS A beautiful fall morning when I got to Union Square Park. The September sun slanted through the trees, where the leaves were already beginning to change. I'm not one of those people who like fall. Fall generally just reminds me that winter and ice and cold and snow are on the way. But this was like a last gasp of summer, a glorious day that made all that wintertime misery seem far, far away.

Union Square Park is at 14th Street near Broadway and Park Avenue South. I took the Lexington Avenue subway there, walked through the park from the station, and found an empty bench at the north end. When I first came to New York, Union Square was a notorious haven for drug pushers, hookers, and muggers. Not too many normal, upstanding citizens ventured inside. But, like a lot of things in the city, the park had changed dramatically over the years. Now there was the Farmer's Market, which sells produce and vegetables; a lot of cute art and antique stands; and outdoor restaurants nearby where people could enjoy the park view. The whole place had a different feel to it.

I looked around and saw mothers sitting with their babies, young people lounging on the grass, and people walking their dogs. Just a nice day in the park for everyone. Except for me. I was on the job. I was there to meet a man who might be a mass murderer, a horrendous child abductor, a fiend so sick that he made his own sister his first victim. Well, at least I thought he was all of these things. Most of them, anyway.

Grayson showed up a few minutes later. He looked around as he strode through the park to see if anyone had spotted him. Amazingly, no one recognized him. Here he was, maybe the next Senator from New York and his face on billboards all over the city, and everyone just minded their own business. New Yorkers—you gotta love 'em.

I thought maybe he'd come with an entourage, even though he promised he wouldn't. But there was no one else. I saw him looking around behind me, too. Probably figured I was with a cameraman or a photographer. When he was satisfied I was alone, he sat down on the bench next to me.

"Fancy meeting you here," I said.

"What's that supposed to mean?"

"I thought maybe we should exchange a few pleasantries before getting down to business."

"Now why would I want to do that with you?"

"Because of all we've meant to each other in the past?"

"You've never meant anything to me."

"What about those sweet nothings you whispered in my ear?"

"Hey, you had your chance with me, honey, and you blew it."

"You're such a romantic, Elliott."

"Cut the crap, Carlson. Just tell me what it is you know—or think you know—so I can get the hell away from you."

"Well, I think that just about completes the pleasantries," I said.

I went through everything I'd found out with Grayson. His face showed no expression as I told him in even more detail what I knew about Sandy Marston and all the rest. That was okay. He had a good poker face. But I had the winning hand. I was sitting there with a full house, and he had nothing.

"Here's what's going to happen," I told him. "First, I'm going to call publicly for an exhumation of all of the bodies that were found in that grave. I'm betting the other five dead kids aren't who you said they were either. Just like Joey Manielli wasn't. I have no idea why you'd want to misidentify them, what you hoped to gain—or hide—by doing it. But I'm pretty sure that's what you deliberately did. I think if I stir up a big enough controversy about it, you won't be able to just stand up and tell everyone to trust you that the other IDs are correct. Sooner or later, those other families are going to demand some answers. And the only way to do that is to dig up every one of those bodies again and find out if you're telling the truth or not.

"Then I'm going to reveal the contents of the package that Sandy Marston and Louise Carbone left behind at her mother's home. Who was that kid in the picture with you, Elliott? What were you doing with him? These are all questions you're going to have to be answering once I put this on the air.

"I'm also going to call for an examination of the 'suicide' letter Marston supposedly left behind. All we have is your word that it was him who told you where to find Lucy Devlin's body. What if you already knew? Because you put it there? That would make it easy to pin the blame on Marston, who wasn't around anymore to defend himself.

"Plus, I want the police to reopen the murder case of your sister back in Pennsylvania. I want you to tell everyone again that story about the mysterious drifter you said was talking to her that last day. The mysterious drifter that no one saw but you. You were only twelve years old when you told the police that story. Maybe they won't believe you as easily this time. Maybe they'll ask you some tougher questions than they did back then.

"I can't prove anything yet, but it doesn't really matter, does it? Because when I throw it all out there, there's going to be a big scandal. And questions about you and your past. A lot of questions. Do you think the people of New York City are going to want to put someone like that in the Senate? Do you really think you can win on Election Day if I put all this out there on the air? Me, I don't think so."

I smiled triumphantly. I wasn't sure exactly what was going to happen next. But I had a pretty good idea of the possibilities.

Either he was going to confess everything, try to explain away some of it by telling me at least part of the truth, or bluff his way through by denying everything.

Whatever one he did was okay with me. I had him dead to rights, no matter what.

Except he didn't react in any of the ways I expected.

Instead, he just smiled back at me.

"You've got it all figured out, huh?"

"Pretty much so."

"You think you've got all the answers?"

"That's right."

"Well, you forgot about one thing."

"Which is?"

"Lucy's mother."

"What about her?"

"This is going to have quite a terrific impact on her—one helluva repercussion for her, I'd say."

"Anne Devlin is dying. I don't think that really matters very much at this point."

"I wasn't talking about Anne Devlin."

"Then who?"

"I'm talking about Lucy's real mother."

I looked around the park. The rest of the people were still eating and reading and enjoying themselves in the warm morning sun. But the day didn't seem so beautiful to me anymore.

We all make compromises in our lives, we all have dark secrets in our past, we all break the rules we vowed to live by sooner or later. Most of the time, if we're lucky, no one ever finds out about our moments of weakness. I'd told myself for a long time that's what would happen to me. But the hard truth is there are consequences—there are always consequences—when we stray from the path of truth and integrity and doing the right thing.

I thought again about how the Lucy Devlin story had come around and found me again after all these years. And if there was anything I could have done to change that, to avoid being in this park right now talking with Elliott Grayson about Lucy Devlin again. Or were Lucy and I indeed always fated to be linked together no matter what?

I don't know the answer to these questions.

And yet I believed that I had somehow caused myself to be in the very situation that I was right now.

Caught up in a web of my own lies, my own transgressions, my own sins.

The same lapses in moral judgement that I always preached so eloquently to others about avoiding.

I realized at that moment Grayson had been playing me the whole time. I was the sucker in the high-stakes card game—feeling all smug and confident with a full house, never realizing my opponent was holding four aces. Four aces always beat a full house. He'd conned me. He sat there with his best poker face and let me tell him everything I knew. He set a trap for me, and I walked right into it.

"I don't know what you're talking about," I said, trying to maintain my own poker face.

But I wasn't as good at the game as he was.

"Sure you do," he said.

"Who's Lucy Devlin's real mother?"

"Why you are, of course."

PART IV

THE WOODSTEIN MANEUVER

CHAPTER 51

I WAS NINETEEN when it happened. A sophomore in college. Young, headstrong, and definitely wild. My father had been very strict with me when I was growing up. No dates, no parties, even no TV—unless he approved of the shows first. When I finally left home and went away to school, I really let loose.

That's how I wound up at a campus fraternity party one night. I'd gone with a couple of girlfriends, neither of whose names I can remember anymore. I was drinking heavily and, as the night wore on, my inhibitions—which were never that strong to begin with—pretty much all fell by the wayside. I remember winning a tequila shooter drinking contest at one point. I remember dancing on a tabletop afterward. I remember lifting up my t-shirt and flashing my breasts while guys cheered.

Most of all, I remember Don Crowell.

He was a senior. President of the fraternity, star of the swim team—a real big man on campus. He was a dreamboat, too. Wavy dark hair, big brown eyes, sensual lips. I'd seen him as soon as I came to the party. I tried to catch his eye, but he never noticed me. Until I started baring my breasts dancing on the tabletop. That seemed to get his attention.

He was drunk by that time. But then, of course, I was, too. So it worked out nicely. We wound up making love in an upstairs bedroom. The lovemaking didn't last very long, as I recall. Not much foreplay, not much cuddling or anything else afterward. He mumbled something about calling me the next day, and then he fell asleep. He never did call, by the way. I left him there in the bed, found a ride, and headed back to my dorm. It was all over so quickly that I hardly even noticed that we hadn't bothered to use protection.

It took me a while to realize I was pregnant. At first, I just wrote the symptoms off as nausea or bad food or the flu. I never even thought about taking a pregnancy test. Finally, one day I went to a doctor, figuring he'd give me some antibiotics to get rid of it. Instead, he came back after the tests and told me the last thing in the world I expected to hear. I was pregnant.

Most young women in that situation would have had an abortion, and I might have, too. After all, a baby didn't fit into my plans. I was going to journalism school, I was going to graduate and move to a big city. I was going to become a famous newspaper reporter. I wasn't ready for motherhood. There'd be plenty of time for that later.

In fact, my father ordered me to have an abortion when he heard the news.

I'd never seen him so angry. He called me a tramp, a slut, and lots of other names I didn't even think he knew. He said I was a disgrace to him and to my mother. He told me how embarrassed they would be if their friends and neighbors and coworkers ever found out about my condition. He wanted to drive me right then and there to an abortion doctor, get the deed done as quickly as possible, and then never talk about it again. My mother listened quietly as he raged on at me, never saying what she thought. Just like she always did.

I suppose that's why I decided not to have the abortion.

Because my father wanted me to so badly.

The result was an irreparable rift between my father and me. He disowned me, he kicked me out of the house, and he refused to give me any money or support. I quit school, moved in with some friends, and gave birth six-and-a-half months later to a baby girl.

While I was pregnant, I made the decision that even though I was having this baby, there was no way I could raise a child on my own.

I made arrangements to have her put up for adoption. It was easy to do. Sort of like donating clothes you don't want to the Salvation Army. There was only one caveat: The adoption hospital said I could never know the family she went to and I could never have any contact with them or my baby. I said that was fine with me. I figured, at the time, it was a small price to pay. But it was a bill that got bigger and bigger as the years went by.

I'd like to say it was an emotional moment when I handed my newborn baby daughter over for adoption at the hospital. That I hugged her and kissed her and promised her I'd see her again one day. That I cried for days afterward. But the truth is, it wasn't like that at all. It was all very perfunctory and routine. I was mostly just glad that the whole thing was over.

I went back to school, graduated with a degree in journalism, got a job at a small newspaper in New Jersey, and eventually moved to New York.

It was not until some years after that when I started thinking again about the daughter that I would never see. I'd done a story about a mother whose baby girl died of sudden infant death syndrome when she was only a few weeks old. Listening to her grief as she talked about how she had held her baby in her arms the day she was born, I suddenly remembered doing the same thing with my own. For some reason, that interview set off feelings of maternal instincts in me. I figured they'd go away after a while, but instead, they kept getting stronger.

I began to think about my daughter all the time. Imagining what she would look like. Wondering what she was doing. Thinking about whether or not she ever knew her biological mother was out there somewhere.

At some point, I'm not sure anymore exactly how or when, I came up with the idea of tracking her down. I was just about to turn thirty, and I guess I was going through an early midlife crisis. I was in between marriages, my first and my second. My first husband and I had tried to have a baby at one point in the beginning without any success. I somehow felt it was punishment for me—a message from God or whatever karma existed out there—for what I had done. I mean, I'd had this beautiful baby girl after only a few minutes of drunken sex at a fraternity party. Then I messed it all up. This was my payback.

Later, in my other marriages, I'd gotten so busy with my career I never really pursued the idea of motherhood. That's what I told myself anyway. But maybe it was about what happened with the baby I'd once had, too. My guilt over giving her up for adoption. And now my penance was that I could not have another child.

At least that's the way I feared it would be for me back then. So, I came up with an idea. Why not find the daughter I actually had? I tried going through official channels, but the adoption agency said their records were absolutely sealed and confidential.

Then, somewhere around that time, I began dating a guy who worked for a federal hospital regulatory agency. I don't remember his name anymore. I think it started with a J . . . Jack or Jim, maybe. Anyway, he was bragging to me in bed about how he had access to any hospital records in the country. In return for me performing certain sexual acts, several of which are still illegal in some states, he agreed to pull my file for me. That's how I found the Devlins.

The story about accidentally meeting Patrick Devlin by chance while interviewing him for a story about city construction was always a crock. It was no accident. I came up with the idea of the story just as an excuse to talk to him. I wanted to find out about the man who was the father of my daughter.

I pretended to be interested in his construction plans so I could find out what I needed to know. After the interview, I asked him if he wanted to join me somewhere for a drink. Sitting in a bar on Lexington Avenue, he told me about his apartment in Gramercy Park, his wife, Anne, and his adorable daughter, Lucy.

I'm not sure how I wound up in bed with him. Some of it had to do with pure physical attraction, I suppose. I always was attracted to muscular, construction-type guys.

But there was another reason I did it, too.

I decided I wanted to see Lucy.

The daughter I'd given up eleven years earlier.

And what better way to do this—as cold and unfeeling as it sounds now to say it—than by sleeping with the man who was now her father.

I think I felt there might be some kind of closure for me in sleeping with the man who had become the father of my daughter. I know that doesn't make a lot of sense, but it seemed to at the time.

I still remember the first time I met Lucy. I'd gone to Patrick's office, and she was there with him. I had to pretend, of course, that Lucy was just the little girl of this man, nothing more to me. He introduced me to her as one of his business clients, and she politely shook my hand.

It was such a surreal moment as I struggled to keep my emotions in check. She had light brown hair like me, freckles like I had when

I was little, and—maybe it was just me—I thought she looked just like a young version of Clare Carlson. I wanted to tell her that. Instead, I just shook her outstretched hand, smiled, and said hello.

Patrick and I had started out first having sex at hotels or some of his residential projects, but then wound up sometimes going to his home during the day. Anne Devlin was away a lot on business trips, and Lucy was at school, so we figured we were safe. Patrick never knew about me being Lucy's biological mother or how I tracked him down. The funny thing, though, was that after a while I forgot about how weird it seemed to be doing it in the house where Lucy lived. It was almost like I started to think that I belonged in that house, instead of Anne. I began to fantasize about it being me and Patrick and Lucy there. It all seemed so perfect.

Until that day when Lucy walked into the bedroom and saw us together.

She wasn't supposed to be home from school for hours. But there had been a gas leak at the school that day and classes were let out early—with the teachers making sure all the children were escorted home safely. And so Lucy was left off at the door, walked inside the house, and heard noises coming from her parents' bedroom. She pushed open the door, saw us in bed together having sex, and screamed like any eleven-year-old might when suddenly confronted by a scene like that. Then she ran out of the room crying.

Patrick went after her and eventually calmed her down. I'm not sure what he told her, how he explained it all—but she finally stopped crying and went to her bedroom. I knew that because I peeked in that room before I left and saw her looking out the window. Like a little angel, I always remembered thinking.

It was the last time I ever saw Lucy.

What had that done to the psyche of an impressionable eleven-year-old girl—to see her father having sex with a woman who wasn't her mother?

Not the mother she knew, anyway.

Did that incident somehow play a role in her disappearance, which came soon afterwards? Had she run away? Had I unwittingly made it easier for a kidnapper to abduct her because of her confused emotional state? Those are the questions that have haunted me over the years.

Of course, it seemed bizarre and strange at first when I spent so much time in that house during the hours, the days, the weeks afterward—covering the story as a reporter for the *Tribune* about the search for Lucy.

I barely spoke to Patrick. I was afraid that one of us might say or do something to give away our secret relationship to Anne. So instead, I wound up becoming extremely close to her. We were like best friends or even sisters, Anne would say. She always laughed about how closely we'd bonded during those troubled times. And why not? We shared something really special together: We were both Lucy's mother. Even if she never knew that.

I always wondered if someone would recognize me from all the time I'd spent there before Lucy disappeared. Like a neighbor. But no one ever did. And, after a while, the relationship just became natural. Me and Anne. Hoping and praying and believing that we'd get a break in the case and Lucy would be found. Anne Devlin kept believing that long after I had stopped. She would never let go of that slender hope she continued to hold onto. And she had made me promise a long, long time ago to help her find the real answers about Lucy, no matter how long it took.

"You owe me, Clare," Anne Devlin had said.

I sure did owe her.

More than she would ever realize.

CHAPTER 52

"How did you find out?" I asked Elliott Grayson.

"I checked the adoption records."

"Those are supposed to be secret."

"Well, you found out about the Devlins from them, right? How did you do that if they were private?"

"I pulled some strings," I said. "I'm a reporter. I know how to get information no one else can obtain."

"I'm a US Attorney, so pulling strings isn't very hard for me either."

"But why?" I asked. "Why would you ever check that in the first place?"

"I'm an investigator. When you started asking new questions about Lucy Devlin, I got curious. So I investigated. And I eventually found the adoption papers with you listed as the biological mother. You must have been just a kid then. Barely out of high school."

"I was in college," I said quietly.

"Anyway, I was able to confirm that you and the Clare Carlson in the adoption papers were one and the same person."

"But you didn't tell anyone else?"

"Not yet."

"Why not?"

"I figured I might be able to use that information to my advantage at some later date."

"Like now."

"Exactly."

He took out a packet of papers and handed them to me. They were copies of the adoption documents. On top was a form I'd filled out before leaving the hospital. I read through the words on the page now, still numb and in shock over what was happening.

NAME: Clare Carlson.

AGE: 19

SEX OF BABY: Female.

There was a picture of me taken at the hospital that day, too.

The young woman in it stared back at me from the piece of paper I was holding—young, confident, so sure that she was doing the right thing.

I remembered exactly, now, when that picture had been taken.

It was right after I handed my baby girl over to a nurse.

The last time I'd seen her until I tracked her down to the Devlins.

* * *

So much has changed since that day more than twenty-five years ago when I gave birth to the baby that would become Lucy Devlin.

My father's dead now. The rift between us was never really repaired. He was a stubborn man. I'm stubborn, too, and neither of us would ever admit we were wrong. Having that baby cost me my father. If I could go back and relive that period of my life, maybe I'd have handled things differently. Or maybe not. It doesn't really matter because we don't get do-overs in life.

Don Crowell is dead, too. I looked him up on the Internet one time just out of curiosity. I'd never told him I was pregnant and—as far as I knew—Crowell went through his life barely remembering me as just one of a series of one-night stands he'd probably had with lots of women back then. He joined the Air Force after college, rose to the rank of major, and flew a number of dangerous combat missions. He later piloted commercial aircraft, safely bringing down a crippled jet to Los Angeles with more than 300 people aboard on a foam-covered runway at LAX. Then, one night as he was walking to a store a block from his house, a drunk driver sped through a red light and mowed him down in the crosswalk. Crowell was killed instantly. Life is unpredictable—you never know what's out there waiting for you.

For years, I'd kept alive the spark of hope that Lucy was still alive somewhere—all grown up, healthy and happy and wondering sometimes about me just the way I did about her.

Then I cried for her when they said they found her body in that grave in Dutchess County.

Now I wasn't sure what to believe anymore.

I'm forty-five years old, a three-time divorcee with no discernable marriage prospects in my immediate future. And, even if I did find someone and get married again, I had no reason to think it wouldn't turn out badly, given my track record with men. I mean, the last guy I was interested in was Elliott Grayson.

What does that say about my judgement?

I'd had my chance to be a mother—when I was very young—and I casually just threw it away.

I thought there'd be more chances, more opportunities for me then.

But it never worked out that way.

And now all that was left were the regrets.

* * *

"Let's you and me make a deal," Elliott Grayson said.

"What kind of deal?"

"I'll give you something if you agree not to run with your story. Whatever it is you've found out—or think you've found out—about me. In return, I'll give you something I believe you want very badly. Something even more important—more valuable to you—than this story."

"You're offering me a payoff?" I asked incredulously.

"Whatever you want to call it."

"No way."

"Maybe we can both save our careers this way."

"Look, I know this will look bad for me if it all comes out. Make me look like a dishonest journalist. A tramp. A backstabber to Anne Devlin who preyed on her feelings to break stories and win a Pulitzer Prize. A terrible woman who gave her baby up for adoption without so much as a second thought. TMZ and the all-news cable channels and the tabloid press will have a field day with me. I'll probably lose my Pulitzer, my job, maybe even my whole journalism career if that happens. But I'm still going to do the right thing. I'm going to tell this story. Whatever it is. And there's nothing in the world you can do to stop me."

I talked about my integrity as a journalist. How I'd spent my entire career following a code of journalistic ethics. How I'd lectured my reporters about this code—about always doing the right thing as a journalist—so many times over the years. The meaning was very clear. I could not be bought no matter what he offered me. My integrity as a journalist was the most important thing that I cared about in my life.

Or so I thought.

"Why don't you at least listen to my offer before you reject it?" Grayson said.

"Because there's no point."

"This is an offer you can't refuse."

"I can't be bought, Grayson."

"Your daughter's still alive," he said. "I know where Lucy is."

CHAPTER 53

"LUCY IS ALIVE," I said, repeating what he'd just told me in shock and disbelief, even as I heard myself say the words.

I had clung to that hope for fifteen years, ever since the day she disappeared. Just like Anne Devlin had. I knew it was a long shot all the way even back at the beginning, and that hope faded away to almost nothing as the years passed without any news. And then, of course, the last flicker of hope died when her body had been found in that grave in Dutchess County.

Except now everything had turned upside down again.

"She's alive and well," Grayson said to me. "She's a grown woman now, of course. Married, with a little daughter of her own. She's very happy."

"What happened to her?" I asked.

"I can't tell you that unless we make a deal."

"Where is she?"

"Same answer."

I nodded.

"What kind of a deal are we talking about?"

* * *

The deal Grayson offered me went something like this:

He would answer my questions as truthfully and fully as he could on Lucy Devlin, the bodies in the New Hampshire grave, the other missing children, Sandy Marston, Patrick Devlin, and even the death of his own sister.

In return, I agreed not to put it on the air or tell anyone else what I knew.

And then—after the Senate election, when he was in office—he would tell me where Lucy was.

Grayson said that when the truth came out, it would show he had always tried to do the right thing. Even if I broke my promise and went public with it after he told me about Lucy and the election was over, he thought he could probably survive the long-term political fallout. But the immediate scandal might torpedo his chance to get elected. His priority at this point was just to keep me quiet until then.

"How do you know I won't double-cross you?" I asked. "I mean, I could just listen to everything, promise you not to tell anyone, and then go ahead and put it on the air anyway tonight. What's stopping me from doing that?"

"Three reasons," Grayson said.

One of them obviously was the information he had about Lucy. He wouldn't tell me where she was. Not until after the election.

"What are the other two?" I asked.

"First, I'd just deny it. Claim we never had this conversation. Everyone knows you've been out to get me, so I'll say you made it up. You'd say you didn't, I'd say you did. It would be a classic case of 'he said, she said.'"

"Second, you have no proof. Without me backing you up, you'd need some kind of evidence to go on the air with the stuff I'm going to tell you. You might eventually track down enough evidence, but that would take time. It certainly wouldn't happen before the election. Again, without proof, it's just your word against mine."

Then—just for emphasis, I guess—he repeated the third and most obvious reason.

"The biggest thing here is your daughter, Clare. I'll tell you where to find your daughter. But I won't do that until after the election. And only if you keep your word to me. If you don't, you'll never see her or know what happened to her. That's the quid pro quo here, Carlson. Your daughter for your story. Do we have a deal?"

I know what you're probably thinking about me right now. How could this woman—who knew that her own child had been kidnapped—have kept on covering this horrible tragedy just like any other story? How could she accept a Pulitzer Prize—the highest award in journalism—and use it to catapult to journalistic fame on the back of her missing daughter?

These were all legitimate questions.

I've asked them of myself many times over the years.

The best answer I can tell you is that it was the only way I knew how to deal with what happened to Lucy. I've always thrown myself totally into my work—the same way as I do now with my obsession each day over breaking news—as a solution for the problems in my life. And so that's what I did with Lucy. I just kept covering the story like a journalist so that I didn't have to deal with the pain and the reality of what had happened. All I had to do was keep filing stories on deadline and getting on the front page. It almost became just another story. Almost.

At some point, I even began to think that the Pulitzer I won was a sort of consolation prize for me. Sure, I had lost a daughter. But fate had rewarded me with this Pulitzer because of that. My daughter in return for fame and acclaim as a journalist—that was the trade-off. And I was good with that. For a long time, anyway. At least that's what I told myself, until all this happened.

But now I had to make a decision.

There's a scene in the movie *All the President's Men* when Dustin Hoffman and Robert Redford interview a Nixon campaign committee official named Hugh Sloan. Sloan's one of the good guys of Watergate, a man of integrity and conscience caught up in the scandal. They ask him about the distribution of illegal campaign funds from Attorney General John Mitchell.

"How did that go?" Hoffman's Carl Bernstein character asks.

"Badly," Sloan replies.

Well, that's how I felt right now.

This was a bad deal. It ran against everything I believed in and had dedicated my life to and taught others to believe in, too. It was an abandonment of the journalistic principles I always held so dear. If I did this, I would never be the same journalist—or the same person—that I was before.

Of course, Grayson was wrong about a couple of his assumptions.

First, even if he denied ever talking to me, there would be a big scandal if I broadcast the story. Enough to ruin his chances to be elected. That's the thing about scandals involving politicians—people always want to believe the worst. Even if there's no proof, they assume a politician is guilty. There was no doubt in my mind that if I ran with this story, it would cost Grayson the election.

Second, I did have proof. Before coming to the meeting, I'd set up a sophisticated taping device we sometimes used at the station to surreptitiously record these kinds of interviews. It was running right now in my purse, taking down everything we said. All I had to do was play that on the air, and he'd be finished.

He was right about the third reason though.

Lucy.

If I sat on this story, at least until after Election Day, he promised to tell me how to find my daughter. The daughter I thought was dead. The daughter I'd lost twice—once the day she was born, and again when she was eleven years old. The daughter that was still out there somewhere for me, if I wanted her.

I thought back again to all those hollow-sounding speeches I made to young reporters about honesty and integrity and moral standards for a journalist.

That's been my mantra to reporters for a lot of years. The "what breed?" story and The Woodstein Maneuver question. I ask the new reporters to put themselves in Woodward and Bernstein's place and think about what they would do if offered a bribe—a huge amount of money—to cover up Watergate, the greatest investigative journalism story of our time. Only a few reporters ask the key question: "How much money?" they want to know. But those are the ones I worry about most. Because there is no compromise, no extenuating circumstances that ever make it right for a journalist to cross that line. And once they do, I warn them, they can never go back.

I could recite that damn speech by heart. I've given it so many times in the newsroom to Maggie and Brett and Dani and Cassie and Janelle and all the other people who work for me. And yet, here I was now ensnared in the same web of lies and dishonesty and moral corruption that I've preached so eloquently about to others.

They say that everyone can be bought.

That everyone has a price.

It just isn't always about money.

"Do we have a deal?" Grayson asked me now.

"Yes," I heard myself say. "I'll do whatever it takes to find Lucy."

The Woodstein Maneuver.

CHAPTER 54

"THE FIRST THING you have to understand is about my sister," Grayson said. "I loved my sister. You're wrong in thinking I had anything to do with what happened to her."

"But, there was no mysterious stranger in the schoolyard, was there?" I asked.

"No."

"Why did you tell the police there was?"

"Christ, I was only twelve years old . . ."

"That's not really an answer."

Grayson looked at me with a sad, pained expression on his face. I knew at that moment he was going to tell me the truth about his sister. Later, when I'd play over in my mind our conversation in the park that day, I'd never be sure how much he told me was fact and how much was fiction. But there was no doubt about his sister. The pain was too real.

"My father was a fireman who saved people's lives and their houses and their possessions," Grayson said softly. "He was a hero in that town. He took part in civic activities, he coached Little League baseball, and he went to church every Sunday. Everyone thought my father was a terrific guy. Except his own family. We didn't think he was so terrific."

"He mistreated you?"

"He beat the hell out of me. Sometimes to punish me. Sometimes because he was drunk. Sometimes because he just seemed to get a kick out of doing it. I never understood then what makes a man do something like that, and I still don't today."

"What about your mother?"

"He beat her, too. Behind closed doors, most of the time. But I could hear it."

"And your sister?"

"Sarah? She got it the worst of all. She was tough, though. She was the only one who stood up to him. That made him even madder, so he beat her harder. I sometimes would lie in bed at night and hear the screaming coming from her bedroom. I felt sorry for her, but mostly I was just glad that it wasn't me getting a whipping that night."

I saw the pain on his face again. I realized it was for the guilt he'd been holding on to all these years.

"By the time Sarah got to be ten or so, things changed," he said. "My father didn't just beat her anymore, he did other things, too. He'd come home after a night of drinking at the bar and force himself sexually on her. I don't think I really understood what was happening at that age, but I knew it was a terrible thing for my sister. I wanted to help her. But I was afraid.

"Finally, this one time, I stood up to him. I told him to leave Sarah alone. He didn't do anything to her that night—instead he concentrated all his anger on me. There was a deep woods behind our house, and he dragged me out into it for maybe a mile. Then he went to work on me—first with his fists, then with a thick tree branch.

"By the time he was finished, I was a bloody mess. My jaw was broken, I had a couple of cracked ribs, and there were bloody bruises all over my body. He left me out there like that in the woods, alone and scared and hurt in the dark. The next morning, after I managed to make it home, I told people I'd gotten lost in the woods and fallen down a cliff. No one ever suspected my father had done it.

"A few weeks later, the screams coming from Sarah's room were worse than ever. The next morning, when I went in to check on her, she was nowhere to be found. I knew in my heart what had happened. She had fought back against my father again, and he'd taken her out into the woods—just like he did with me. I searched the woods until I found her body. I'd never seen a dead person before, and this was my own sister.

"I ran back to the house and found my father drinking a beer at the kitchen table. When I told him about Sarah, he dragged me back to the spot in the woods where I'd found her body. He made me help cover her up with leaves and dirt. Then he said I should go to school as if nothing had happened. He said that when anyone asked me about Sarah, I should tell them that I saw her talking to a strange man in the schoolyard. He said if I told anyone the truth, then I'd wind up like her. I did what he wanted. I was just a scared twelve-year-old kid."

It was the second time he'd used the phrase, "I was just a scared twelve-year-old kid." I had the feeling that he'd said it many times to himself over the years, trying to justify what he did. But he hadn't quite managed to pull it off.

"What happened after that?" I asked.

"A few months later, my father moved us to a new town—this time in Tennessee, where he got a job in another fire department. And everyone there thought he was a great guy, just like they did back in Clarion. After a while, I even almost believed that night in the woods with Sarah had never happened. But deep down I knew. I wanted him to pay for what he did to her. I didn't know how or when, but he had to be punished.

"When I was older, I promised myself, I'd reveal the true story to everyone. But I never got the chance. One night my father rushed back into a burning building, the furnace exploded, and he was killed. He saved four people before he died, and they eulogized him at the funeral as a true hero. I suppose I could have come forward then, but it would have been pointless. No one would have believed me anyway.

"I guess that's probably why—after I went through my motorcycle gang phase—I decided to go into law enforcement. It was too late to do anything about what he did to Sarah, but maybe I could help other families. Child abuse is going on every day all over America. Everyone says there's nothing that can be done about it. Well, I decided to try. I got myself assigned to a department at the FBI that specialized in missing and abused and murdered children. I became an expert in these cases. I arrested a lot of predators and I put a lot of people in jail. It was very satisfying work for a while. But it wasn't enough.

"One day we got this really heartbreaking letter at FBI headquarters from a little ten-year-old girl in Virginia. It was a helluva thing. Her name was Lisa Fenton, and she actually sat down and wrote us a letter telling us about all the terrible things her father had done to her. She said she had watched this show about the FBI on TV, and they were always helping people. She asked us if we would help her. I went to see Lisa Fenton. After talking to her, I was sure she was telling the truth. But I couldn't do anything. Her parents denied it all and said Lisa was always making up stories. The father was a big corporate lawyer in Washington, and he had a lot of political clout. My boss said there wasn't enough evidence to make a case, and I knew he was right. So we let it drop.

"A few months later, the parents brought Lisa to the emergency room of a local hospital. She had internal bleeding and she'd been battered around the face and head. It turned out she'd resisted her father's advances that time, and he'd gone a little crazy—as he put it. He was crying and saying how sorry he was, and his wife kept insisting how much he really loved his daughter. We wound up prosecuting him after all, but it was too late to save Lisa. She died a few days later from her injuries.

"That one really got to me. Lisa Fenton was the same age as my sister, Sarah, had been, she fought back like Sarah and she even looked a little like Sarah. And, worst of all, she had come to me for help, and I'd let her down. Just like I did with Sarah. That's when I decided I needed to do more than just put these bastards in jail."

It was all starting to make sense to me now. These weren't any black-market adoptions at all, like I had thought. There was no money involved here. This was about Elliott Grayson, the vigilante.

He had spent a lifetime scarred by the memory of not being able to save his sister. So he tried to save as many other children as he could to somehow make up for it. At first, he used the law to do this, but it wasn't enough. That's when he crossed the line between being a lawman and a lawbreaker.

Now he was somewhere in between.

"These cases of abuse you were dealing with had already happened," I said. "It was too late to save the young victims. You wanted to get the child out of the family where they were being abused. You found children who were in bad family situations, with no hope and no way out. Then you 'abducted' them—and found them different, better homes with parents who were desperate to have children."

"Something like that."

"Why was Sandy Marston helping you?"

"We used to ride together. Different motorcycle gangs. But we met up a couple of times and hung out together for a while."

"And the two of you just decided to save the world together?"

"Look, bikers aren't always what you think they are. I was a good one, and there's a lot of good guys there. Hell, Marston was the valedictorian of his high school class, did you know that? He should have gone to college, but he never did. His father had a bad gambling habit and lost all his tuition money one weekend in Atlantic City. Marston was so distraught he ran away, joined the Warlock Warriors, and never looked back after that. But he was a very intelligent man. He wrote poetry, you know. I'll bet he never told you that."

Maybe that was the side of him that had attracted Louise Carbone.

"Okay, Sandy Marston was a sensitive and misunderstood genius," I said. "But why did he do all this stuff for you? Taking all these kids for you, driving them cross country to new homes. What was in it for him?"

Grayson looked across the park where a young boy of about eleven or twelve and his father were throwing a football back and forth. The father would throw a pass, and the boy would run out and catch it. Each time he did, the boy would do a celebratory touchdown dance like they do on TV, and then the two of them would exchange high-five congratulations. Grayson wiped something from his eyes as he watched them. Maybe a tear as he thought about him and his own father. Maybe he was thinking about how he never had the chance to throw a football around with his father when he was growing up. Maybe he was thinking about how lucky that little boy in the park was. Or maybe he just had something in his eye. Sometimes I overanalyze things.

"When I first started working in law enforcement, there was a big federal drug bust against the Warlock Warriors gang for dealing and distribution of marijuana, cocaine, and a lot other stuff. They took Marston into custody. I pulled some strings, got him out of jail, and told him I could keep him out of it. In return, he had to help me."

"He was your snitch."

"At first. He gave me information about drug deals and other things he heard people were up to. He really helped my career skyrocket. I got this reputation as a guy who knew more than anyone else in the department. In return, I gave him and his people in Hell's Kitchen a wide berth, made sure they didn't get hassled by any authorities. I got the NYPD to go along with me. It wasn't hard. That kind of thing happens all the time. One hand washes the other. I was his rabbi, his protector. Even that time he got arrested—back with the little girl he was checking up on before Lucy—I was able to keep the jail term to a minimum. Marston was my snitch. I owned him. I took care of him. It's the way things are."

"Then he became more than a snitch. You used him more and more in dealing with these kids."

"How did you ever figure that out anyway?"

"Joey Manielli."

"Of course. I'd heard about him popping up in the system. I hoped no one would notice. But yes, that's what happened. I had access to all sorts of information around the country. When I heard about a particularly bad family situation, I looked into it. The really bad cases . . . well, that's when I did something."

"Let's talk about the other five bodies in that grave," I said.

"What about them?"

"They're not who you said they were either, right? Just like Joey Manielli wasn't."

He nodded.

"It just happened. I heard about the kids' bodies being found, and I made sure I got put in charge of the task force investigating it. We dug up the bodies, and that's when I got the idea. The children I'd found new homes for . . . well, their families were still looking for them. If some of them were dead—or at least people thought they were dead—then they'd be safe for good. So, I gave out the wrong IDs."

"But you didn't figure on one of them turning up somewhere—letting people know he or she was alive—like what happened with Joey Manielli?"

"They had new names, new identities. That's all I could do. Some of them were too young to even remember much about their real parents or homes. Manielli was the anomaly. He'd gotten those fingerprints taken after the car theft when he was twelve. It was just a bad break that someone discovered that."

"But other stuff like that could have happened," I pointed out. "Arrests, medical issues. Even more likely, one of them could have gone looking for their past lives and families as they got older—for revenge or maybe just curiosity or a lot of other possible reasons people want to know about their ancestry."

"Look, I'm not saying it was a perfect plan. It was flawed. I know that. I wish now I'd never done any of it. But at the time I just wanted to save these children and let them have a chance at living normal lives—away from the hellish homes where they were trapped. I knew it was dangerous, but I took the risk because the welfare of these children was the most important thing to me. I saved six lives. I'm proud of that, even if I'm not proud of everything I had to do to accomplish that. Anyway, this all happened a long time ago. After a while, I stopped. It just became too difficult to pull off. And I guess I realized I was wrong to take the law into my own hands like that, even though I believed I was doing the right thing for those kids."

I nodded. It all made sense, sort of.

"What about the six real children in the grave?" I asked Grayson. "Who were the bodies?"

"Other missing children."

"Who killed them and put them in that grave?"

"I don't know."

"And what about their parents? Still sitting at home waiting for word? These people didn't do anything wrong, they just lost their children. Because of you, they'll never have any kind of closure in their lives. Didn't you feel guilty about that?"

"I did what I had to do," he said. "I wanted to save the six who were alive. As for the dead ones, I figured it wasn't the worst thing in the world that their families still clung on to hope they might be alive somewhere. Is hope—even false hope—the worst thing in the world to give someone?"

I thought about Alice Devlin waiting all those years for Lucy to come home.

I wasn't sure about the answer to that.

"Like I said, this all happened years ago," Grayson said. "I hadn't thought about it in a long time until that e-mail and the phone call to my office from Louise Carbone, which I'm sure Marston set up."

"Marston probably figured he could score big now that you were running for a high political office. He'd been holding onto this stuff for years, and now he was trying to blackmail you. He thought you'd be willing to pay him off to make sure none of this came out before Election Day. But you couldn't give Marston the money he wanted. He was too much of a loose cannon out there. As long as he was around and knew what he knew, you couldn't be sure about being elected. I think Marston suddenly realized that, realized what you might be capable of doing to win the Senate seat. That's why he and Louise took off the way they did. To get away from you. But you set them up, made it seem like they were responsible for Lucy's death. I helped you do that, even though I didn't realize it at the time. Then they both conveniently died in that shootout. They had to die, didn't they? Because otherwise Marston would have told everything he knew. About Lucy Devlin. About all of it. You could never let that happen."

"That's ridiculous."

"All right, you tell me what happened in Idaho."

"I made up the suicide letter with the confession about Lucy, I admit that. But the shooting was an accident."

"Who was the little girl that you dug up and claimed was Lucy?"

"Just another missing kid whose body we'd discovered."

"What's her name?"

"It doesn't matter."

"I'll bet it matters to her family."

"I did what I had to do," he said defiantly. "What I didn't do was kill Sandy Marston and his girlfriend deliberately."

I wasn't sure if I believed him or not. It could have all happened the way he said it did, of course. But I remembered what my friend Cliff Whitten had said about Grayson. That he'd do anything to get what he wanted—lie, cheat, break the rules, and violate any legal standards—because he thought he was in the right. The problem is when you do this, sometimes you make things worse than they were in the first place. Maybe he decided that Marston and Louise were expendable. Maybe he decided that, in the big picture of things, they really didn't matter that much. Maybe he thought of all the great and noble things he could do in Washington if they weren't around to ruin it. Maybe. I'd probably never know for sure.

Of course, I'd saved the most important question until last.

"What about Lucy?" I asked.

"She was the same as all the rest of them. Marston befriended her, got her to go away with him on his bike that day. She really was at that motorcycle convention in New Hampshire, just like the letter said. But she was with Marston, not me. I wasn't there. I guess Marston and his girlfriend just told you that to get me involved. Eventually, we placed her with another family. A good family. She's a grown woman now, married, a mother—happy, healthy, with her whole life to look forward to. I don't know how much of this she knows. You'll find out when you meet her. If you meet her."

I ignored the implied threat.

"But why take her?"

"Like I said, it was the same reason as the others. It was a bad situation inside that house. She wouldn't have survived it."

There it was. The truth I could never believe about Patrick Devlin. Anne Devlin had suspected something bad was happening between him and Lucy, but I assumed it was just her imagination. I'd slept with the guy, I thought I knew him—at least back then. But I thought now about the anger in his eyes when I'd first raised the accusation with him. The way he'd punched the wall of that construction shed. Had he punched Lucy that way, too, when he got mad or wanted his way with her?

"I never thought Patrick Devlin was capable of something like that," I said.

"I'm not talking about Patrick," Grayson said.

"But you said she was abused in that house."

"She was."

"Then who—"

"There were two people in that house with Lucy."

That's when the horrible truth finally hit me.

"I had to save Lucy from her mother," Grayson said. "Anne Devlin."

CHAPTER 55

"I WANT TO know about you and Anne and Lucy and what went on inside that house," I said to Patrick Devlin. "Not the sugar-coated American dream version. Everyone—including me—has bought that story for a long time. But that's not really the way it was, right? The dream didn't just die the day Lucy disappeared; it was a nightmare long before that."

We were sitting in the den of his house in suburban Boston, a spacious two-story Cape Cod with gray shingles and a view of a big yard and swimming pool in the back.

I'd flown up there right after my meeting with Grayson. Devlin didn't seem surprised to see me this time. Or mad at me anymore. Maybe he'd been thinking about everything since our last conversation and realized it wasn't over. Maybe he'd already decided he had held onto his secrets for too long.

Devlin introduced me to his wife and children. The wife was a pleasant-looking blond woman of about my age, who offered me coffee and something to eat. I never knew if she realized what I was there for, or if it would have mattered if she did. The children were a young boy and a girl. They were blond-haired, too, and happily played video games on iPads while Devlin and his wife and I made small talk. Neither of them looked anything like Lucy. Devlin finally told his family that he and I had some business we needed to discuss in private.

Then he led me into the den, closing the door on them as easily as he did on Anne and Lucy and his other life years ago.

"How did you find out?" he asked after we sat down.

"That's not important. The only important thing is this: Why did it happen?"

"Lucy was adopted. That's when it all really started. Of course, you didn't know that. No one ever knew about the adoption."

I acted as if this was the first time I'd learned this.

"You and Anne couldn't have children?" I asked.

"We tried for a long time, but nothing happened. Then the doctor gave Anne the bad news that she could never have a baby. She was very upset and disappointed, almost suicidal for a while. I told her we could adopt, but she said that wasn't the same. She said she needed her own child. Someone that came from her own flesh and blood, not some other woman's. But eventually she changed her mind and we adopted Lucy."

"How come this never came out before?" I asked.

It was a question that had always bothered me. When a child disappears—or is abducted—the person who gave the child up is part of the investigation. I always figured someone would track it down to me back then. But they never did.

"The police asked at one point if there was any issue involving adoption or other parents that might want custody or anything like that," Devlin said. "Anne said no. She said we were the only parents Lucy had ever had."

"Why didn't she tell them the truth?"

"Because she didn't know the truth anymore. The only way Anne would accept adopting a baby was if she truly believed the baby was hers. She never told anyone about the adoption. She even made up a whole story about the birth and hospital and everything that happened, which she'd tell people. After a while, she began to believe it herself. When the police asked if there was any adoption or other custody issues, she wasn't really lying when she said no. She just refused to acknowledge that the adoption had ever happened."

So far, it sounded bizarre, but not terrible.

"The thing is that at some point the fantasy began to overtake the reality for Anne. Lucy became the focus of everything in Anne's life, an extension of herself in a way. At first, she showed that by almost smothering Lucy in love. Lucy could do nothing wrong in her eyes, Lucy was the perfect little girl. But later, as Lucy got older, that all changed. Anne became obsessed with her in a different way. When she got really crazy, she'd tell me that Lucy was evil. That she wasn't really our daughter. That she had the devil inside her."

"The devil," I repeated.

"Yes."

"Why the devil?"

"I've thought about this a lot over the years. The simplest answer I can give you is Anne had some emotional issues of her own that she took out on Lucy. As Lucy grew up and became a pretty and adorable girl, Anne became more and more jealous of her. That's the only way I can describe it.

"She also became convinced that I was more interested in Lucy than I was in her. When I would play with Lucy or hold her on my lap, Anne would get upset. She'd ask me why I wanted to pay attention to a little girl when I had her. Sometimes she would even call me a pervert or a sex addict or other horrible names. In her mind, she was in competition with Lucy for my attention.

"Eventually she became consumed by jealousy over Lucy. The better Lucy did in school or the more people told her what a wonderful daughter she had, the angrier Anne got. Sometimes she'd take that anger out on me, which I could deal with. But most of the time she directed it against Lucy. That's when things got out of control."

I tried to picture Anne Devlin like that. It seemed difficult to match with the woman I'd known over the years. But then I'd found out a long time ago that people aren't always what they seem.

"One day I came home early and found Lucy in tears," Devlin said. "There were bruise marks and burns all over her body. Anne had tied her to a scalding radiator and beat her. I found out later it was because someone at the store had told Anne how beautiful her daughter was, but hadn't complimented her. When they got home, Anne went on a jealous rampage against Lucy.

"It began to happen more and more after that. Anything could set Anne off. If Lucy said the wrong thing or came home from school a few minutes late or even if she wanted to watch a TV program Anne didn't like. Sometimes I'd be there to stop it. Too many times I wasn't. I'd discover the evidence when I got home, the bruises and the scars and the blood in the house. Afterward, Anne would be terribly apologetic. She'd promise it would never happen again. She'd smother Lucy in love again for the rest of the night, sometimes for days afterward. Until the next time.

"I didn't know what to do. I didn't know where to turn. If I went to the police, I didn't think they would believe me. Or they might think I did it. Lucy was in no emotional or mental condition to tell the truth. She was too confused about what was happening to her. She was constantly trying to please her mother. But the harder she tried, the worse everything got.

"At one point, I went to an old friend I knew in law enforcement. Someone I'd known years before. I told him off the record what was happening. He agreed with me that the police wouldn't believe me and probably think I was the one hurting her. Even if they did accept my story, they couldn't protect Lucy. He said things like this happened all the time, all across America. He said they only took a child away from her mother temporarily anyway and sooner or later Anne would get her hands on her again. He said all I could do was try to protect Lucy as best I could and hope for a miracle."

"Was it Elliott Grayson you talked to?"

"Yes. I knew him from my days riding with motorcycle groups, and we'd kept in touch after that. He just told me to hang in there. He said maybe something would happen to change what seemed to be a hopeless situation."

Of course. That was how Grayson had found out about Lucy. Patrick Devlin didn't know it, but he had alerted a self-proclaimed vigilante to his daughter's plight.

"That time with you was the worst," Devlin said. "After Lucy walked in on us in bed, she told Anne about me and sex. Anne thought she was talking about me and Lucy having sex. I openly admitted to sleeping with someone else there that day—I never said it was you—but Anne wouldn't believe me. She was convinced I'd been with Lucy. That night I had a late meeting. When I got home, I found Anne in Lucy's bedroom. Lucy was screaming. Anne was beating her with a big strap. She said she wasn't going to stop until all the evil was beaten out of her. She called it an exorcism. She said she was beating the devil out of our daughter. Well, I stopped her in time, but I knew it would happen again and again unless I did something. I was prepared to do anything to save my daughter. As it turned out, I never got the chance. Because Lucy disappeared."

Elliott Grayson, I thought.

"Didn't you ever imagine that Anne might have killed her and just gotten rid of the body?"

"No, I knew it wasn't Anne."

"How?"

"Because her anguish was so real. It was almost like she had some kind of reverse guilt because of all the terrible things she'd done to her. After Lucy was gone, Lucy turned into the greatest little girl in the world. At least the way Anne remembered her. She dedicated her life to finding her. Who knows what would have happened if she did—I used to have nightmares about that. I wanted to know what happened to Lucy, but I was afraid about what Anne would do to her if she was found.

"After Lucy disappeared, Anne and I stayed together for a while, but we weren't really husband and wife anymore. All she cared about was this crusade to find Lucy. That consumed her. I don't think she cared one way or the other about whether I stayed with her or not. Me, I tried to put the tragedy of our lost daughter behind me. I got married again, I had my children here—my life is pretty damn good. I've tried to pretend that Lucy never existed. I never quite succeeded, but I pretended to myself that I did. Until now. And that's really the whole story."

Except it wasn't.

Of course, Devlin didn't know that I was Lucy's biological mother. He didn't know that Lucy was still alive. And he didn't know that Elliott Grayson, his old friend, had been the one who took Lucy away that day to try to save her from Anne's jealous and irrational rages.

But there was something else Patrick Devlin did know that he hadn't told me yet.

I could sense it from the expression on his face and the way he talked.

"What else?" I asked.

"What do you mean?"

"There's more, isn't there?"

I had a feeling—a reporter's instinct, I guess—what it was about.

"What were you really doing in Mountainboro, New Hampshire, recently?" I asked.

"I told you before . . . I was just curious after that mysterious e-mail about a Lucy sighting there."

"I think it was more than just curiosity. It's time to tell the whole truth, Patrick. This is just you and me talking—I'm not a reporter here anymore. The reasons for that are kind of complicated. But the bottom line is I'm not going to be putting any of this on the air, at least for the time being. What happened in Mountainboro?"

Patrick Devlin looked out the window of his house. Toward the swimming pool and the big yard and all the other things in his life now. Maybe he was thinking about how far he had come over the years. Or maybe he was thinking about Anne and Lucy and the life he had lived before this one.

"I went back to the gravesite," Devlin said. "Where those six kids had been buried. I decided to go back there after you called that day and told me Anne was dying. I wanted to see the spot again, but it's a shopping mall now. Helluva thing, huh?"

"I still don't understand . . . why did you want to go back there?"

He looked at me sadly.

"I guess because I wanted to pray for mercy and forgiveness and some kind of peace after all this time."

"Who were you praying for?"

"Those six dead kids. Lucy. Anne. And most of all, I guess, for myself."

"Why you?"

"I'm the one who buried the bodies."

CHAPTER 56

ANNE DEVLIN WAS back in the hospital again, and this time it looked as if she wasn't getting out.

The doctors said she probably had only a few days left.

When I went into her room, she looked even frailer than before lying in the hospital bed. But I didn't feel pity or sadness for her anymore. Just anger.

It had taken me nearly five hours to get there. An hour's ride to Logan Airport in Boston. An hour and a half in the air until we landed at LaGuardia. Another hour or so in a cab sitting in rush-hour traffic back to Manhattan. I spent much of that time thinking about what Patrick Devlin had told me.

The answer was right there in front of me all the time. Someone should have seen it. Me. The cops. The families of the victims. But nobody ever did. Maybe because it was so unbelievable, so ludicrous, so hard to accept. Or maybe because it was so obvious that we all just blew past the warning signs.

There were six bodies in that grave in New Hampshire. Six children whose parents had gone through the same kind of grief Anne Devlin had when she lost Lucy. I'd thought they were all victims.

But Anne Devlin wasn't a victim anymore.

She was a killer.

* * *

"She told me how she killed those six children," Patrick Devlin had said. "She picked out her victims by hanging out at schools and parks and shopping malls to watch other mothers with their children. She looked for ones that seemed particularly happy. She said that happiness was what set her off, that she wanted them to feel the same pain and experience the same loss as she did.

"Afterward, she would follow them home and then stalk the children until she had an opportunity to approach them alone. It apparently wasn't that hard to get them to go with her. She was a nonthreatening, friendly, pleasant-looking woman—not a rough motorcycle guy like Marston. Sometimes she even told them about losing Lucy to get their sympathy.

"She brought them back to our town house. During the day when I was at work or while I was away on business trips, she said. She brought them up to Lucy's room and pretended they were Lucy—letting them watch Lucy's favorite TV shows, play her games, and even feeding them favorite foods like Oreos and Cheerios that Lucy loved. But, in the end, she said she had to kill them because 'they weren't the real Lucy.'

"Some of them she strangled, some she beat to death—and one she even stabbed with a kitchen knife. She said it took her hours to clean up the blood that time before I got home. Afterward, she buried the bodies in the backyard of the town house. You remember how she had that big garden back there? It had a high wooden fence that prevented people from seeing into the yard. It wasn't hard for her to plant those small corpses in the ground without anyone knowing.

"Afterward, she would befriend the grieving parents and act as if she was comforting them—while all the time she was the cause of their children being gone. It gave her a kind of high, she claimed. Some sort of relief from the pain of losing Lucy."

I'd heard about cases like this before—when the victim becomes the predator. I remembered a murder case in New York a while back in which a Son of Sam–type gunman killed and wounded a dozen people in random attacks, then disappeared for a long time. When the shootings started up again a few years later, the shooter turned out to be one of the original wounded victims—who had decided to do to others what the unknown shooter had done to him. There's a fine line between sanity and insanity in all of us, I suppose. Anne Devlin had very obviously crossed over that line.

"She was crying when she told me what she had done to the children," Devlin said. "She talked about killing herself, about joining them in heaven, about being with Lucy again in another world. Most of all, she kept talking about how sorry she was. About how she would never do it again. About how she couldn't go to jail because then she wouldn't be home when Lucy came back and walked in the door. She pleaded with me to help her."

It was hard for him to explain what happened next.

"I told her I wanted to see the bodies. I guess I needed to convince myself that it had really happened and wasn't just another figment of her imagination," Devlin said. "But it was all too real. She dug up all the places in the backyard where she'd put the bodies. They were there, just like she said.

"I'm still not sure why I did what came next. Maybe it was because I still cared for her on some level and wanted to protect her. Maybe I was protecting myself because I was so deeply involved in it by this point. Or maybe I just wanted it all to go away, and the nightmare wouldn't end until the bodies were gone. If they were never found, then no one would ever be sure that they were dead or be able to tie the deaths in any way to Anne. All I knew was I couldn't leave those bodies lying there in the backyard of our house.

"I remembered the remote area of New Hampshire around Mountainboro from the bike conventions there. I drove there with the bodies piled in my trunk. I had to put them all in plastic bags to make the trip. It was a horrible nightmare; many of the bodies were in very bad shape by then, of course. But I did it. I buried them as deeply as I could. All six of them. Well, five actually, at first. A few weeks later Anne remembered a sixth victim she hadn't told me about. I had to go back and bury her, too. That was the toughest moment for me. After I drove hundreds of miles with those corpses in my trunk, I had to go back and bring one more."

The one on top. The one who'd been identified as Becky Gale. I'd wondered if it was significant that she'd been buried separately from the others. But Anne Devlin had simply forgotten she'd killed that one until later. Sometimes facts are just meaningless like that. Not everything has significance.

"When it was done, I never set foot in that town house again. I just couldn't, knowing the horrors she had committed there. I sold the place as quickly as I could, finalized our divorce, and never talked to Anne again. I was always haunted by the fear she might kill again and I would be responsible for the new deaths by not having her put away. But I don't think she ever did. I think what happened was a burst of rage and insanity that ended when those bodies were in the ground.

"I made a new life for myself," he said, looking around at the pictures of his wife and children. "I moved on, something Anne could never do. She dedicated the rest of her life to the pointless quest of finding Lucy, and now she'll have to die knowing Lucy was dead a long time ago. She spent a lifetime chasing after a dream that was already gone. Me, I've just tried to forget. I try all the time to forget about those six bodies. Six lives Anne had taken away out of her insane grief over losing our own daughter. Maybe that's why I went back to Mountainboro. To see the place where I buried those bodies a long time ago. To make sure I never do forget."

* * *

The same nurse was on duty as the last time I was in Anne Devlin's hospital room. I remembered when I saw the name Joyce on her name tag.

"She's in a tremendous amount of pain," the nurse told me when I arrived this time. "We're giving her morphine and a lot of other painkilling drugs, of course. But after a while they lose their effectiveness. She's suffering terribly. I wish there was more we could do, but we can't."

She left and I walked over to the bed where Anne Devlin lay, hooked up to breathing and feeding apparatus and monitors that flashed her vital life signs. Her eyes were closed, but she opened them as I got near. She smiled when she saw it was me. She knew who I was, that was important.

"Clare, I wasn't sure you'd come back in time," she said in a weak voice. "The doctors seem surprised I'm not dead yet. But I'm still here, hon. How are you?"

This woman was talking to me like I was her friend, but I didn't even know her anymore.

"I talked to your husband today," I said.

"I don't have a husband."

"Patrick."

"Oh, him."

"He told me about Mountainboro."

"What's Mountainboro?"

"The place where he took the bodies of the six children you murdered."

She looked at me blankly, as if she hadn't heard—or at least didn't understand—what I was saying.

"I had a dream about Lucy last night," she said suddenly. "We were together again, just the two of us. Me and Lucy. She was more beautiful than ever. I think Lucy is prettier than any other little girl I've ever seen. We talked and she told me how happy she was to see me. She said she's been waiting for me all this time. All those years that I was looking for her, she was right there. I was just looking in the wrong place, she said. That's when I realized where I was. I was in heaven. I was in heaven with Lucy and we were going to be there together forever and ever. I woke up then. But I think maybe that was a vision from God. A sign that I was really going to meet Lucy in heaven again when I die. What do you think, Clare?"

I leaned close to her so I could be certain she'd hear every word I said.

"You're not going to heaven."

"Huh?"

"You murdered six children."

"Do you think Lucy still likes Cheerios? I've got to make sure that there's enough in the house when she comes home."

"Six innocent children," I said. "Six children who will never get to live the lives they should have. Six families whose lives were destroyed, too. All because of you."

She still didn't seem to be listening. The nurse had said that the painkilling drugs made her delusional a lot of the time.

"Let me tell you about the day I brought Lucy home as a baby..."

"No, let me tell you about Lucy," I said. "You're the reason Lucy's gone. You beat her, you abused her, you turned that house into a nightmare for that child. She would have died right there if she would have stayed. The same way those six children died. The ones you killed because you couldn't stand to see them having a happy life if you couldn't have Lucy."

She heard me now, I could tell that from the look in her eyes. She smiled. A scary smile. A smile so indifferent to the suffering she'd caused that I wondered if Patrick Devlin was right about her being finished with the killing. Or were there more bodies out there? Dead children no one knew about yet?

"Why should they have their children if I couldn't have Lucy?" she said, and I knew it wasn't just the painkillers talking.

This was the real Anne Devlin.

"I used to see those mothers with their kids, looking so happy and pleased with themselves. And there I was all alone. It just wasn't fair. Why did Lucy have to go away and leave me? Well, if I couldn't have her, I decided they couldn't have their children either.

"You want to know something? Afterward, I really enjoyed getting close enough to them to see the grief I was responsible for. They'd cry and look up to God and ask: why? But I knew why. I'd done this. I'd let them understand the pain that I felt. It felt good, so good.

"I did it for Lucy, you know. That's the real reason I killed them. Those children died in memory of my Lucy."

It wasn't supposed to end like this. I always figured that when I found the person responsible for all the killing, it would be different. The guilty person would be an obvious pervert, a twisted sex addict, some obviously terrible individual. There'd be a dramatic confrontation—a shootout, a chase—and then eventually this person would be brought to justice. That was the way it always happened in books and movies. But all I had was this sick woman lying in a hospital bed.

I wanted to tell her that Lucy was still alive, but that she would never see her again. I wanted to tell her that I was really Lucy's mother. I wanted to tell her that it had been me who slept with her husband before Lucy disappeared. I wanted to tell her anything that would hurt her.

The nurse named Joyce came in and looked at her. Anne Devlin had closed her eyes now and seemed to be asleep now.

"She's in the most terrible pain," Joyce said, adjusting some of the monitoring devices.

"My father died of cancer some years ago," I said, just trying to make conversation. "I remember that was very painful."

"We know how to prolong life a lot longer now because of modern medicine," she said, "but we can't stop the pain."

"She seems relatively peaceful now."

"That won't last. It's only because we gave her so many painkillers. In an hour or so, they'll have worn off and she'll be in agony again. That will be the pattern until she dies. Only the periods of pain will get longer and the peaceful ones shorter, until it's all pain and suffering until the end. The quicker that happens the better. Death would be a blessing for her at this point. Do you understand?"

Joyce looked me directly in the eye when she said it. I suddenly realized this wasn't idle conversation anymore.

"What are you saying?"

"Mrs. Devlin has no family, no other visitors. Just you. We can't pull the plug on her here without family authorization. It's against regulations. She has no living will, no power of attorney that allows anyone to end her suffering. That's such a shame. If someone were to just take her off life support, then it would be so much better for her. But I can't do that. I'm a nurse. Do you understand now?"

I understood.

Joyce cared about being a nurse, she cared about humanity, she cared about her patient.

Of course, she didn't know what her patient had done.

"I used to see those mothers with their kids, looking so happy and pleased with themselves," Anne Devlin had said to me a few minutes earlier. "And there I was all alone. It just wasn't fair. Why did Lucy have to go away and leave me? Well, if I couldn't have her, I decided they couldn't have their children either . . . I'd let them understand the pain that I felt. It felt good, so good."

I stared at the woman in the bed for a long time after the nurse left the room. Each breath was laborious now, her body shaking as she fought to hold onto the last vestiges of life. I could make it a little easier for her to go now. I could end it all right here and now, and no one would care. The nurse had practically pleaded with me to do it. To send her to the other side.

"Do you think I'll see Lucy in heaven, Clare?" she had asked.

I thought about Lucy on the day she was born and holding her in my arms in the hospital. I thought about her as an eleven-year-old going off to school that last day. I thought about all the pain this woman had caused her and all those other families over the years.

"Go to hell," I said to Anne Devlin.

Then I walked out and left her there to die alone.

CHAPTER 57

I HAVEN'T PUT any of this on the air yet.

I'm sure that I won't make any decision until after the election when Grayson has promised to tell me the truth about Lucy.

And, even if he does, I'm not sure what I will do about the story after that.

I've thought about it a lot. I've come at it from all different directions, making a case to myself for both sides of the argument. There've been days when I decided to go ahead and tell everything right now, no matter what the consequences, on that night's Channel 10 newscast. Other times I convince myself I should destroy all the evidence I've accumulated—the tape recording with Grayson in the park, the stuff I took out of Louise Carbone's house, even my notes on the story—so that I can't ever take that fateful step.

I've considered, too, the possibility of going on the air with just a part of the story—how Anne Devlin murdered those six innocent children—without revealing anything that might jeopardize my arrangement with Grayson. But I quickly conclude that this is not a valid option for me. If I ever do tell this story to a TV audience, I must tell it the same way I've done it here—from beginning to end, with nothing left out.

In the end, I have done nothing.

Instead, I remain in a kind of perpetual limbo, unsure how to deal with the Hobson's choice that I face.

* * *

Elliott Grayson won the Democratic nomination for the Senate in a landslide, as expected. He currently has a twenty-five-point lead over the Republican nominee in the upcoming general election. Unless something goes catastrophically wrong for him, Grayson will be the next US Senator from New York. People have already begun talking about him as a potential candidate for President four or eight years down the line.

Watching him give his victory speech in front of the cameras on primary night, I was struck by how different he seemed than the anguished man I talked to in Union Square Park that day. I wonder which one is the real Elliott Grayson, or if there even is one anymore. After all of this, he remains a contradiction to me. I loathe him, but I am also fascinated by him. I believe that some of the things he has told me are true. But that not all of them are. I'm convinced that he's been motivated to carry out some of the things he's done for good, moral reasons, but that he also has the capacity to be truly evil. The question is which will win out in the end: the good or the evil?

Grayson continues to promise that he will tell me how to find Lucy once the November election is over.

But what happens then?

I have given Grayson my word that I will keep his secret and not air the story if he tells me how to find Lucy—and my word, even after all this, is somehow still sacrosanct to me as a journalist.

But there are other problems, too.

If I do wait until after Election Day in November, find out the truth about Lucy—and then go ahead anyway with the story, how do I justify sitting on this information so long? My secret deal with Grayson would eventually be discovered. There'd be countless questions, justifiable ones, about my lack of journalistic ethics. I could be destroying my own career as well as his. Even worse, there could be a scenario where he survives the scandal and I don't.

I only have Grayson's word, too, that he even knows where Lucy is or that she is still truly alive.

For all I know, he could have made up the whole story as a trick to keep me from going public with what I know until he gets to Washington as a US Senator. Lucy might have been that little girl they dug up, just like he first said, or she might be lying in another grave somewhere.

My journalistic instincts tell me to be skeptical, but my heart wants so desperately to believe him.

And so, I am left in the unenviable position of having made a Faustian bargain with a man who I believe is evil, and yet I must depend on his honesty and integrity and conscience to tell me the truth that I want to hear.

* * *

Anne Devlin lingered on for nearly a week before she finally died.

All the newscasts eulogized her as a tragic figure—a loving mother who suffered the worst loss imaginable and devoted her life to the memory of her lost daughter. We did that on Channel 10, too.

"Somewhere up in heaven, Anne Devlin is holding Lucy in her arms at long last," Brett Wolff intoned in a sober voice.

"Well said, Brett," Dani said. "I don't mind admitting that I have tears in my eyes tonight."

After the newscast was over, I went home and got myself drunk, ate every bit of junk food I could find, and threw up for much of the night. By the next morning, I was all right again. I had purged myself of whatever guilt I felt for allowing that on the air.

It's amazing how much we're able to compromise everything we believe in and yet still live with ourselves.

* * *

Things are pretty much back to normal at Channel 10. We finished first in the October ratings sweeps, beating out the other stations by the biggest margin in our history.

This was due in large part to a two-week series we ran called "Bedroom Secrets of the Stars" in which Brett and Dani revealed whether celebrities like to sleep in pajamas, in their underwear, or in the nude. It concluded with a report in which Brett and Dani and Cassie and Janelle all talked about their *own* bedroom secrets—and posed on camera in sexy nighttime wear.

That series was pretty much my idea, and Jack Faron was ecstatic with me when the ratings went through the roof. He's never really asked me too many questions about what happened that day in the park with Grayson. I simply told him afterward that there was no story there, and we ran an innocuous piece on Grayson that had no impact whatsoever upon the election. I suspect Faron knows there's more to it, but he never brought it up again. I think he's just happy not to have to make any tough decisions about taking on a man as powerful as Elliott Grayson. Jack Faron's a good TV executive, but . . . bottom line . . . well, he's still a TV executive.

Me, I'm riding high again at Channel 10, and I suppose I should be happy about that. Instead, I feel lost, I feel confused, I feel like a failure—even if other people can't understand why.

"Are you okay?" Maggie asked me the other day.

"I'm fine."

"You don't seem fine."

"I'm telling you, Maggie, there's nothing wrong with me."

"Okay, if you say so."

"You don't believe me?"

"I just think you seem different."

Maggie was right, of course.

I was different.

For a long time, I had told myself I was a real journalist—a person of intelligence and principles and serious values who just happened to be working in the world of TV news.

But that wasn't true anymore. I had lost something in the Lucy Devlin story, something I could never get back again. I can never make myself whole as a newswoman again, no matter how hard I try.

I feel an emptiness inside me now each day when I go to work that I fear will never go away.

* * *

Janet keeps trying to fix me up for dates and push me to maybe even try marriage one more time, albeit with little success. She says it's because I'm not trying hard enough. I say it's because she's got lousy taste in men. She says that's really funny coming from me since I've made so many bad choices when it comes to the men in my life. Hard to think of a snappy comeback for that one.

Why is it that I've had this attraction all my life to men like Don Crowell and Elliott Grayson? And then pushed away Sam and the other husbands I had? Why not a nice, uncomplicated relationship with a good guy? Why couldn't I settle down and be happy with someone like that? I'd lost out on Sam, but there had to be other good guys out there just like him.

I thought about Louise Carbone and how much she and I were alike in some ways. She'd had a chance to live a normal life with a good husband and a daughter she loved. But she'd thrown it all away to join the Warlock Warriors and ride off with Sandy Marston. She just couldn't handle the idea of living the rest of her life like everyone else in Lodi, New Jersey.

I understood that.

Of all the people involved in this, Big Lou is the one I feel the worst about.

I miss her.

There are still a lot of unanswered questions.

Such as who were the children actually buried in that mass grave up in New Hampshire?

If Grayson knows, he won't say. And Devlin told me that day at his house, he never found out their identities. I went back over the list of people Anne Devlin "befriended" following Lucy's disappearance. I made a list of people with children who were never found and remained classified as missing after all these years. I assume that some of them might be in that grave, but I can't be sure. I can't be sure either that Anne Devlin didn't kill other children besides those six whose bodies might turn up sometime in the future or else never at all.

I also continue to wonder about the deaths of Sandy Marston and Louise Carbone.

Why did Marston come running out of that farmhouse waving a gun when he knew he would be cut down by sharpshooters surrounding the place? Okay, probably because he'd killed a guy in a bar and he knew he had nothing to lose. But what if it hadn't happened that way? Again, we only had Grayson's account of the incident, and I knew now that he had lied about so many other things.

And what about Big Lou? The young federal agent who shot her to death even though she was unarmed got promoted and received a big pay raise. I tried to talk to him, but he stuck to his official version of the story. Did Grayson buy him off for his silence? I have no proof of any of this.

But I believe in my heart that Grayson saw an opportunity to keep Marston and Big Lou quiet about what they knew and he'd taken it. I didn't know exactly how he did it, and I probably never will. But the deaths of Marston and Big Lou seemed too convenient for his Senate campaign to be just a coincidence.

I am suspicious, too, about other things—and not convinced that either Elliott Grayson or Patrick Devlin told me the whole story of everything they know.

For one thing, who was the body of the little girl found in the Dutchess County grave that was supposed to be Lucy Devlin? And where did the body come from? Did Grayson somehow know about the murder of another little girl and keep it secret, knowing he might need it to pull off that subterfuge? Or—and I hesitated to even consider the possibility—was that body really Lucy, just like Marston's note claimed, and Grayson was lying about her being alive to keep me quiet about the rest?

Also, did Patrick never suspect that it was Grayson who had helped abduct Lucy after their conversation about the horrors going on in that house with her mother? And, it also seemed awfully coincidental that it was Grayson who oversaw the exhumation of the six bodies that Patrick buried in New Hampshire if there really was no connection between either of the men on all this.

The biggest question, though, the one that continues to haunt me, is who wrote that original e-mail. The one to Anne Devlin that started it all with the claim of seeing Lucy with a biker named Elliott in Mountainboro, New Hampshire. Without that e-mail, none of this would have happened and the secrets of Lucy Devlin and the others might have remained hidden forever.

I've run all sorts of possibilities through my mind.

It could have been Teddy Weller, Grayson's primary opponent, who wanted to smear him politically. Maybe even Grayson himself, since the results helped him get elected. Maybe Sandy Marston or Big Lou to help in their extortion efforts against Grayson. Maybe Patrick Devlin did it as some sort of penance for dealing with his guilty conscience over those kids' bodies he helped his wife bury in that grave. Or maybe even Anne Devlin herself, to ensure that she stayed in the public eye because she reveled in playing the tragic mother in search of her long-lost daughter.

Any of these was possible, I suppose.

But there's one other name I've been thinking about, too.

What if Lucy sent that e-mail?

Okay, it sounds crazy, I know. But think about this:

All of the people I've mentioned would have known some of the things in that e-mail. About the motorcycle convention in Mountainboro. About Elliott Grayson. About the birthmark on Lucy's shoulder. About how much she loved Cheerios and Oreo cookies. But, as far as I can tell, none of them would have known about all these things. There was only one person who did. Lucy Devlin herself.

Maybe she found out about Anne Devlin dying of cancer.

Maybe she'd seen another interview with her before I'd done mine and came up with the idea for the e-mail.

Maybe she found out she was adopted and decided to put all these events in motion in the hope she could find her real mother after all these years.

Maybe Lucy Devlin just didn't want to be forgotten.

CHAPTER 58

I HAVE THIS dream about meeting my daughter again. Two dreams, actually.

The first dream is the happy one. Lucy has grown up and become a beautiful woman. She looks a lot like me, but prettier—and she has all of my good qualities and none of my bad ones. When we meet for the first time, she tells me she's watched me on television and always admired me from afar. Even before she knew I was her mother. She tells me all about her own child, an adorable little girl, too—and how I'm a grandmother now. Then I take her in my arms and I hold her. I tell her that I'm sorry I left her for so long. I tell her that I'll never leave her again. I tell her she's the one good thing I've ever done in my life.

The second dream is more perplexing. In this one, I'm sitting in a car outside a house that I've never seen before. Grayson has told me Lucy lives inside, but for some reason I can't go up and knock on the door. Instead, I just sit in the car and do nothing. Eventually Lucy comes out of the house. Again, I want to run to her, but I can't—my legs won't move. I simply watch as she walks away down the street outside of her house, just like she did that long-ago day in New York City, and disappears on me all over again.

In the letter Louise Carbone had sent to her own daughter, she said: "We make a lot of decisions in our life, and sometimes wish later that we could take some of them back. To go back in time and change everything and make it right again. That's what I wish I could do. But it's too late for that now."

I know that's true for me, too. I can't change the past, and I can't change the things that have occurred because of the decisions I made. I changed Lucy's life irrevocably when I gave her up that first day in the hospital. The person she is today, whoever that is, would be nothing like the person she might have been if I hadn't set all of this in motion back then. It's too late to go back and try to undo all that.

I fear that is the meaning of the dream about not being able to get out of the car. That I know deep inside that it is too late for me to become a part of Lucy's life, and for her to be a part of mine. That the best thing I can do—the only logical choice I have—is to leave things as they are. That I can't ever fix the damage I've caused, no matter how hard I try.

And yet . . .

I'm not a particularly religious person, but I am a spiritual one. I believe that there is a God and an order to the universe and a reason for everything that happens to us. So many different events had to come together to get me this close to Lucy. The original e-mail; Anne Devlin dying of cancer; the Senate candidacy of Elliot Grayson; the bizarre series of events that took place over a period of years in the tiny town of Mountainboro, New Hampshire; the revelations about what Patrick and Anne Devlin did; the fact that Grayson—the person who orchestrated the abduction of their daughter—was the one who helped dig up the bodies buried there. I can't believe all of this was simply coincidence. I believe that some sort of higher power in the universe has drawn me and Lucy together after all this time for a reason.

In the end, I guess that the feeling I'm most left with—even more than the guilt, the sadness, and the regrets—is hope.

Hope that maybe it really isn't too late.

Hope that I get one more chance to put the broken pieces of my life back together again.

Hope that this time I can do it right.

EPILOGUE

Once her daughter is safely home from school again, the mother tells herself she must stop worrying so much.

Yes, there is danger and evil out there in the world—but there is also much that is good.

Sometimes it leaves a mother uncertain over what to do.

She suffered so much in her own childhood.

So she knows she must be careful now not to overreact and not to be overprotective and not to do anything that might prevent her daughter from having a normal life.

In the end, the mother tells herself, you just have to trust your instincts and believe that everything will work out all right.

On the TV screen in front of her, reporters are interviewing Elliott Grayson—who's just been elected to the US Senate.

At one point, as she knows they will, they ask him about breaking the Lucy Devlin case.

Afterward, the newscast goes to a broadcaster named Clare Carlson who does a recap of the whole story.

She is fascinated by all of it.

Especially fascinated by Clare Carlson.

Yes, she decides, sometimes you just have to trust that everything will work out all right in the end.

Then, the woman who a long time ago used to be Lucy Devlin, goes to her own daughter.

She hugs the little girl tightly and tells her how much she loves her.

There might be a lot of uncertainty in this world.

But there is one thing Lucy Devlin knows for sure.

There is no greater love than a mother for her daughter.

Nothing that a mother wouldn't do for the sake of her daughter.

Nothing at all.

31901062957826

9 781608 092819